PRAISE FOR "THE SENECA SCOURGE"

"Fun, fast, original, and won't strain your emotions."

— *SCIENCETHRILLERS*

"*The Seneca Scourge* by Carrie Rubin was impossible to put down."

— TRUDI LOPRETO FOR *READERS FAVORITE*

"I love, love, love, LOVED this book. 4 out of 4 stars ... well written, well thought out, well planned, and just a great book altogether."

— *ONLINE BOOK CLUB*

"Rubin masterfully blends medical thriller, mystery, and sci-fi into a thoroughly enjoyable read."

— AUDREY KALMAN, AUTHOR OF *TINY SHOES DANCING*

PRAISE FOR THE BENJAMIN ORIS SERIES

THE BONE CURSE: "A strong medical thriller—inclusive, skillfully written, and inviting."

— *FOREWORD REVIEWS*

THE BONE HUNGER: "The reveal is a real shocker, and Rubin's winning lead is well-suited to sustain a series. This is just the ticket for Robin Cook fans."

— *PUBLISHERS WEEKLY*

THE BONE ELIXIR: "The author's pithy writing keeps the story popping all the way to the rousing final act. A chilling supernatural tale with indelible characters."

— *KIRKUS REVIEWS*

THE SENECA SCOURGE

THE SENECA SCOURGE

CARRIE RUBIN

INDIGO
DOT
PRESS

Indigo Dot Press
indigodotpress@gmail.com

Second edition 2025
First published in 2012 by Whiskey Creek Press

FIC031040 FICTION / Thrillers / Medical
FIC030000 FICTION / Thrillers / Suspense
FIC028000 FICTION / Science Fiction / General

ISBN 978-1-958160-15-2 (trade paperback)
ISBN 978-1-958160-16-9 (ebook)
ISBN 978-1-958160-17-6 (kindle)

PROLOGUE

Thomas Lamb once read somewhere that a human sneeze could spray thousands of germs at one hundred miles per hour up to twelve feet away, the particles lingering in the air for minutes, waiting to be inhaled. If that were the case, he pitied his fellow passengers.

Using his dark slacks for tissue, Thomas wiped the mucus off his hands and brushed crumbs from the tray table. He ignored the sideways glare from his seat companion and settled back into the cramped chair. He felt awful. The cold started yesterday—nothing major, just some sniffles and a dry cough—but today it had escalated. Now his entire body ached, and he suspected a fever. At least the Nairobi to London flight was over, and in a few hours he'd be back in Boston. Shortly after that, his coastal town of Seneca.

Home. It'll feel so good.

If only the coughing would stop. He'd been pretty embarrassed at London Heathrow, especially that last sneezing fit where he had to give up his seat and rush to the bathroom for more toilet paper to wipe his nose. He'd half expected the Japanese tourist on his left to snap his photo, and if not him, then surely the Australian tour group one row over.

But Thomas had wielded no control over his symptoms. Every time he finished with one coughing or sneezing bout, another one surfaced. Luckily, he'd been able to contain himself through customs or they might not have let him board. And damn if he wasn't getting home.

Unable to sleep, he started flipping through lecture notes he'd drafted on the earlier flight, but his exhausted brain couldn't keep up. Looked like his geology students would have to get by without him for another few days. He filed the notes back into his bag and then excused himself and headed to the bathroom for one last stop before landing. On his way he stifled another cough and smiled at an attractive Middle-Eastern woman with a young child on her lap. The little boy smiled back, and Thomas knelt down to shake his hand, thinking of his own son stationed in Afghanistan.

After a brief exchange with the mother, Thomas proceeded to the bathroom. When he finished, he reached for the soap, saw it was out, and skipped the water altogether. Coughing, he made his way back to his seat, squeezing past a South American flight attendant and a jersey-clad Canadian student.

Good Lord, I hate these crowded planes.

Finally, he slumped back into his seat, closed his eyes, and took a big breath.

Pretty soon he'd be home.

1

The thing about an outbreak was, nothing signaled that first patient, nothing as convenient as a neon sign suspended from the neck flashing *Hey, I'm the index case. Stop me before I spread.*

It wasn't until a second or third case occurred that an outbreak was declared, and even then suspicions might not be roused. Not until the cells of infection branched out, gaining momentum in multiple social directions, did the pattern come into focus.

On a mild Monday afternoon in early November, Dr. Sydney McKnight's unenlightened focus centered on Thomas Lamb, her ICU consult. Although not particularly thin, the gray-haired man looked frail in the bed sheets, his face pasty and furrowed. An endotracheal tube coursed through his mouth, attached by a long tube to a mechanical ventilator, the body of which produced a steady stream of artificial breaths every five seconds. *Pop, hiss. Pop, hiss.*

From his left wrist dangled an arterial catheter for ease of blood gas collection; from his right shoulder, a subclavian venous line for IV fluids, medications, and other blood draws. His right index finger housed the probe for the pulse oximeter, and sticky leads on his chest mapped a constant tracing of his heart on the cardiac monitor. Sydney had learned from his chart he'd recently developed an arrhythmia.

As she proceeded through her physical exam, Mr. Lamb either too ill or sedated to respond, she couldn't help but wonder how he would spend the beautiful November afternoon were he not held hostage by a hospital bed and a collection of life-saving machines. A walk through Boston Common? A long lunch in a neighborhood pub with his wife? Planning a lecture in his office?

Sydney slipped the stethoscope underneath his gown and let it rest on his chest. Harsh ventilator breaths greeted her. She waited for a spontaneous breath of his own, but when it came, it wasn't much better, his lungs sonorous and coarse.

Her exam shifted to the patient's heart, the stethoscope rising and falling with each expansion of his chest, but between the noisy ventilator pops and the man's own ineffectual breaths, the cardiac sounds barely resonated. Next, Sydney palpated his belly, examined his head and neck, and performed a quick neurologic exam, the best she could, anyway, given Mr. Lamb's unresponsive state. When she finished, she felt no more enlightened than when she'd entered the room. She needed to talk to the patient's wife. The ICU staff had already completed a thorough history with the woman, but questions remained, particularly about the geologist's recent trip to Africa.

After giving Mr. Lamb a final glance, Sydney left the room. She had planned to walk over to radiology to study his x-rays, hoping that by the time she returned, his wife would be back, but her plan was interrupted when she spotted Dr. Jones, the new infectious disease attending, leafing through the patient's chart behind the ICU desk. Despite all the beeping machines, ringing phones, and simultaneous conversations, he looked up when she approached.

"Hello, Sydney, what did you learn?"

Sydney hesitated in confusion. "I'm sorry. I thought Dr. DeWitt was my attending. I was going to finish my workup and page her."

"No need. I told her I'd take this one. It will be a good way to get my feet moist. She was grateful, actually. She seems awfully busy."

Moist?

Sydney tightened her blonde ponytail. "Oh, okay. Well, I examined Mr. Lamb and was about to go see his x-rays. I'm hoping his wife will be back soon so I can talk to her and try to obtain more information."

"Great. Give me a moment to finish examining his chart, and then we'll go view his films."

Sydney nodded, and in a few moments, Dr. Jones stood and indicated he was ready to go. Sydney eyed his pinstripe suit and black silk tie and was once again surprised by his formal attire. Standing next to him in her barely hospital-acceptable chinos and black GAP sweater, she felt like a lost little orphan.

Once in the radiology department, Sydney escorted Dr. Jones to the ICU x-ray board. They sat down on two of the three chairs that fronted it. Using a foot pedal, Sydney guided the whirring, rotating panels to bed five, their patient, where four chest films hung, all taken within the last twenty-four hours and each showing a progressively worse stage of disease.

Sydney shook her head. "Wow, his lungs are almost whited out."

Dr. Jones's face registered similar disbelief. He grabbed an x-ray from the light board and ran his fingers over the surface, gently flipping it one way and then the other, as if the image was a delicate work of art. Sydney was about to ask what he was doing, but when she heard him mumble something about cavemen beneath his breath, she thought she understood.

"Don't worry," she said. "All x-rays will be digitalized soon."

Dr. Jones seemed not to have heard her and returned the film to its place. "Doesn't look good for Mr. Lamb, does it?"

"No, Dr. Jones, it doesn't."

"Please, call me Casper," he said, still staring at the x-ray.

Finally, he stood and headed back towards the unit. Sydney followed along like a dutiful student, amused at the thought of calling him Casper out loud, the name no odder than the man himself. When they returned to the ICU, she was relieved to see Mrs. Lamb back in her husband's room.

After reaching for masks and gloves, the two physicians entered the small space, still as gloomy as it had been minutes before. Sydney introduced herself to Mrs. Lamb, and Casper did the same. The woman gave them a polite but transient smile. She looked to be in her late forties, dark hair, tall, mildly overweight. She wore a Michigan State sweatshirt and a faded pair of jeans, and her makeup-free face suggested she'd slept little in the past couple of days. After a few moments of sympathetic exchange, Sydney dived into the history.

"Mrs. Lamb, I know from the chart your husband's been ill for about a week now, starting with what seemed like a cold and then developing into fever, chills, and coughing—"

"Relentless coughing," she said, her voice weary.

"Right. I was wondering if you could take us through the timeline once again, particularly in relation to his trip to Africa. As infectious disease consultants, we're especially interested in the foreign travel."

"My husband was in Kenya. He's a geologist and was studying soil samples in a village near Nairobi—Hunchakos I think it was called. He returned home five days ago but had started feeling ill two days before then."

"So he was already sick when he got on the plane?"

Mrs. Lamb gave Sydney a defensive look. "Yes." She grabbed a tissue and wiped her nose. This was followed by a brief cough.

"Do you know where else he might have landed?"

"I know he had a layover in London. Switched planes, I think. Then I'm pretty sure he flew directly into Boston."

"Did he give you any indication as to how he might have caught the illness?"

"No. Like I said, it started as a cold, then everything spiraled downhill after that. His fever spiked and his coughing increased. He felt weak and shaky. I finally convinced him to go to a clinic three days ago, where they did some kind of flu test. Even though it was negative, they gave him a prescription and told him to follow-up if he didn't improve. Well, as you can see, he didn't improve. The next day we went to the emergency room, where they hooked him up to oxygen right away and admitted him. We started out on the general ward, but before I knew it, we were up here in the ICU, my husband hardly able to breathe and now clinging to life on a ventilator."

She reached for another tissue and dabbed her eyes. More sniffling, nose wiping, and coughing followed.

"Mrs. Lamb, are you getting sick too?"

"No, no, I'm fine. Just a little scratchy throat and cough. Probably my allergies. Stress always makes them worse."

"Hmm." Sydney felt a wave of unease. "Maybe you better get yourself checked out. Get a prescription like your husband. I assume it was Tamiflu they gave him?"

Mrs. Lamb nodded. "Lot of good it did him."

"Tamiflu works best if given right away. It can shorten the duration of illness and help prevent spread of the virus."

Sydney realized she sounded like a pharmaceutical rep and tried again.

"It certainly would be reasonable if you got yourself tested and started the medicine."

"But the ICU doctors said they're not even sure Thomas has influenza."

"That's true, his influenza antigen test was negative, but

since his course is still compatible with the disease, they want to wait for the culture results."

"They said he might have something like Severe Acute Respiratory Syndrome, some new strain. Isn't that the one with the high mortality rate?" Mrs. Lamb's voice cracked, and she wiped her eyes again.

"Yes, and I suppose we need to consider that, but it seems unlikely, given there's been no new cases of SARS for years." With her gloved hand, Sydney gave Mrs. Lamb's forearm an awkward pat. Then she shot a look at Dr. Jones as if to say *Feel free to jump in anytime.*

When he didn't interject, Sydney turned back to Mrs. Lamb. "I don't suppose either of you had a flu shot, did you?"

Mrs. Lamb shook her head.

Sydney didn't press the issue. The woman was distressed enough. But it was unfortunate, considering a schoolteacher like Mrs. Lamb was a perfect candidate for the vaccine.

They talked a little more, and Sydney reassured her they would do all they could to find the exact cause of her husband's illness and try additional treatments if necessary.

Mrs. Lamb nodded and thanked them, but she didn't look especially convinced. Sydney turned to Dr. Jones, waiting.

Casper must have realized Sydney was staring at him expectantly, because he said, "I'm sorry, is there something you need?"

"I'm waiting for you to do your exam."

"Oh, right." He looked around the room as if searching for something.

"Here, you can use mine." Sydney cleaned her stethoscope with alcohol. "There's supposed to be a stethoscope left in all respiratory isolation rooms, but I don't see one in here."

"Right." Casper took the stethoscope. It dangled in his hands like a dead snake, and for a moment he just stared at it. Sydney watched as he put the ear tips in his ears—backwards —and placed the diaphragm of the scope on the patient's chest. He slid it from one position to the next, his movements awkward.

"Sorry, my scope is kind of old. Bought it used for a great price in med school, but since it still works, I see no need to replace it."

"No, no, it's fine." Casper handed it back to her, seemingly relieved to have the relic out of his hand. "I trust you completed the rest of the exam."

Sydney nodded and once again swiped her stethoscope with alcohol. She was fastidious when it came to infection control.

"Then no need to repeat it," Casper said.

The comment pleased her. Nothing irked worse than staffing a patient with the director of the infectious disease department, Dr. Burke. He always had to go back into the patient's room to do another complete physical exam, as if Sydney were a medical student rather than a fully trained, soon to be board-certified physician who could be practicing medicine completely on her own were she not doing an infectious disease fellowship.

Thinking of Dr. Burke, a.k.a. "Dr. Tomato Head" to the residents, Sydney's mind traveled back to their encounter a few weeks ago. She was no less miffed by the exchange now than she had been at the time, Dr. Burke having asked—ordered, really—Sydney to forego her current research project and instead team up with Dr. Jones.

"But I've already laid the groundwork. MRSA is an important topic in the field of infectious disease," Sydney had said, her interest in methicillin-resistant *Staphylococcus aureus* strong.

"As is West Nile virus."

"That's what this new guy is working on?"

"Yes, that's what this *new guy* is working on. Dr. Jones is a distinguished physician and researcher. Not only is he board-certified in internal medicine and infectious disease, he holds a PhD in virology."

"But Dr. DeWitt is planning on me."

"Dr. DeWitt is a very busy researcher herself. She could do with one less fellow to handhold. After all, you were the one who approached her. By dropping your research project, she can spend more time on the others."

Sydney had steadied her voice. "Dr. Burke, I've been planning this project since my residency."

"You're only three months into your infectious disease fellowship—"

"Four, but who's counting?"

"Okay, Dr. McKnight, four months. No need to raise my blood pressure any higher than it already is. Now, you have two years and eight months left of your fellowship. Did I at least get that right? Plenty of time to start a new project."

"But this isn't fair. I—"

"Fair, Sydney? You want *fair*? How fair was it when you ordered a five-thousand-dollar test on my patient? The one I distinctly told you not to. The one his insurance company didn't authorize."

"But he needed that study. If—"

"And how fair was it when you fudged a diagnosis to justify an admission?"

"That woman was clearly suicidal. She needed inpatient care. I can't help it if the psychiatry resident didn't agree."

"There are rules, Dr. McKnight. Rules meant to be followed. By me, by you, by everyone. It's not always about you." He had paused and glared at Sydney from across his desk. "I pulled strings for you, remember? You're an excellent clinician, but because of your shenanigans, I had to fight to keep you here."

And there it was. That constant reminder of what he'd done for her. Godly Department Head Spares the Wayward Disciple.

"But I know little about West Nile research," Sydney had said, sinking back in her chair.

"You'll learn."

And so she would, fractured ego or not. Sydney had relished the chance to work with Dr. DeWitt and knew nothing about the new guy. Dr. Burke said Dr. Jones's references were glowing, but if that were the case, why had Sydney never heard of him? She was probably more up to date on medical journals than the faculty, so why had she never come across his name? And what kind of name was it, anyway? Casper Jones? It sounded like a stage name.

When she'd met him for the first time two weeks ago, she'd realized it wasn't just his name that was suited for Hollywood. The man was in his thirties, at least six-two, and clearly physically fit. Closely cropped hair blanketed his head like soft moss, and dark eyes complimented his light brown skin. When he smiled, his whole face came alive, highlighted by two perfectly positioned dimples. It was as if God had hollowed them out as an afterthought, the finishing touch to a masterpiece.

His Tinseltown look hadn't lessened Sydney's frustration by the research exchange, though. Nor her suspicions of the man.

Hearing Dr. Jones's voice, Sydney's reverie broke, transporting her back to the present.

Her cheeks warmed in embarrassment. "I'm sorry, did you say something?"

"I said I think we're finished in here." Casper smiled beneath his mask at Sydney and Mrs. Lamb.

Sydney nodded and said goodbye to Mrs. Lamb, at which time she and Dr. Jones discarded their protective gear, washed their hands, and left the room to discuss the case with Crystal, the resident on duty. The young woman with an auburn ponytail sat behind the desk, charting on patients, seemingly oblivious to the bustling ICU around her. A muscular medical student named Joe hovered by her side.

"Hey, Crystal," Sydney said. "Can we talk about Mr. Lamb?"

"Oh, sure." Crystal smiled and bounded up in her chair, her eyes sparkling despite the long hours she toiled. She grabbed a notepad and pen. "What do you think is wrong with the guy?"

Sydney looked at Casper, who indicated with a brief nod that she continue.

"There's still a good chance this is influenza, a bad case that's progressed to Adult Respiratory Distress Syndrome—ARDS. Even with a negative antigen test."

"But it could be something like SARS as well?" the medical student piped in.

"It's possible." Sydney frowned. "If it *is* SARS, it will be the first case in five years."

They all fell quiet, each no doubt pondering the significance of that.

Crystal broke the silence. "The viral cultures should be back soon. Then we'll know for sure. Until that time, is there anything else you think we should add?"

"It's a good idea to continue the antiviral as well as the antibiotics, in case there's a bacterial component. It also might be wise to check some blood work for immune deficiency, including an HIV test. And whatever you do, don't stop the respiratory isolation. We don't need the pathogen visiting the other wards." Sydney eyed Casper. He nodded in agreement.

Crystal added the blood work to her to-do list.

"Have you guys considered steroids in case it is ARDS?" Sydney asked the ICU resident.

"My attending mentioned it, but he wants to wait for the viral cultures."

Sydney looked at Casper. "I guess that's all I can think of for now. Do you have anything else you want to add?"

"No, I think you've covered it. The cultures will bear our truth."

Sydney glanced at Crystal, but if the overworked redhead was similarly bemused by Dr. Jones's word play, she didn't show it, her gaze locked only on the beautiful man before her. Even the medical student looked transfixed as Casper continued his instructions.

"I want you to be sure to call me if anything develops with Mr. Lamb tonight. And I especially want to know the results of the culture."

Sydney nodded. "Hopefully with that knowledge, we can keep this an isolated case."

At that, Casper's face darkened, and while Sydney assumed it was out of concern for the patient, she couldn't be sure. In fact, a sudden and unexpected sense of foreboding enveloped her.

It was probably just her fatigue talking.

2

———————

S ydney startled awake to the shrill of her pager and blinked repeatedly at the clock, trying to register the numbers. 12:30 a.m.

She sat up and shook her head, as if the jostling would rouse her brain. Annoyed her call night had gotten off to such a poor start, she silenced the pager and read the number through unfocused eyes.

The ICU.

An image of Mr. Lamb surfaced, and after a mouth-stretching yawn, Sydney grabbed the phone off the nightstand and dialed the number. Crystal answered.

"He's worse," she said. "He's lost all spontaneous respirations, and his heart rate's becoming more irregular. Is there anything else from an infectious disease standpoint we should add?"

Sydney worked to free the frog in her throat. "What were the results of his HIV test?"

"The antibody test was negative."

"It might not be a bad idea to add Bactrim anyway, in case this is *Pneumocystis jiroveci*. I'll check with Dr. Jones and get back to you."

After paging Casper, Sydney called Crystal once again and told her to go ahead with the Bactrim. Then she turned off the light and hoped to slip back into oblivion. Unfortunately, sleep didn't come easily, and images of Mr. Lamb, surgical masks, and whited-out chest x-rays swirled in her brain.

Eventually she drifted off, and the next thing she knew, her pager screeched again, and her heart rate shot up anew. It was the ICU, and she had a sinking feeling the news wouldn't be good.

"Dr. McKnight? Mr. Lamb died. I'm sorry to wake you, but I thought you'd want to know." Crystal's voice lacked its usual bounce.

"Yes. Thank you. I'm sorry we weren't more helpful." That's what came out of Sydney's mouth, anyway, but her brain launched right into the self-blame game.

"Dr. McKnight? You still there?"

"Yes. What happened exactly?"

"We couldn't oxygenate him anymore. We did a CAT scan of his lungs, and it was nothing but white frosting. He became even more acidotic and shocky and eventually went into complete heart failure. My attending and I ran a full code, but it was of no use. Sorry I can't give you better news."

"Thanks for calling me. Sounds like you guys did all you could. How's Mrs. Lamb doing?"

"She doesn't look too good, but I guess that's to be expected, right?"

In lieu of an answer Sydney said goodbye and let the phone fall to her lap. She berated herself for not going into the hospital. While she'd been tossing and turning in bed, a man had been dying. Maybe she could have done more to diagnose him. Perhaps if she had conducted a literature search, or cross-checked his symptoms on the Internet, or…

She forced herself to stop. She hated when she did this to herself. The constant rehashing, the tireless *what ifs*. People died in the ICU almost every day. She knew that. Yet it was difficult for her not to take personally.

Liz Rierdan, another first-year infectious disease fellow and one of Sydney's few friends, constantly reminded her of this. An odd pair they made, considering Sydney played the Black Russian to Liz's Sunny Delight, but they had survived residency together and had forged a tight bond. Even their appearances contrasted. Where Sydney was tall and sinewy with long blonde hair usually coifed in a ponytail, Liz was short and petite with messy black curls that redefined the concept of entropy. And for Liz, unlike Sydney, optimism ruled, such that "Oh, don't worry, everything will be all right" was the norm. Even when Sydney had complained about her research swap, Liz merely replied, "Just be happy you get to play beakers and Bunsen burners with a Taye Diggs lookalike. Remember, I'm stuck deciphering DNA with Dr. Tomato Head Burke."

Sydney sighed and got up for a drink of water. She debated whether to call Casper. He had said to call him for anything. A patient dying was probably "anything."

She paced around her tiny one-bedroom apartment, until she finally retrieved the phone and dialed Casper's number. When he answered, she filled him in on Mr. Lamb's death.

"I wish we could've helped him more," Sydney said.

"There's nothing different we could've done. He was on multiple medications—none of them helped. Viruses can be scary. That's why I'm here."

"What do you mean?"

"You know…that's why I went into virology. To hopefully come up with a cure."

"Sorry, I think that's years away." Sydney murmured a goodbye and disconnected.

A glance at the bedside clock told her it was already 5:00 a.m. Tuesday was her day off from running, but now, wide awake, she decided to alter her schedule. Maybe the fresh air would clear her head. The weather remained remarkably mild for November, and she hadn't yet retired to her treadmill.

Slipping out of her shorts and T-shirt, she pulled on a navy running suit and clipped her pager and cell phone to her waistline. She grabbed her keys and pepper spray and, after a swig of orange juice, headed out the door. The air had a wonderful fall scent, but instead of the invigoration Sydney usually felt, she experienced only a sadness. Mr. Lamb would never smell autumn air again. At least not on this earth.

Once back at her apartment, she showered, skipped the makeup, took advantage of the ponytail, and ate a quick bowl of cereal with fruit. She made it to the hospital by six-thirty and beelined to the ICU. Her general-ward patients would have to wait.

Like a permanent fixture, Crystal sat behind the desk, but her eyes weren't as sparkly today.

"Did you even see your call room last night?" Sydney asked.

"For about thirty minutes."

"You poor thing. I definitely don't miss those days."

Crystal rubbed her eyes and yawned. "Mr. Lamb's culture came back."

Sydney brightened. "When?"

"Just pulled it up on the computer five minutes ago."

"Well?"

"Influenza."

"Really?"

"Yep. But I don't understand this part." She handed Sydney a hard copy of the report.

Sydney frowned. "Influenza, type C?"

"Weird, isn't it? I didn't think influenza C was clinically relevant."

Sydney took a seat and pursed her lips. "It usually isn't. I can't believe the lab checked for it."

"Do you think it's a mistake?"

"I don't know. Influenza C *has* been cultured from people with the common cold, but I've never heard of it causing such significant disease. It could be a fluke, I suppose." She looked back up at Crystal. "Are you sure no other viruses were identified from his nasal aspirate? Metapneumovirus? Adenovirus? Coronavirus?"

"No, this was the only one."

"Strange." Sydney tapped the lab report against her palm.

"Maybe the guy had a cold, caused by Influenza C, but his real demise was from bacterial superinfection," Crystal offered.

"Maybe. But his sputum and blood cultures were negative for bacteria, right? And none of the antibiotics helped either."

"I know. It doesn't make sense. Plus, his immune work-up was normal, meaning he wasn't immunocompromised."

Sydney leaned back in her chair, trying to fit the pieces together.

"Why did his initial antigen test come back negative?" Crystal asked. "After all, he had influenza, just not the type we expected."

"The quick tests look for types A and B, not C. Besides, they're not a hundred percent accurate."

"What should we do?"

"Wait for the autopsy results, I guess. Maybe the pathologist will find some other infectious agent that the blood tests and nasal aspirate didn't pick up. In the meantime, I'll alert the health department. I'm sure the influenza C is a red herring, but an epidemiologist might find it interesting." Sydney wheeled her chair closer to the counter. Rubbing her neck, she added, "God, I hope I didn't miss anything."

"There's nothing you could have done. Nothing cures a virus."

Crystal's words reminded Sydney of Casper, and as she reached for the phone to page him, she imagined how surprised he'd be by the culture results.

Actually, he wasn't.

"But don't you think it's odd? Influenza C doesn't cause this type of illness."

"Hmm."

Sydney continued, perhaps hoping to create a spark. "I'm going to call an epidemiologist at the health department. The result might be reportable."

"Yes, you do that."

"Then again, it's not like a second case is likely to occur."

Another, "Hmm." Sydney wondered if Casper was paying attention. Then he said, "Will there be an autopsy?"

"I'm sure there will be. Why?"

"It would be nice to see a sample of his lung tissue, don't you think?"

After hanging up, Sydney flipped through the ward clerk's Rolodex to find the number for the health department. Not expecting to reach a human being so early, she entered the number in her cell phone for future reference and rounded on a few patients before going to morning report. Finally, at half past eight, she made the call. While on hold, she thought about Casper's nonchalant reaction to Mr. Lamb's culture result. The guy was a virologist. He should be salivating at anything new and unusual.

After a few more minutes of transfers and holdings, Sydney was connected to an epidemiologist. She'd expected voice mail, so she was surprised and pleased when Dr. Steinberg came on the line. Sydney had worked with her as a resident during a local meningococcemia outbreak. Abrupt and sharp, the woman had a strong Bronx accent acquired from her earlier days in New York.

Sydney identified herself and told Dr. Steinberg about Mr. Lamb's illness, as well as the unexpected influenza strain.

"Did you say influenza C?"

"Yes. I wasn't sure whether to report it or not."

"Probably a red herring."

"That's what I thought."

"Influenza C causes colds, not ass-kicking symptoms like those of your friend Mr. Lamb."

"I know. I'm sorry, maybe I shouldn't have bothered you."

"Bother schmother. Of course you should bother me. I'm not saying I'm not interested. I'm just saying influenza C is unlikely to do that. In fact, I don't think it's ever happened."

"Maybe our lab made a mistake."

"Yes, I'll definitely want a nasopharyngeal swab to repeat our own culture. What about vampire juice? Got any of that left over?"

Sydney assured her there should be several vials available—the poor man had blood drawn all night for various tests—and that she would have the lab send one out. Dr. Steinberg also asked to be kept abreast of the autopsy result and any other new developments.

Sydney thanked her for her help and finished by saying, "Whatever it was that caused this man's demise, it happened quickly. We certainly don't need any more cases like that."

"Well, that's the thing."

Sydney's shoulders tensed. "What's the thing?"

"Nothing else came up positive on this guy, right?"

"Right."

"No other virus, no bacteria, no fungus, no nothing."

"That's correct."

"Well, let's say—in a hypothetical situation, of course—that influenza C *was* the cause of this poor man's death."

"Okay…"

"Then we'd have one hell of a pisser on our hands."

"I'm sorry?"

"Think about it, Dr. McKnight. New influenza strain. A strain never linked to serious disease in the past. No effective vaccine." Sydney imagined Dr. Steinberg flipping up fingers as she went. "Does the Influenza Pandemic of 1918 ring any bells? And that was with a typical A strain."

Sydney closed her eyes. "Plenty of bells."

"We've all been waiting for the next pandemic—expecting it really—and a mysterious, non-vaccine preventable, new and unfamiliar strain of highly infectious influenza has all the makings of just such a nasty and horrific event. And it… Well, really, need I say more?"

The chill in the epidemiologist's voice sparked a shiver down Sydney's spine.

No. No, you most certainly need not.

3

The day was long.

The night would prove longer.

Sydney finally left the hospital at 7:00 p.m. and, considering her poor sleep on call the night before, she was exhausted. Perhaps she should've skipped the morning run after all.

She pulled into her apartment building's lot only to find her personal parking space occupied by a beat-up Ford Escort. Her chest tightened, anger bubbling up inside her. She considered waiting outside for the offender, but soon fatigue took over, and she settled for a spot two blocks away. Clutching her keys, she locked her Jeep and marched down the dark and sparsely populated sidewalk, each step more agitated than the last. Cigarette smoke wafted from a nearby apartment window, and somewhere down the block, a dog barked until a sharp word from its owner silenced its yapping.

When Sydney reached her brick, multi-unit complex, she discovered Mitch Price waiting outside the door, a dopey grin on his face. The first inklings of a headache materialized, and she massaged her forehead to soothe it.

Mitch was what most people would call Sydney's

boyfriend, though she didn't see it that way. To her they were two doctors passing time during their residencies and now fellowships, she in infectious disease, he in pulmonary medicine. Sydney had assumed Mitch saw their relationship that way as well, but lately she worried he sought more.

"Mitch, what are you doing here?"

"And hello to you too, princess."

"Don't call me that. You know I hate it."

"Wow, someone's in a good mood."

"Sorry. Long day."

"Yeah, I heard about the patient in the ICU. Weird."

"Word travels fast."

"Hey, I'm a pulmonologist. It's my job to know about lungs."

Sydney let them into the building and then to her apartment a few feet down the hallway. She flipped on the light and waited for Mitch to enter. As she hung her jacket and purse on the wrought-iron coat rack behind the door, she decided maybe it wasn't so bad having him there after all. She could get his opinion on Mr. Lamb.

Making her way to the kitchen, she asked, "What do you think happened to his lungs? ARDS? Bacterial pneumonia?"

Mitch shrugged and plopped himself onto Sydney's new couch, his artificial leg striking the glass coffee table in the process. The prosthetic was a gift from his childhood, a result of a bone-destroying tumor in his femur, and although he'd had the thing since the age of twelve and was completely adapted to its titanium presence, Sydney felt bad for him. She knew that was irrational—stupid, even—considering he managed fine with the substitute limb. Still, it was always there between them. Or not there, she supposed, for those occasions calling for its removal.

And there it was now, up on her light-colored couch along with his shoes—soiled shoes dotted by dirt and pebbles. Sydney opened her mouth to object but then hesitated.

Although not much for material possessions, she'd taken care to make her apartment stylish and clean, filling it with contemporary furniture and modern artwork. Her favorite piece, a twisting black and white sculpture she'd purchased from the Museum of Modern Art in New York, adorned a corner of the living room, and although its meaning remained lost on her, it made for a great display. After the homes she grew up in, she craved pretty surroundings and strived to make the apartment a space she could be proud of, pint-sized or not.

Finally, compulsiveness got the best of her. "Um, would you mind slipping off your shoes?"

"Oh, sorry." Off came the shoes. "As for your question about what happened to that patient, I'm not sure, but if I had to guess, I'd say ARDS. He was on enough antibacterials to cover pneumonia. He wasn't immunocompromised, was he?"

"No."

"Diabetic?"

"No."

"Then maybe just a nasty flu strain and a boatload of bad luck."

Sydney figured he was probably right. She grabbed a couple of Heinekens from the fridge and joined him on the couch, squeezing into the only space his body didn't occupy. "It's sad. He was only fifty-one."

"Wife?"

Sydney nodded.

"You can't cure everyone."

"I know."

They sipped in silence for a moment, and then Mitch said, "I paged you twice today. Why didn't you answer? I used our code so you'd know it was me."

Sydney's bottle halted halfway to her lips. "Sorry, just

busy." She rose from the couch. "Hey, I'm hungry. How about you?"

"I grabbed a slice of pizza on the way here. Sorry, should've brought you one."

Sydney returned to the kitchen to make herself a sandwich. It didn't take long before Mitch dove into his research, a topic Sydney seemed to know more about than her own. She spent the next ten minutes chewing wheat bread and turkey, while hearing everything she never wanted to know about cystic fibrosis obstructive lung disease. She supposed she should pay more attention. He was likely to make a big discovery someday.

She watched him reposition his glasses and take a deep breath, ready to begin the next discourse. Before he had a chance, she shimmied over to the couch and brought the subject back to Mr. Lamb.

"I called an epidemiologist, you know."

Mitch looked at her, his lips parted and his eyebrows raised, as if trying to shift conversational gears. "Oh?"

"She was very interested. In fact, she called me back this afternoon. Said she's investigating whether there have been any recent unexplained viral-type deaths among otherwise healthy people, either here in Massachusetts—particularly Seneca where Mr. Lamb was from—or in the Kenyan village he recently visited, although that could prove more difficult."

"She really thinks influenza C was the cause?"

"No, but in the unlikely event it was, she wants to be prepared. She's requested Mr. Lamb's autopsy report and has promised to keep me posted."

"Hmm."

Sydney leaned forward on the sofa and rested her elbows on her knees. "It's going to be challenging. The guy's been all over, including airports. Who knows if we'll ever identify the source?"

"Hey, it's not your problem." Mitch's voice grew soft and

dreamy, and he buried his nose in her hair. His hand found her thigh.

"What do you mean, not my problem? Of course, it's my problem. I'm an infectious disease fellow."

Mitch's nose brushed her ear, his breath hot on her skin. "I mean, it's not your problem *tonight*."

He kissed Sydney's neck, one hand teasing her ponytail, the other sliding up her thigh and onto her belly, where it soon landed inside her sweater.

She held her breath, wanting to remove his hand. She knew his actions were understandable, considering they hadn't been together for the past ten days other than a few lunches at the hospital. Still, her own interest level was low. It had been over six months since she'd finally relented to their first date—persistence was definitely his strong point—and at the time, none of the other female residents could understand her hesitancy. He was attractive, smart, nice. Yet as the dates wore on, Sydney realized there wasn't any spark, and she found herself hanging in for the companionship. Over the past month, she knew she should break it off, especially now that Mitch sought more than she had to offer. It was only fair. But given their schedules, they hardly saw each other—their six months of dating were more like two to normal people— and she would always lose the nerve, fearful of hurting his feelings.

His hand crept higher. Sydney exhaled slowly, arms still at her side, unable to reciprocate. Her inactivity did little to quell him, and soon his fingers grazed her breast and cupped it, and his lips were on her own.

She swallowed a lump of refluxing sandwich. "Mitch, um, I'm—"

"I know, I know," he panted, his lips pressed against her skin.

"No, I mean, I'm not really—"

Sydney was interrupted again, this time by her pager, and

she'd never been so happy to hear its obnoxious beep. She jumped off the couch to answer it.

"Oh man, Syd, come on. It can wait. You're not even on call."

"No, I should answer. Might be important."

It was Liz, her tone unusually somber. Sydney cradled the cordless phone against her ear and struggled to refasten the bra Mitch had managed to unclasp.

"We've had two admits tonight, both with fever, cough, and respiratory distress, similar to your patient with influenza C. And that's not the worst part."

"Oh?" Sydney's pulse quickened.

"One of them is Mr. Lamb's wife."

Sydney sank back down to the couch, ignoring Mitch's questioning gaze. "Who's the other?"

"A twenty-five-year-old medical student."

"He works at the hospital?"

"Yes, but not right now. He's currently doing a rotation in an outpatient clinic. The same clinic Mr. Lamb visited four days ago."

"Oh, God," was all Sydney could think of to say.

"You're sure this was influenza C?" Liz asked.

For a moment, Sydney couldn't answer, every hair follicle on her skin prickling with anxiety. Finally, she said, "According to the lab report, it was. The epidemiologist is running a confirmation test."

"Weird. Influenza C doesn't do this kind of thing. Must be a mistake."

"Probably. But that's not really what bothers me."

"What does?"

Sydney paused and, out of habit, slid her fingers down the back of her neck and found the dime-sized mole that lived there, the one she'd had since birth, the one she kept hidden with turtlenecks, collars, and hair. "What bothers me is that Mr. Lamb died within eight days of the first sneeze."

"Might just be him. Doesn't mean the virus will be as severe in the others."

"Maybe." Sydney's tone didn't carry much conviction. She stood and sought out her jacket and purse. "I'm coming in."

"Don't be ridiculous. You were up half the night on call. I've got things under control. I only called to keep you informed."

"I have no doubt you have things under control. You probably have them both cured by now. But I feel like I should. I owe it to Mrs. Lamb."

Liz continued to protest, but at some point she must've realized Sydney wasn't budging, and the objections ceased. Sydney told her she'd meet her on the ward in thirty minutes. As she replaced the phone on its cradle, Mitch frowned.

"What are you doing?" he asked, as if Sydney had just planned a fun-filled trip to Disney World rather than the hospital.

"I'm going in."

"Well, I can see that, but why? Liz is on call, not you."

Sydney pressed her lips together and planted both hands on her hips. "A man died from a rare strain of influenza, one that in no way should do what it did. He was my consult. Now there are two more. If the same thing happened to your cystic fibrosis patients, you'd be hitting the pavement quicker than rain."

"I suppose," he said, apparently seeing her logic but still disappointed.

"I'm sorry. Some other time, okay?" *You've got to tell him, Sydney.*

Mitch sighed, stood up, and came toward her for a kiss. He grabbed his own jacket and headed for the door. "Aren't you coming?"

"I will in a second. I think I should call Dr. Jones first."

"That the new guy?"

"Yeah."

"How's he working out?"

"Okay, I guess." Sydney was still a little foggy on that herself.

After Mitch left, Sydney turned the phone back on and pulled Casper's number from her purse. Even though Dr. DeWitt was on service, Casper had made it clear he wanted to be kept in the loop. She dialed the number, and he answered almost immediately.

Sydney relayed what Liz had told her. When she finished, her attending said, "Interesting."

"Scary was the word that came to my mind."

"I'll see you there."

"What? You're coming in?"

"Of course."

"But Dr. DeWitt is on service. You certainly don't need to."

"And neither do you."

Sydney didn't know what to say. His decision to go to the hospital and see the new patients contradicted his laissez-faire attitude about their disease.

"No. I guess you're right." After a pause, she added, "But I have this terrible habit of putting my nose where it doesn't belong."

4

On the drive to the hospital, Sydney wondered if going in was such a good idea after all. Fatigue consumed her. What could she do differently than Liz? But despite her physical exhaustion, her neurons sparked with curiosity, and the thought of two new patients with the same virus as Mr. Lamb made remaining at home impossible.

She parked the Jeep in the employee ramp, scoring a spot right next to the connecting skywalk. She hustled toward the entrance and nearly plowed into a man loitering nearby. Alarmed, her safety feelers pricked up, but the man, wearing white scrubs beneath a black leather jacket, seemed disinterested and turned away. Sydney rushed past him and hurried over to the main hospital building, making a quick stop in the cafeteria for a cup of coffee before entering the stairwell to access 3 North. As she rounded the final flight of stairs, she heard voices. Looking up, she was surprised to find Casper, along with the man she'd seen in the parking ramp, standing near the stairwell door.

"Remember what you're here for," the man said to Casper. "There's no time to—"

Casper spotted Sydney, his startled expression cutting the

man off mid-sentence. For a moment, the three of them stared at each other in silence.

Casper cleared his throat. "Sydney, glad you're here. I was just about to see the new patients."

Sydney looked at Casper and then his companion. As she'd noticed in the parking lot, the man wore white scrubs, like those of the orderlies, but until tonight she'd never seen him. He was an inch or two shorter than Casper but equally solid and handsome, and he had that same light brown skin. If it weren't for the longer hair and absent dimples, Sydney would've thought the two men were related.

She dropped her eyes to the man's chest and found an orderly's ID badge. She extended her hand. "Hi, I'm Sydney McKnight. I don't think we've met. Are you new?"

Sydney's gesture spurred the stranger into action. Face warming, he shook her hand. "Yes. I'm Jackson Bryant. Just started a couple of days ago. Dr. Jones here is giving me some tips."

Casper nodded, his own smile forced, not his usual butter-melting beam.

"Giving you tips? In the stairwell?"

They chuckled, Casper adjusting his tie and Jackson rubbing his chin.

Casper said, "Just ran into him on the way to the ward. I wanted to review our respiratory isolation precautions, particularly in regard to these new patients."

"Yes, and thank you, by the way." Jackson started down the stairs. "Nice meeting you, Dr. McKnight. I better get back to work now."

Sydney's gaze followed him, and she wondered why she hadn't encountered him in the hospital. Then again, he was only recently employed. "How did he know I was a doctor?"

"He's probably seen you on the ward."

"I haven't seen him."

"Well, doctors tend to be ignorant of what goes on around them, right?"

"What did he mean—"

Casper had already opened the door and stepped into the hallway leading to 3 North. "Come on. They're probably waiting for us."

Sydney nodded, still staring at the empty stairwell. After another sip of coffee, she climbed the last few steps to join Casper. Before she could take another stab at her question about Jackson, Casper launched into a discussion of the patients. She was relieved by his revived interest.

When they reached the ward's front counter, located midway down the carpeted hallway in the newer wing of the hospital, a subdued group greeted them: Liz, two female nurses, a resident, and a medical student, the latter two of whom were male. A ward clerk perched nearby as well, but other than her phone chatter and an incoming fax, the station was unusually quiet. Liz looked up from a chart, her eyeglasses smeared and her hair a curly mess. When she saw Casper, she straightened and began cleaning her lenses. In fact, everyone seemed to straighten for the man. Even the guys. With Casper decked out in his usual crisp suit, the rest of the crew resembled misfits in jeans or scrubs.

"So, what's the news?" Sydney asked, annoyed to find herself running a hand over her ponytail.

"It's not great." Liz pulled her chair closer to the desk. Sydney joined her, and the two women scanned the lab reports. "Mrs. Lamb's blood gas shows signs of respiratory failure, which is consistent with her clinical status. She's on high amounts of oxygen and is starting to tire."

"What about the medical student?"

"He's not as bad off, at least not yet. He's on room air but complains of chest pain with the cough. His name is Chip Reynolds. I'll let Terry give you the details."

Terry was the fourth-year medical student on duty. He was

taking an elective in infectious disease and probably questioning his choice of rotation right about now.

Everyone turned to face him, their chair wheels chafing against the carpet. Terry's face reddened from the sudden attention. Still, his presentation was swift and efficient. Sydney learned that Mrs. Lamb had been ill for three to four days, initially with a cough and sniffles but then with fever, chills, and weakness. The fever spiked higher yesterday afternoon—Sydney suspected that was probably shortly after she'd seen the woman—and Mrs. Lamb's symptoms took a dramatic turn for the worse, at which point family members insisted she visit the emergency room. She went in earlier today, only hours after her husband had died. She required oxygen and was promptly admitted. Over the last few hours, she'd worsened even more.

Hearing the report, Sydney felt ill herself. She'd interviewed Mrs. Lamb yesterday afternoon. She'd noticed her coughing. Mrs. Lamb had blamed it on allergies.

Sydney berated herself for not doing something more at the time. Why hadn't she insisted Mrs. Lamb get checked out? What kind of doctor was she?

A little voice told her to chill. They didn't even know what her husband had at the time. There was no way to predict the outcome.

Crap.

Sydney tuned back in to hear about Chip Reynolds, the unfortunate med student who evaluated Mr. Lamb in clinic four days ago. He'd been ill for about twenty-four hours, making the incubation period of the virus as short as two to three days, certainly consistent with influenza. His clinical history matched the others, only his symptoms were milder, and his blood oxygen level remained high. The only reason he'd been admitted was because of his association with Mr. Lamb. Otherwise, the ER doctor would have sent him home.

"How did Chip Reynolds make the connection to Mr.

Lamb so quickly?" Sydney asked Terry. "He sees sick patients all day long. He could've just caught a cold. What made him think to go to the emergency room rather than sleeping it off?"

"That's probably what he would have done, but he's working with Dr. Denver, the Lamb's family physician. Dr. Denver received news of Mr. Lamb's death this morning. He knew Chip was suffering from a cold, so he urged the student to get evaluated."

"Bet the poor kid almost messed his pants," the resident said, shaking his head.

They all sat in silence for a moment, absorbing the new information and its significance. The nurses had gone back to their charting, but Sydney could tell they were listening.

Liz, ever the optimistic infectious disease fellow, chimed in. "Hey guys, before we declare Armageddon, let's look at the facts."

"Which are?"

She crossed her arms over her scrubs and leaned back in the chair. "Mr. Lamb had an unusual strain of influenza, one that doesn't normally cause significant disease. Even if Mrs. Lamb did catch it, it's likely the virus would end with the two of them. For all we know, Chip Reynolds is spending the night in the hospital for nothing more than a bad cold."

"But if it is the same virus?"

"Even if it is, it doesn't mean Chip's course, or even Mrs. Lamb's course for that matter, will be the same. They both might recover fine. You can't calculate a mortality rate based on one patient."

"No, you can't, but if it turns out it *is* the same virus, one that's highly contagious and lethal, well…" Sydney didn't finish the sentence, the implication clear. "Has everyone been practicing careful precautions with these patients—gloves, masks, gowns if necessary?"

Everybody nodded, at which time Casper spoke up, startling them with his tone. "She's right. We all need to be meticulous, extremely meticulous, around these patients. It's important we act as if each encounter is a potentially life-threatening event." He smacked the counter with his palm for emphasis.

Sydney had never seen him so intense—jaw rigid, nostrils flared. He looked at each of them in turn, holding their gazes for a few nerve-racking seconds.

"And we need to make sure the nurses know this as well. And the phlebotomists, and the respiratory therapists, and anyone else who enters these rooms."

At the mention of nurses, Kyra Washington, Sydney's favorite RN and another name on her rather meager friendship list, strolled up to the counter. "We have both patients in negative pressure isolation rooms."

"Absolutely, and anyone else who comes in with similar symptoms will need the same." Casper scanned the group again. He plucked the stethoscope hanging around the student's neck and gripped it in his hand. "And absolutely no sharing of these. Make sure the exam equipment in each room stays put. Everybody understand?"

Everyone nodded. No one would have dared dispute him.

"Sydney?" Casper's voice was less stern now. "Why don't you call the epidemiologist and update her on the new patients."

Sydney nodded and reached for the phone to page Dr. Steinberg. While she waited for the epidemiologist to respond, she listened to Casper and Liz discuss their treatment plan with Kyra. The resident and student remained nearby. Liz asked about their other attending physician, Dr. DeWitt, but Casper assured her he'd be taking all the new patients with these symptoms, at least for now, and that Dr. DeWitt had readily agreed, given his familiarity with the first case.

Dr. Steinberg returned Sydney's page within five minutes.

Apparently, she wasn't taking the night off either. Sydney told her about the latest admissions.

When Sydney finished, the epidemiologist said, "This isn't good, Dr. McKnight."

"No, it isn't."

"You sure Chip Reynolds was linked to Mr. Lamb?"

"Yes."

"What about their influenza antigen tests?"

"Negative, like Mr. Lamb's, but viral cultures are pending."

"Make sure the lab specifically checks for influenza C again, and please send me blood and nasal samples from both patients."

Sydney assured her she would and then listened as Dr. Steinberg reviewed all the same infectious disease precautions Casper had just stressed. "Influenza can be an airborne disease. If we have some deadly new strain circulating, we need to be exceedingly careful."

"I'm well aware of that." Sydney's dread mounted.

The two physicians fell quiet, neither wanting to verbalize what the other must surely be thinking.

Finally, Dr. Steinberg broke the silence. "Mr. Lamb had been all over, most notably from Nairobi to London to Boston. On airplanes. In airports. All the while he was coughing, potentially spreading the virus. Plus, you tell me Mrs. Lamb is a schoolteacher. Let's hope she wasn't symptomatic the last time she was in class." Dr. Steinberg started thinking aloud. "Let's see, today is Tuesday. She was at the hospital with her husband yesterday. Her symptoms started Saturday. So, if she hasn't been to class since Friday, we might be okay."

"Um, Dr. Steinberg?"

"Yes?"

"The resident caring for Mrs. Lamb learned there was an open house at her school on Saturday. Hundreds of elementary students and their families were there. So was Mrs. Lamb."

A long pause followed. Kyra must have seen the apprehension on Sydney's face, because she edged up behind her and gave her a little hug, a collection of gold bangles jangling against her dark skin. Although the nurse had no way of knowing the conversation on the other end of the line, Sydney's tensed shoulders likely told her all she needed to know.

Finally, the esteemed epidemiologist spoke. "Shit," was all she managed to say.

Dr. Steinberg finished their conversation by promising to alert all Massachusetts hospitals, clinics, and emergency rooms. She would also call the Centers for Disease Control and Prevention.

"Do you think calling the CDC is premature?" Sydney's throat was thick and dry.

"After what happened with SARS? No way."

Sydney hung up the phone and massaged her temples, the temporary soothing from Kyra now gone, the nurse called away to attend to a patient. It was almost 9:40 p.m., and Sydney's body was exhausted. Unfortunately, her mind still fired like an M-16.

She turned to Liz and Casper, who had moved onto a different discussion, and filled them in on the phone call. Sydney asked Casper which patient he wanted to see first.

He stared at her for a moment. "Oh…well…I'm sure Liz has already examined them." He began rummaging through lab sheets.

Sydney gave Liz a funny look, but Liz held up her hands as if to say *Don't ask me.*

Sydney tried again. "But Dr. Jones, every patient needs an attending note, and I'd like a baseline exam myself."

Casper opened Chip Reynolds's chart and flipped through its contents, making Sydney wonder if he'd even heard her.

After a long pause, he put the chart back on the desk and sighed. "Okay, then. Why don't we start with the medical student?"

Casper followed Sydney to room 328, where each of them pulled a long, yellow gown from a cart by the door and slipped it on. Casper's fit snug over his suit, while Sydney's was loose and awkward. Next came blue respiratory masks, followed by gloves.

Casper pushed open the door. "After you."

It took only a few minutes to understand why Casper had chosen the research tract over the clinical and why he seemed reluctant to see patients. His bedside manner was below par. He'd barely said two words to Chip Reynolds, a strawberry-blond kid with a giant medical textbook open in his lap. The poor guy was probably boning up on influenza in between coughing fits. Casper's technique didn't improve in Mrs. Lamb's room either.

Liz was waiting at the front counter when Casper and Sydney returned. She asked if they'd learned anything new.

Sydney shook her head. "Guess there's nothing left to do but wait."

"Go home," Liz said to her. "You look tired."

"I don't know. Maybe I better stick around."

"You'll be on call again before you know it. More patients like this might come in. If you don't get sleep, you won't be helping anyone."

Sydney nodded and attempted a smile. Liz was right. She was always right.

After a quick goodbye, Sydney headed down the hallway, its freshly renovated walls adorned with paintings by local artists. The rest of the group had already dispersed, including Casper, who lingered near the water fountain halfway down the corridor. He didn't drink from it, just turned it on and off like a toddler unable to restrain himself. When Sydney approached, he looked at her and frowned.

"Why would anyone drink from these things? They're an infectious disease waiting to happen." He continued flipping.

"Well, you're not supposed to plant your lips on the thing. Just lean over the stream, grab your drink, and go. What, no water fountains in New York?"

Casper smiled, his dimpled visage more suitable for television than the hospital. "Speaking of drinks, why don't we go to the cafeteria for a soda?"

"A soda? Now?"

"We can discuss the patients in more detail. Merge our brains and map out a plan in case of an epidemic."

Sydney hesitated, thinking it best she go home. Liz was right. She needed sleep. But how does one say "no" to a research attending? Sydney didn't want him calling her a slacker. "Sure, okay."

"Good." Matter settled, Casper headed off down the hallway.

Five minutes later they were seated in the cafeteria—closed except for the vending machines—drinking caffeine-free diet soda. While Sydney sipped, Casper guzzled, like a man stranded at sea. Not until he'd nearly finished the can did he make eye contact with her. He smacked his lips and smiled but said nothing, making Sydney squirm in her seat.

"Um, Dr. Jones—"

"Casper."

"Oh. Right. It's much easier to call you that in my head than out loud."

He shrugged. "It's my name."

"Where does it come from, anyway?"

He hesitated for a moment. "Old family name."

"It's very unique."

More silence. Sydney decided to get back to the patients. "So, do you think Chip Reynolds has the same virus as the Lambs—"

"Why medical school?"

"Pardon me?"

"Why did you choose to go to medical school?"

"I thought we were going to discuss the patients."

"We will, but I'm curious about you."

Sydney raised her eyebrows. He was curious about her? She wasn't the one making love to a soda or fondling water fountains.

"Look, if we're going to work together, I feel you should bulb me a bit on your background."

Sydney narrowed her eyes at his word choice, but before she could inquire, he repeated his earlier question. "Why medical school?"

Sydney shrugged. "I guess the expected response is that I dreamed of being a doctor ever since I was a little girl."

"And did you?"

"No."

"What did you dream about?"

"Surviving."

"I'm sorry to hear that."

"Why?"

"Seems like such a waste of a childhood."

Sydney took a drink of soda. "I suppose it was, but I brought it on myself."

"Oh, I doubt that."

"No, I was pretty wild."

"Wild? How so? Were you cruel to your parents?"

"Okay, getting back to Chip Reynolds. Do you think—"

"Sydney, I don't mean to make you uncomfortable." Casper peered at her so intently she had to look away. "I just want to understand...learn more about you."

"Why?"

"I guess, to quote you, I like sticking my nose in places it doesn't belong."

"Lucky me."

"So, what happens to make a child turn 'wild'? Was it your father?"

"Never met the guy."

"Really?" Casper seemed surprised.

"Don't suppose my mother even knew his name."

"Oh, you mean like a sperm lender?"

Sydney barked a laugh. "No, like a mother too wasted on drugs to remember who she slept with."

"Oh." Casper didn't look horrified, merely curious. He slipped off his suit jacket and draped it over an empty chair. "And what about your mother now? Do you two get along?"

"My mother died when I was eleven. Heroin overdose."

"I'm sorry."

Sydney plucked the tab off her soda can. "History."

"Who raised you then?"

"Foster parents. A fabulous slew of them."

Casper frowned. "Foster parents?"

"You going to tell me you don't know what they are either?"

He sat up straighter. "No, of course not, but why so many?"

"Because I was hell on wheels. Truancy, shoplifting, tattoos, you name it."

"Well, how did you end up a doctor? You must've had *some* positive role model."

"Me, myself, and I."

Casper looked confused, but Sydney didn't clarify. Nobody knew about her time in juvie, and she intended to keep it that way. In reality, it was a blessing. Scared her straight and landed her once and for all with a decent foster family, one that made sure she finished school with a vision in mind. Now at thirty-one, she barely recognized that girl, though some traits never wiped clean.

"You must have worked hard—and been very brave."

Sydney swallowed. "Look, Dr. Jones, I better go."

"Please. It's Casper, remember?"

Before Sydney could say anything else, a faint beeping sounded. Her hand automatically flew to her pager, but its display was blank. "Do you hear—"

Sydney didn't get a chance to finish, because Casper excused himself and hurried off to the bathroom. She sat there, looking around. After a few minutes, she grabbed her purse and was about to leave, when Casper returned, looking a little sheepish.

"I'm sorry, I didn't mean to rush off like that."

"What was that about?"

Casper hesitated. "I had to check my blood sugar."

"You're diabetic?" The fact he had the disease didn't surprise Sydney as much as the fact he'd divulged it, the tidbit being the first personal piece of information she'd learned about the man.

"Since the age of five."

"Wow. Must've been terrible having a childhood filled with shots."

"Oh?"

"Your insulin injections. Not to mention all those finger pricks."

"Oh, yes, right. Not a lot of fun."

Casper seemed uncomfortable, as if the topic embarrassed him, so Sydney decided she'd better change the subject.

Sure, fine to talk about foster care and tattoos, but leave the old diabetes alone.

They finally got around to discussing the patients but covered no new ground. Sydney suspected the whole cafeteria rendezvous was a ruse to get her to reveal her past, though why, she had no idea. One would think she was as fascinating as a woman who'd circled the earth in a flying teacup.

When eleven-thirty rolled around, she stood to leave. Gathering her purse, she said goodbye, but Casper insisted on walking her to her car. On the way, they spoke little, and it wasn't until she'd climbed into her Jeep that he said her name.

She closed the car door and rolled down the window. "Yes?"

"Be careful with this virus, okay? More careful than you've ever been before."

Sydney's stomach tensed. "What do you mean?"

Casper slipped his hands in his pockets. "Just watch yourself, that's all."

With that he walked away, leaving Sydney even more confused and unsettled than before. His words replayed in her brain the entire drive home, and by the time she entered her apartment, her head spun and she felt an alarm out of proportion to the night's events. She decided sleep would be her best medicine, and after a quick cleanup, she collapsed into bed. She'd barely closed her eyes when her pager went off.

Groaning, she pulled herself up and checked the number. Unfamiliar. She debated whether to answer but knew she'd never get to sleep if she didn't. Maybe it was Casper. Maybe he'd forgotten to tell her something.

She found the phone and dialed the number. Dr. Steinberg answered.

"Dr. McKnight, sorry to bother you so late, but I thought you should know."

Sydney was beginning to hate those words. "Know what?"

"I spent the evening alerting state medical facilities. They've all been told what to look for. Unfortunately, I've already received a call." Dr. Steinberg hesitated, as if reluctant to continue.

"From whom?"

Sydney heard Dr. Steinberg take a deep breath and then exhale loudly.

"The children's hospital," she said. "There are two possible cases at the goddamn children's hospital."

5

––––––––––

Three feet away Dr. Peyton's secretary sighed and frowned, her fourth cycle of each. Leaning against the wall, Sydney refused to let it bother her. If the pathologist wouldn't return her pages, she'd come to his office and find him in person, even if it meant lurking near his secretary's desk in the vestibule like a stalker.

The pathologist was known for his eccentricities, from riding a moped in winter to garnishing every meal with alfalfa sprouts, but he was equally well known for his proclivity for a certain four o'clock news program, and that meant he should arrive shortly. Sydney supposed being head of a department had its advantages.

She knew Dr. Peyton had performed Mr. Lamb's autopsy that morning, and she was itching to know the results, even if they were preliminary. She prayed Dr. Peyton had discovered something to shed light on the devastating new virus. She felt justified using the word "devastating," because that's what it was. She didn't care that n equaled only a few cases. In her own personal research study, the small sample size was suffi-cient to reach a conclusion: the virus was bad news.

Not only had Mrs. Lamb required a ventilator last night,

Chip, the medical student, seemed close to follow. The two kids at the children's hospital were equally ill. By last report, one was struggling in the pediatric ICU on a respirator, and the other was requiring four liters of oxygen and tiring quickly. It didn't take Dr. Steinberg long to learn both children were fourth-grade students of Mrs. Lamb's. It also didn't take long for her to receive four e-mail responses from worried local physicians, all of whom had treated patients with the exact symptoms listed in the previous night's electronic medical alert. The first two were seen in a competing hospital's ER and admitted. The third was an elderly man sent to the VA hospital, and the fourth was another child admitted to the children's hospital yesterday, where doctors discovered she was a cousin of one of Mrs. Lamb's students. A link between the other three had yet to be determined.

In the meantime, Dr. Burke, the director of the infectious disease department, put Casper and Sydney in charge of monitoring the cases. They were to act as a contact source for all other medical personnel, including Dr. Steinberg as well as the investigators from the CDC, who were scheduled to arrive tomorrow. And, of course, influenza C, or whatever the virus turned out to be, would be their new focus now. No West Nile virus for the time being.

Sydney checked her watch and stood straighter against the wall. It was two minutes before four. Dr. Peyton would be there soon. The helmet-haired secretary gave another troubled sigh, and Sydney fought the urge to be rude.

Finally, with one minute to spare before his beloved news show, Dr. Peyton arrived, all hundred and twenty pounds of him, dressed in a plaid sport coat and red bow tie, his thinning hair attempting the classic yet never acceptable comb-over.

He gave a start when he saw Sydney. "Dr. McKnight. To what do I owe this honor?" He eyed the clock hanging above his faithful sentinel's head and frowned.

"I won't take much of your time, Dr. Peyton, but I need

information on Mr. Lamb. I paged you three times and left messages with your secretary, but I didn't hear back. It's really important."

The pathologist let Sydney into his office but made no attempt to disguise the fact that her visit was of great inconvenience. "I have little to tell you. I need to review the slides as well as the blood tests. These things take time, you know."

"Time isn't exactly on our side. We might be at the start of the next SARS storm."

"I thought Mr. Lamb had influenza."

"I was being metaphorical."

"Well, for influenza, it's the worst lung involvement I've ever seen."

"Meaning?" Sydney asked impatiently. Maybe too forcefully as well.

Dr. Peyton shot her a look, and she realized she'd better be careful. He took a seat behind his immaculate desk, posture straight, hands folded in front of him. "The lungs were completely destroyed."

"What do you mean?"

"Well—and remember, this is only the gross tissue I can comment on. We'll have to wait for the microscopic exam."

Sydney shifted her feet, not having been invited to sit down.

"For the sake of description, I'd say his lungs looked like beet soup. Some areas were relatively maintained, others were lobulated chunks of tissue, and some were almost liquid in nature. I've never seen anything like it. Not influenza, not SARS, not anything."

"But that doesn't make sense. How could a virus cause such significant macroscopic damage?"

"Beats me, but it's the worst destruction I've ever seen. No wonder the patient died. There aren't enough ventilators or oxygen in the world to aerate those lungs."

Alarmed, Sydney gaped at the pathologist, while he simply glanced at his watch. "Was there anything else?"

"But…well…there are still so many unanswered questions."

"And they'll have to wait until the microscopic samples are ready. Maybe even then we won't get answers, at least not the ones we want."

Sydney shook her head. What kind of virus could wreak so much damage in such a short time? "Do you think it's hemorrhagic disease?"

"Again, I need the microscopic evidence, but it seems unlikely considering only the lungs were involved. Other than damage from lack of oxygen, all the other organs were intact."

"Unbelievable." Sydney crossed her arms over her abdomen, as if giving her lower torso a hug.

"I'll keep you posted," Dr. Peyton said.

Sydney stood motionless a few seconds longer, but then, sensing her dismissal, she nodded and left. It didn't compute. Influenza didn't cause such gross destruction of the lungs. But unless it was a mistake, Mr. Lamb's culture *had* confirmed influenza C. She hoped the other patients' cultures would soon be available, because then the medical providers would know better what they faced.

Before heading back to the ward to update Casper on the autopsy results, Sydney opted to visit the morgue and see the tissue herself. The death motel was her least favorite place, but it would be helpful to witness Mr. Lamb's pulmonary destruction firsthand. She hadn't been there for over a year, not since she observed the autopsy of a young patient with Epstein-Barr virus who'd died unexpectedly during her shift, but she knew some of the residents and figured they'd allow her a peek.

She wasn't disappointed. Mekhi Tresner, a third-year pathology resident, had just exited the area but graciously escorted her back to the room where Mr. Lamb's organ samples were being prepared for both gross and microscopic evaluation.

"I've never seen anything like it." Mekhi's words echoed Dr. Peyton's earlier comment.

The resident donned a pair of gloves and a respiratory mask and handed Sydney the same. Then he brought over a small section of lung and plopped it on the counter in front of them.

"You see here?" He pointed to an area on the left. "That's about the only normal tissue we could find in this section. The rest is broken down, almost liquefied in nature."

Studying the burgundy, pulpy mess, Sydney had to agree. She remembered what healthy lungs looked like from medical school: pink, aerated, lobular. Mr. Lamb's lungs were none of those things.

"Have you guys found an organism? Other than influenza C, I mean?" Mekhi asked.

"No. So far that's all we've got."

The resident shook his head. "Influenza doesn't do this."

"Tell me about it. Burke's scheduled a six o'clock meeting tonight for the infectious disease staff. Maybe someone will have an idea."

Mekhi continued to poke and prod, and after a few more minutes of watching, Sydney had had enough. She thanked him, made him promise to page her with anything new—figuring his bow-tied attending wouldn't remember to—and bolted out of the cold, depressing dungeon. Or at least that's the way it felt to her, and the fact that she'd just seen the soupy lungs of a man she'd met only two days before didn't make the place any easier to warm up to. A man who up until a short time ago was living, breathing, walking, and talking.

Weary and disheartened, Sydney stopped in the cafeteria for a shot of caffeine. As an afterthought, she grabbed a can of soda for Casper, who'd apparently just discovered diet root beer. Once back on 3 North, she started the search for him.

Instead, she found Kyra, dressed in her usual colorful scrub top, along with two other nurses and a ward clerk.

Kyra smiled when Sydney approached. "How are you holding up?" she asked.

"I'm all right. More importantly, how is Chip Reynolds? You're his nurse this shift, right?"

Kyra's smile faded. "He's not doing too well. I was telling the resident I think he might be ready for the ICU."

"Damn it." Sydney sank into a chair behind the desk and opened her soda, its pent-up hiss matching her frustration. She grabbed Chip Reynolds's chart and looked over his vitals.

Kyra reached over Sydney's shoulder and pointed to the patient's oxygen saturation levels. "See? I can't keep his sats up, no matter how much oxygen he's on. He does okay for a while, but then the numbers dip down again."

"How does he look?" Sydney asked, remembering what she always told her students: Don't treat the numbers, treat the patient.

"Not good."

So much for her adage.

"He's trying to put up a tough front, but he's working hard to breathe and complaining of a lot of chest pain. His cough keeps getting worse too."

Sydney rubbed her sore neck for a few moments and then stood. "I'll go see him."

After the tedious process of gowning, gloving, and masking, she entered the room and found Chip asleep, his chest muscles retracting with every breath and the hollow of his neck caving in and out. A stethoscope dangled from his IV pump. She cleaned it and placed it on the flimsy hospital gown covering his chest. Nothing but coarse rhonchi, wheezes, and crackles came back to her. In less than twenty-four hours, Chip had gone from a relatively normal lung exam to a man in need of a ventilator. She replaced the stethoscope and stepped away from the bed, discarding her precautionary yellow costume along with her gloves and mask in the receptacle bin just inside the patient's door and washing her hands.

Returning to the front desk, Sydney gave Kyra a grim look. "You're right. He needs to go upstairs. I'll page the resident."

Sydney also put a call into Dr. Steinberg, and by the time she'd spoken with the epidemiologist and got the patient ready for transfer, it was five o'clock. She still hadn't talked to Casper.

"Have you seen Dr. Jones?" Sydney asked Kyra.

"He was here a while ago. Said he was going to his office, something about needing a 'lounge.' I assume he meant a nap." Kyra must have caught the look on Sydney's face, because she added, "And no, I don't think he's as strange as you make him out to be. Talks a little weird, wears fancy clothes, but there's nothing wrong with being a little different."

Sydney pondered the RN's words. "Thanks, Kyra. By the way, I know we don't tell you enough, and God knows you nurses are overworked, but you're awesome. I can't imagine life in this place without you."

Kyra smiled and put a hand on Sydney's shoulder. "Thanks, doc, but don't worry, I'm not going anywhere."

Sydney grabbed Casper's now marginally cool can of soda and headed down the hallway toward the stairwell. The infectious disease offices were located on the sixth floor, giving Sydney another three flights of stairs to add to her day's dismal exercise regime.

Once outside Casper's office door, she heard shuffling from inside. She knocked and thought he said, "Come in," but judging by his surprised expression when she flung open the door, she must have misheard. A small jar with red contents filled his hand, but he quickly tucked it inside a drawer away from Sydney's view.

"Sorry, I thought you said to come in."

"No, no, it's fine. You startled me, that's all." His smile was in place, but it didn't quite meet his eyes.

"What's that?" Sydney nodded toward the desk drawer.

Casper shrugged and clasped his hands together. "Nothing. Just some research." He unclasped his hands and ran them along his desk, as if brushing off crumbs.

"What kind of research?"

More desk brushing.

"Okay, now I'm really curious. What kind of research?" Sydney took a seat and pushed up the sleeves of her sweater.

"It's nothing, really. You've just caught me in a bit of an embarrassing situation."

"How so?"

He hesitated and leaned forward. "Let me ask you something. From what I've heard, you seem willing to bend the rules for the betterment of a cause. Is that a fair statement?"

Sydney studied him through narrowed eyes and wondered what exactly their director head, Burke, had told him. "Depends on the cause," she responded cautiously.

"You're not averse to short cuts, are you?"

"I'm assuming this little Q&A has something to do with that bottle in your desk drawer?"

"Maybe."

Uncomfortable, Sydney glanced away. What was it about the man that made her want to share a soda one moment, and then turn and flee the next? Was she the only one to notice his idiosyncrasies?

Her mind went back to earlier that afternoon. She'd stolen a few minutes for a quick lunch in her office, not having time for a proper meal in the cafeteria. While she was chewing on a protein bar, a thought had occurred to her, and she'd bolted up in her chair. The articles. Where was his name on the research articles?

Curious, she had whipped open her desk drawer and grabbed the stack of West Nile virus papers Casper had given her shortly after they'd met. She scanned each and every one for his name but found no Casper Jones. A few listed a *Jones, P.M.*, but no Casper. Why would he have given her articles he hadn't authored? He was, after all, the expert in West Nile disease.

Deciding it was probably a coincidence, Sydney had turned to her computer and clicked open the internet. Scrolling to PubMed in her bookmarks, she'd proceeded to do a literature search on Dr. Casper Jones but again found nothing—not a single article, reference, or quote.

At the time she had tried to explain it away. Certainly there were lots of explanations—obscure journals, searching error, different research interests in the past—but now in his office, caught in the middle of yet another odd Casper Jones moment, Sydney wondered if there was more to the story.

Once again, she considered telling Dr. Burke, but what would she say? Her division head would think she was playing games, or worse, sabotaging Casper, trying anything to get out of the research.

She studied Casper's bookshelves. Still empty. Walls still barren. Not a plant or photograph or knickknack to be found in his office. Just the same microscope and computer she'd seen before, as if he were vacating rather than moving in.

She turned back to him. "What's in the bottle?"

"It's really no big deal. We've managed to make a volcano out of an anthill."

She watched him pull the glass jar from the drawer and place it on his desk. A closer inspection revealed a dark red substance suspended in fluid.

"Looks like a tissue sample," she said. "So what?"

"So what, indeed. See? Not a big deal."

"What is it, exactly?"

"A sample of Mr. Lamb's lungs."

Sydney's brows shot up. "Wow, I'm surprised Dr. Peyton

gave it to you so quickly. He hasn't even dictated his report yet."

"Well…that's where the short cut comes in."

"You didn't tell him? But how'd you get it?"

"Is it just me, or is that guy a little weird?"

Sydney allowed a small smile. "Definitely a weird one."

"He acted like Mr. Lamb's body belonged to him and him alone. He didn't even want me looking over his shoulder."

Sydney pointed to the small jar on Casper's desk. "I saw the lung tissue up close myself. Pretty ugly."

"Indeed."

After a long pause, Sydney said, "So, you stole a chunk of lung. That's a new one for me."

"I'd like to say 'borrowed.' I merely borrowed a sample while Dr. Peyton was making a phone call."

"How'd you sneak it past the pathology tech?"

"Her? She was no problem."

Sydney eyed his Hollywood face. "Hmm, I suppose not, but do you really think it's wise confiscating tissue that might be biohazardous? After all, we still don't understand Mr. Lamb's infection. It could be anything."

Casper leaned forward, his expression growing darkly serious. "Look, we need to find out what's going on with these patients. The quickest way for me to do that is to study the virus and the tissue it's destroying. Believe me, I was very careful with its retrieval, but I don't have time for Dr. Bowtie to cross all his T's and dot his I's before he hands over the gold."

Sydney supposed he had a point.

"Are we fused on this?" Casper asked.

She frowned. "Are we what?"

"Together. Are we together on this? I'm thinking of the patients, that's all. I can't sit idle while people die. Waiting a few hours to follow protocol might seem reasonable to some, but to me it seems dangerous."

"Why didn't you just ask Dr. Peyton for a sample? Maybe he would've given you one."

"And maybe he wouldn't have."

After a few moments, Sydney raised her palms. "Your secret is safe with me, Agent Jones."

Relieved, he tucked the jar back into the drawer and asked for an update on the patients. She told him about Chip Reynolds.

"Did you call Dr. Steinberg?" he asked.

Sydney nodded. "She's working closely with the CDC. They'll have someone here tomorrow. Hopefully the virus will be contained in Boston."

Casper said nothing, so Sydney continued. "The other patients' viral cultures aren't back yet, but like Mr. Lamb, they all tested negative on the rapid antigen tests. In the meantime, Dr. Steinberg is trying to track down Mr. Lamb's whereabouts in the past two weeks. With his wife now on ventilatory support, she can't be of any help, and their only son is on his way home from Afghanistan. He's been serving there for the past eighteen months."

"Afghanistan?" Casper's expression was blank.

Sydney blinked. *Um, yeah, that little war we're having?*

Out loud, she said, "Dr. Steinberg's biggest concern is Mr. Lamb's plane ride back from Africa, not to mention Mrs. Lamb's school kids, their parents, their parents' coworkers, and so on and so on."

"And don't forget Chip Reynolds, the medical student, and all the patients he saw in clinic. I'm sure he wasn't wearing a mask."

Sydney nodded, her head weary from the possibilities.

After a few more minutes of sharing information, Sydney stood and prepared to leave. "Oh, I almost forgot." She reached underneath her chair for the diet root beer. "For you. Something to drink during Dr. Burke's meeting." She glanced at her watch. "In ten minutes."

Sydney handed her attending the can, and his eyes lit up.

"It's warm now. Sorry." Once again, she had that feeling of wanting to please, but at the same time, she was flooded with uncertainty. Like the nice man down the street you wanted to trust but instead got a knot in the stomach from.

Casper flipped open the lid and gulped.

Embarrassed by his reaction, Sydney headed back to her office and tried yet again to decipher the guy. He was likable, pleasant, confident, dedicated enough to patients to steal lung tissue, even if his bedside manner was lousy. Yet he was also dark and secretive.

It occurred to her that could very well be the basis of her curiosity. She'd always been attracted to darkness. In fact, Liz liked to joke that only lightning bolts and thunder could put a smile on Sydney's face. Was that all it was? Was she looking for mystery where none existed?

She didn't have time to ponder. Mitch was at her desk, his size tens propped up on some papers she needed for the meeting.

"Hey, there." He tossed the latest *New England Journal of Medicine* on the desk and rose to embrace her. "I've missed you."

Sydney pulled away. "Sorry, been busy. These influenza cases are becoming a nightmare."

"I know. The ICU consulted us this morning."

"Did you see Mrs. Lamb?" Sydney was eager for any suggestions.

"No, Mark did, but he told me about her. We're going to discuss the case during rounds tomorrow."

Sydney sat down in the chair, while Mitch took a seat on the edge of the desk. He looked good today—black slacks, ocean blue shirt. The bright color suited him and contrasted nicely with his dark hair and glasses. He was one of those people who could pull off black frames, the rectangular lenses a perfect complement for his oval face.

You need to tell him.

"Brought you something." Mitch unfolded a paper towel on her desk to reveal a thick brownie. "Figured you could use a little chocolate." He gave Sydney a sheepish grin, as if the treat were a peace offering, though he wasn't sure why.

"Thanks," she said, feeling guilty about her thoughts of breaking up with him.

She offered him a chunk, but he held up his hands. The meeting started in less than five minutes, definitely not enough time to end things with a boyfriend. So instead, in between bites, she told him about Mr. Lamb's autopsy. "What do you think is going on with these patients? Why is the lung tissue so completely destroyed?"

"I don't know, but remember, the findings are only from one patient so far. The other cases might not be as bad."

"I doubt it. So far everyone's following the same path as Mr. Lamb."

"Maybe it's hemorrhagic disease," Mitch suggested.

"I wondered about that too, but Dr. Peyton said all the other organs were intact."

"Maybe the damage stays localized to the lungs. Or maybe there's a destructive enzyme involved."

"But that's not typical of influenza."

"I know. Bizarre, isn't it?"

"Very. But once we're able to confirm whether it's truly influenza C, we can determine its genetic makeup."

"We?"

"The CDC, Dr. Steinberg, Casper, me. We'll be do—"

"You mean Dr. Jones?" Mitch narrowed his eyes. "First name basis. Wow."

"Yeah…well…he likes to be called Casper."

"I'm sure he does. Especially by pretty ID fellows."

Sydney paused, opened her mouth, but then decided to let it slide. "Dr. Jones and I—he's a virologist, you know—will be researching the virus. In conjunction with the CDC and their scientists, of course."

The suspicion was gone. Instead, Mitch looked at Sydney as if she'd just performed a striptease. And perhaps she had. For Mitch, the image of Sydney doing research on a deadly new virus was probably far more titillating than a thong and pasties.

He swept his fingers through her hair and leaned in closer. "I'm impressed. Maybe even a little jealous."

"Don't be. I'm the low woman on the totem pole. I'll probably be making sandwich runs. My job will mostly serve as liaison to the epidemiologists."

"Either way, it looks good on a resume."

Sydney finished the brownie and glanced at her watch. "I better get going. I've got a meeting in about two minutes."

Mitch's fingers grazed her cheek. "I wish I could see you tonight, but I'm on call."

Sydney said nothing, relieved for the temporary reprieve, but also wondering when she'd get the chance to tell him. He worked tonight. She worked tomorrow night. There never seemed to be a good time, and he deserved more than a quick, "Oh, by the way…"

Mitch hopped off the desk, a little unsteadily, and Sydney pictured the titanium limb inside his slacks. What if he thought it was that?

When she still hadn't responded, Mitch said, "Oh come on, Syd, what's going on?"

Sydney gave him an apologetic look and then glanced at her watch and exhaled. "Nothing. Just a lot on my mind."

"Well, sure, with the new patients and all. I understand." He grabbed his briefcase and started for the door. "I'll call you, okay?"

Sydney nodded, feeling lower than a thief in an orphanage.

Next time, Sydney. Absolutely next time.

She scooped up her papers and hurried to the meeting.

"Sydney, hold on. I want to speak to you a moment."

Sydney closed her eyes, recognizing Dr. Burke's voice behind her. Although she'd considered telling him about Casper and the failed literature search, the meeting had lasted over an hour, and now she just wanted to get home.

Despite two epidemiologists, one pathologist, one pulmonologist, five ID attendings, and five fellows, they really hadn't learned anything new. Liz and Sydney had presented the patients, while Casper had reviewed influenza C and its improbability of causing such deadly disease, as well as the need to uncover the virus's genome as quickly as possible. The epidemiologists had talked about past epidemics, including mistakes made and future blunders to avoid. Dr. Steinberg had stressed the importance of isolation as well as staff vigilance with infectious precautions. But mostly, Dr. Burke had wanted everyone to understand their roles and to keep in constant communication with each other. He'd also been insistent that no one other than the hospital's designated spokesperson talk to the media, with the exception of himself, Dr. Steinberg, or one of the two CDC investigators arriving tomorrow. He didn't want mixed messages or false alarms.

Sydney turned around with a sigh she hoped wasn't audible. "Yes?"

Dr. Burke sat back down at the oval conference table and motioned Sydney to join him. While they waited for the others to file out, Dr. Burke jotted a few notes, and Sydney stared at the interactive whiteboard, reminded of the lecture on community-acquired pneumonia she was supposed to give to the residents next month.

Once the last person left, Dr. Burke capped his fancy pen and slipped it into his suit pocket. He cleared his throat with an authoritative air. "So, how are things going with Dr. Jones? You two getting along?"

"Well…sure."

"Splendid." The department head smiled and leaned back in his chair, his face and scalp their usual red hue. "Have you had a chance to begin your research?"

"Not really. Dr. Jones has me reading articles first."

"Of course." Dr. Burke smoothed his striped tie. "I realize this outbreak will set your research back, and I'll take that into consideration during your review. But who knows, if this turns out to be influenza C, you may have yet another research project. One far more interesting and uncharted. I'm sure Dr. Jones would love to get his name on one of those papers." Dr. Burke smiled, and Sydney imagined him fantasizing about having a groundbreaking virologist on staff.

She also imagined him reading her mind, considering he'd just verbalized the exact thought on it. She took a deep breath. "Say, I was wondering, when Dr. Jones sent you his CV, did he include a list of his publications?"

"Of course. Why?"

"Well, I was curious how many times he's been published."

Dr. Burke narrowed his eyes. "What are you getting at?"

"Nothing. I'd just like to read some of *his* articles, that's all."

"I'm sure you already have. He's been published extensively in the field of West Nile virus."

"That's just it—all those articles he gave me? None of them list his name."

Dr. Burke's complexion seemed to redden even more. "Are you trying to stir up trouble? Because if this is your way of getting out of your new research alliance, you can—"

"No, really, it's not like that. It's just that, well…" Sydney squirmed in the vinyl chair. "You see, when I did a literature search on him, I didn't find any Casper Jones publications."

Dr. Burke's nostrils flared, and his tone took an acerbic turn. "Did you ever stop to think he might publish under a different name?"

"No. Why would I?"

"Because then you would realize Dr. Jones publishes under his birth name: Patrick Michael Jones."

"Oh," Sydney said. No, she hadn't thought of that. It certainly explained the *Jones, P.M.* on some of the articles she'd found. But despite her embarrassment, something flickered in her brain. Something Dr. Jones had said last night in the cafeteria during their late-night soda stop. He'd told her that Casper was an old family name. He never mentioned anything about Patrick or Michael. "But—"

"Dr. McKnight, I'm certainly not about to discuss the qualifications of our newest virologist with you, but if it will help you sleep better at night, you can rest assured that Dr. Jones had nothing but glowing evaluations from his peers at Mt. Sinai. We were extremely fortunate he chose to come here after his latest sabbatical in China. Now, if you have nothing else enlightening to share with me, I have a lovely wife and a warm dinner waiting for me at home."

He rose and gathered his things.

China? Casper had never said anything about China. Then again, he never said anything about anything. "But…did you actually talk to his references?"

Judging by Dr. Burke's expression, Sydney had pushed it too far. His piercing gaze was like a laser beam, and she swore she felt her corneas burn.

"Listen, Sydney, you will work with Dr. Jones, and you will work with him amicably. And until you show me proof of any impropriety on his behalf, I don't want to hear another word about it. Is that clear?"

Sydney nodded, sinking in her seat, her lifelong ability to bite back and fend for herself always disappearing in the ring with Dr. Burke. She waited for the inevitable.

"Don't give me any more ammunition against you. With your behavioral track record, you're lucky to have scored a fellowship at all."

And there it was. Right on schedule.

He started toward the door but then stopped. "You know, this could be the biggest blessing our hospital has ever had. Dr. Jones, a renowned virologist, arriving just before a mysterious outbreak. What a coincidence."

Sydney pursed her lips.

Yes, coincidence.

Her thoughts exactly.

Sydney flew up the empty stairwell, her Doc Martens thudding against the concrete. Even though Crystal had paged her first thing that morning, she needed to see the report with her own eyes.

In moments, she burst through the double doors of the ICU and power walked to the desk, which was already brimming with its usual mayhem. Residents charted notes. Nurses darted from room to room. Respiratory therapists whizzed by with ventilators and nebulizers. All the while the ward clerk answered phone calls and faxes, oblivious to the noise around her.

Sydney scanned the unit for Crystal. Spotting her near a patient room, she hurried over, nearly colliding with a nurse on the way.

"So it's really influenza C, then?" Sydney was still breathless from her sprint up the stairs.

Crystal nodded and lowered her mask. "Here, I'll show you."

Back at the counter, Crystal pulled two white sheets from a clipboard and handed them to Sydney. "The top one is Mrs.

Lamb's, the bottom Chip Reynolds. Both of their nasal aspirates tested positive for influenza C."

Sydney stared at the reports. "Unbelievable."

"I know. The lab supervisor called me directly. He, too, thought Mr. Lamb's initial culture was a mistake, but when these two turned up with the same finding, he became alarmed."

"He's not the only one." Sydney's mind tried to process the illogical report in her hand.

"What do you think it means?" Crystal asked.

"I'm not sure. Not much is known about influenza C. Like I said before, it's been cultured from people with the common cold, maybe even pneumonia, but outbreaks have rarely been reported, and certainly not with this serious of disease."

"Where does it come from?"

Sydney shrugged. "One report I found said it's been isolated from pigs, but whether that's significant in this case, I don't know."

"How likely is it…I mean…what are the odds we'll have an epidemic on our hands?"

Sydney put down the reports and rubbed her eyes. "Good enough to bet everything I own."

"Well, they can make a vaccine, can't they?"

"That could take months. Maybe longer. And who knows how safe or effective it would be?"

A voice interrupted them. "There you are. I'd recognize that pessimism anywhere." Liz smiled and put her arm around Crystal. "Don't listen to this depressing, blonde stickpin. If you asked Sydney whether the glass was half-full or half-empty, she'd say, 'What's the point? We're all going to die anyway.'"

"Very funny," Sydney said. Still, she saw Crystal relax, and soon the auburn-haired resident seemed back to her sparkly self.

"You coming to the ward soon?" Liz asked Sydney.

"After I check on Mrs. Lamb and Chip Reynolds. Why?"

"There were four new consults overnight and two admissions. We're swamped."

Sydney's throat tightened. "Any more influenza cases?"

"Possibly. Two of the consults, anyway. I haven't gone to see them yet."

Reaching over the counter, Sydney grabbed Chip Reynolds's chart. In a voice calmer than she felt, she said, "I'll be down in a few minutes. Here, you might want to share these with Kyra." Sydney showed Liz the medical student's latest vitals. "She was his nurse yesterday. She'll want to know how he's doing."

"Sorry, can't do that."

Sydney looked up at Liz in surprise. "Why not?"

"Because Kyra isn't here today. Called in sick." Liz eyed a box of doughnut holes on the counter and helped herself to two. She must've seen the look of concern on Sydney's face, because she added mid-bite, "Oh, come on. Kyra's probably cuddled up in bed with her husband, playing hooky for the day."

Sydney swallowed, certain she was the one with dough in her throat. She closed Chip's chart and headed to his room, her legs heavy and uncooperative.

Playing "hooky for the day" was *so* not Kyra's style.

***

"Sydney, this is Dr. Mayfield and Dr. Tillman. They're from Atlanta."

Sydney looked up from her charting as Dr. Steinberg made the introductions. She stood and shook each of their hands.

"Dr. McKnight is the fellow who initially cared for Mr.

Lamb. She and I have been in constant communication since." Dr. Steinberg gave Sydney a sympathetic smile and added, "I doubt she's had much sleep in the past few days."

Sydney waved the comment off. Standing side by side, the two women's physical appearances contrasted sharply. Whereas Sydney was tall and fair, Dr. Steinberg was petite and brunette, with the kind of smooth olive skin that lilies like Sydney could only dream of. Though they both wore their hair long, Dr. Steinberg's was eighties big, Sydney's sixties straight, and the epidemiologist's crisp Ann Taylor suit clearly outsmarted Sydney's scrubs.

Sydney greeted the CDC investigators. Dr. Tillman, a tall, middle-aged man in a corduroy blazer was dressed more casually than his partner, Dr. Mayfield, a younger, squatter man in a suit and tie.

"It's always terrifying to be in the heart of the storm," Dr. Tillman said. "But you've all done beautifully, and hopefully by contacting us so early, we can contain this outbreak before it gets any worse."

Sydney tried to share his confidence but found it difficult. "I was just finishing the second of two consults, both with similar symptoms to our other patients."

"Have they been appropriately isolated and cultured?" Dr. Tillman asked.

"Yes, and also started on antivirals, antibiotics, beta2-agonists, and steroids."

Dr. Tillman turned to Dr. Steinberg. "So that brings the total to what?"

"Counting Mr. Lamb, five here. Plus six at the Children's Hospital, two at the VA and four more at Memorial—as per my last update this morning."

"Seventeen." Dr. Tillman turned to Dr. Mayfield. "Trent here will scour the nation and other countries for similar cases. So far, we haven't been alerted to any others."

"But that doesn't mean they don't exist," Dr. Mayfield said. "Especially given Mr. Lamb's international travel."

"Right, and our scientists will begin deciphering the virus's genome. At least with an influenza virus, we know something about it, even if it isn't the expected type A or B."

"Like what?" Sydney handed the chart in her arms to a nurse who'd requested it. She thought about the organisms contaminating the plastic binder and wondered when the hospital would make the switch to electronic records. Then again, keyboards also harbored pathogens.

"Well, influenza C is an RNA virus with well-documented proteins and glycoproteins. A couple of outbreaks occurred in Japan, but the cases were mostly colds and mild lower respiratory tract infections." Dr. Mayfield rubbed his fingers over a short, well-groomed beard. "What we don't know, however, is the particular strain circulating here."

"Unveiling an organism's genome can take weeks," Sydney said. "What do we do in the meantime?"

"We try to find out what makes this strain so deadly. Clearly, it's not the typical influenza C virus. Hopefully between culture samples and biopsy—or autopsy—tissues, we'll be able to discover just that."

"And then what?" Sydney asked. "All that's important to know, of course, but we still won't have a treatment. People will still die."

"That's where our precautions come in. The most crucial act at this moment is containment. You're well aware viruses have no easy cure. The only way to treat this thing is to stop it. Quarantine, masks, handwashing."

Sydney thought of SARS. She thought of the fear and panic it provoked. And yet that outbreak was a mere drop in the bucket compared to what influenza could do. She shifted her weight and went for the half-full glass. "Well, let's hope the virus remains local."

"Yes," Dr. Tillman said. "Let's hope."

At that point Dr. Burke came by to escort the investigators to his office, leaving Sydney to return to work. Her mind wandered to Casper, who she hadn't seen all morning. He was probably in the lab, but she didn't have time to find out, because the next two hours were spent on rounds with a group of internal medicine residents, all of whom looked nervous outside the isolation rooms of the two newest patients. Instead of risking all five to exposure, Sydney brought in only the two responsible for the patients' care, making sure they understood the precautions.

The first patient was a thirty-three-year-old teacher from Mrs. Lamb's school. By the looks of her respiratory effort, she would soon be in the ICU. The other was a seventy-two-year-old man named Duncan—he'd insisted Sydney call him by his first name—with no personal relationship to the Lambs, but his primary care physician was Dr. Denver, the same physician with whom Chip Reynolds was working. Although Duncan hadn't been examined by Chip, he had visited the clinic last week for a bad back. From a bad back to a deadly virus, it seemed.

As Sydney put on a gown, she reminded herself they didn't yet know Duncan's diagnosis. His culture would take some time. Maybe he caught some other bug, perhaps a simple cold from his granddaughter or an easily treated pneumonia from a fellow parishioner at church. But his constellation of respiratory symptoms, deteriorating blood gases, and poor oxygen saturation did little to support her theory.

"Hello, Duncan." Sydney strived for cheerful as she entered the room. It was only the third time she'd been by, yet she got a bubble in her throat when she looked at him. It had taken little time for the staff to fall in love with the kind man. "Came back for that exam I didn't get a chance to do earlier."

"Ah, there's my newest sweetheart. Glad you're back." His

voice carried a pleasant Scottish lilt. He smiled at Sydney, as did his silver-haired wife by his side. He reached up and plucked the oxygen prongs out of his nose. "Do I really need these things? They're more uncomfortable than a pliers up my nose."

"I doubt that." Sydney returned his smile underneath her mask, hoping he couldn't see her worry. She glanced at the hard-working chest muscles beneath his gown and sat beside him. With gloved hands, she slipped the prongs back into his nostrils. "I'm afraid you do. See that machine on your right? That measures your oxygen level. We want it above ninety-two percent, preferably higher."

"Such a good doctor you are. When I get out of this place, you'll have to come to my house for dinner. My wife makes the best beef stew you'll ever taste."

Sydney struggled to return his hopeful gaze. "I'm sure she does." She grabbed the stethoscope hanging near the bed and auscultated his lungs. They sounded coarse and harsh.

"Is my heart still ticking, then?"

Sydney couldn't help but laugh. "Still ticking." She turned to the resident by her side. "Duncan, this is Dr. Pete Summers. He's one of the interns, and he needs to do another complete history and physical on you. He'll be your primary doctor, so just have the nurses page him if you need anything, okay?"

"Are you leaving me, sweetheart?" For the first time he looked worried.

"No, not at all. It's just that I have a lot of patients—none as wonderful as you, of course—and I want to make sure you always have someone at your disposal."

"Ah, such a lovely girl, and smart too. Your grandparents must be proud."

Grandparents? Sydney wondered. *Were they even aware of me?*

Sydney's mother, in one of her rare lucid moments, had claimed they weren't. Nothing, she said, and that included

Sydney, could make her reconnect with "those stupid assholes" who'd disowned her, their only child, years before. Or at least Sydney thought those were her words. Time had a way of blurring her unpleasant memories, which, in reality, were most of them.

Sydney asked Pete to do a more detailed history. "Find out everywhere Duncan has been the last few days and everyone he's come in contact with."

As Sydney was about to say goodbye to her new favorite patient, he reached for her hand. "So, doc, you think I'll be all right, then?" His eyes, so sparkly before, now looked tired and scared.

Sydney's chest tightened, as if she were the one who couldn't breathe. She patted Duncan's hand and smiled at him and his wife. The woman had so far remained quiet, although the anxiety in her eyes spoke volumes. "I certainly hope so, and I'll be expecting that beef stew shortly after."

After leaving Duncan's room, Sydney spent the rest of the day in a dark cloud, weaving in and out of patient rooms. Only her non-influenza C patients were doing well.

The next four days remained similarly dismal. As Sydney sloshed through the hospital, frustrated and weary from the virus's toll, her patient load had doubled and the ratio of non-isolation to isolation rooms had flip-flopped. Not only at Boston General, either, but in other cities around the world. Two days after Sydney had met Duncan, he was transferred to the ICU, the man now heavily sedated and hooked to machines. His wife had also been admitted, and from the pattern Sydney detected—that the old succumbed more quickly than the young—the woman would soon be in the ICU with her husband. Also that same day, Mrs. Lamb had died, and though Chip was still alive in intensive care, his survival seemed tenuous at best.

Sydney's despondency, along with the growing knot in her

stomach, didn't stop there. Kyra, her favorite nurse and one of Sydney's few friends, had contracted the virus.

Sydney had suspected the worst when Kyra missed two days of work in a row, but she'd refused to face it. She couldn't imagine one of their own falling ill. But then Kyra had been admitted the night Sydney was on call, bringing an end to Sydney's denial.

And now, in what seemed like a surreal dream, Sydney was writing Kyra's transfer note to the ICU. The overflow ICU, actually, since the real unit had surpassed capacity. For the hundredth time since Kyra had been admitted, Sydney thought back to her first day of residency, over three years ago. She was clueless and terrified, sporting her stiff white coat and clutching her *Washington Manual.* She'd been ordered by a senior resident to place an IV in one of her patients. Unfortunately, Sydney had never done the procedure in medical school and was horrified to make that fact known. Plus, she'd heard plenty of rumors about the friction between nurses and first year residents. It was no secret they dreaded the interns' arrival every July, and now they'd think she was an idiot.

But then Sydney met Kyra. The nurse had seen her floundering in the supply room where Sydney was pretending to know what she was doing.

"Hey sweetie, are you planning on placing an IV or carving a pumpkin?" Kyra had laughed, but instead of berating Sydney in front of the other nurses, she gathered the supplies and walked Sydney through the procedure. She claimed she did this with all the new residents, wanted them to learn the right way, the "Kyra Washington way," but Sydney knew Kyra was saving her hide, and it wouldn't be the last time either. She—

Out of nowhere, a voice broke Sydney's thoughts, and she nearly jumped off her seat.

"Do you want to write the fluid orders or have the ICU docs do it?"

"Oh, sorry." Sydney blinked at the nurse who'd asked the question, trying to make sense of her words. "Just dozing off a bit." She studied the young woman. "Are you new? I don't think we've met."

"No, but I've never worked this floor before. I'm normally a GYN nurse, but your ward was short-staffed, so the supervisor had to start pulling. I'm a little out of my realm." Her voice sounded anxious underneath her mask. "I'm a little scared too. I've heard a couple of nurses have fallen ill with this virus."

"Just follow good precautions," Sydney said, trying to reassure her. "And yes, I'll write Kyra's fluid orders."

Saying her friend's name weighted Sydney's spirit again. It was true, a few nurses and hospital staff had acquired the virus, but Sydney wasn't acquainted with them. With Kyra getting sick, however, the virus had penetrated Sydney's personal world, isolated though it may be.

With a heavy heart, she completed the medical orders, closed the chart, and headed to the fourth floor, home of the makeshift ICU.

In the stairwell, she got an unexpected surprise: Casper, dressed in his usual formal suit, was deep in another tête-à-tête with the orderly named Jackson. The same orderly with whom Sydney apparently never shared shifts. The two men stopped talking when Sydney entered.

Beyond curious, she stared at them but then decided she was too tired and out of sorts to question their motives. "You two really need to find a new meeting place," she simply said.

After another moment of silence, Sydney shook her head and marched up the single flight of stairs. Somewhere in her mind, a bell went off, a bell questioning the improbability of their strange unions, but she was in such a state she didn't care. It was 7:00 p.m.

She'd had about eight hours of sleep in the last fifty-six hours. Kyra was sick. What did Sydney care about a bizarre, clandestine encounter between two equally bizarre men? For all she knew, Casper was gay. He'd been working at the hospital almost three weeks now, and although plenty of female attention had been tossed his way, he seemed disinterested. Maybe that solved the mystery. Two beautiful men taking what time they could together.

None of my business.

Moving on, she stepped into the overflow ICU. Despite the evening hour, the unit was packed, both with patients and staff. Phones rang, machines beeped, and voices rose to outdo them. Sydney scanned the room for Crystal but couldn't find her. In fact, Sydney couldn't identify any residents, everyone looking eerily similar in their blue masks. Only hair color and body habitus would help her now. She waited a few more seconds and finally spotted a masked Doug Newton exiting a patient room. As one of the ICU fellows, he was currently doing a research month, but the high volume of patients had pulled him back on service. Registering who Sydney was, he waved, scribbled an order in the chart outside the patient's room, and joined her at the counter. As always, given his young age, his paucity of hair surprised her.

"You as tired as me?" he asked.

"Probably. Say, do you know what room Kyra Washington is in?"

"That the new transfer?"

"Yes." Sydney struggled to think about her friend in those terms.

"410. The room I just left. Sorry, the names are starting to blur."

"How is she?" Dumb question considering Sydney had written her transfer orders only a short time before.

"I just finished intubating her."

Sydney closed her eyes. Now her friend was on a ventilator. A lump the size of a walnut formed in her throat. She thanked Doug and trudged to room 410, but as she was about to begin the tedious job of gowning and gloving, her pager went off. The 111 code after the number indicated it was Mitch. That was their signal. Sydney hesitated, her right hand still clutching the yellow gown she was about to put on. She hadn't seen him much the past few days, other than during patient care, but he'd finally cornered her yesterday morning and asked when they could get together. She had told him hospital duties were consuming all her time—which was true—and that maybe they should wait until the outbreak was under control. He seemed to accept that, or rather had no choice but to accept that, because shortly after, Dr. Burke had called Sydney away to inform her of a staff meeting that afternoon, a meeting to discuss possible shift-work assignments should the outbreak get worse.

Sydney clipped her pager back onto her scrub bottoms and decided to ignore the call. At least for now. She wondered if relationships ever dissolved on their own, just evaporated into thin air with neither party the wiser. If so, ignoring pages was probably a good first step.

Now, with a pang of guilt added to her already taxed spirit, she proceeded with gowning and gloving and then rested a hand on Kyra's door. There really wasn't anything from a medical standpoint for her to do. The ICU staff would take over most of Kyra's care now. But she wanted to see Kyra one more time before she went home, wanted her to know she was there. Same went for Chip Reynolds, who Sydney planned on visiting next. Even though he was unconscious and barely alive, she didn't want his mother thinking she'd abandoned ship.

After a deep breath, she entered Kyra's room. Her heart sank a rib's length when she saw her. Kyra opened her eyes when Sydney approached, the intubation tube snaking down her throat. She appeared sleepy, and Sydney hoped her sedation level was adequate.

"Hey, kiddo, you comfortable?" She patted Kyra's arm.

Kyra nodded but of course said nothing, not with a tube in her trachea.

Sydney tried to smile underneath her mask. "Nice jammies."

Kyra had made it perfectly clear that if she was transferred to the ICU, it would be in her yellow silk pajamas or nothing.

Kyra blinked.

Sydney swallowed.

After a few moments of silence, Sydney broke her non-platitude rule. "It's going to be okay. You'll be one of the lucky ones who gets better. You'll see."

So far Sydney had only encountered one of those "lucky ones," a young woman whose husband was in the other ICU. She was admitted two days ago with the same symptoms but today had nothing more than a bad cold. Although her culture wasn't back yet, it was everyone's assumption that she didn't share the same virus. Sydney secretly hoped she did. That meant there might be hope.

Sydney stuck around a few minutes longer, having little to say but not wanting to leave Kyra alone. The hospital had discouraged family members from coming. In fact, the CDC had already initiated quarantines, and Sydney knew Kyra's husband and children were biding their time at home. Sydney also *knew* Kyra's husband, and if the time came for her to die, it would take a meteorite the size of Texas to keep him away.

Finally, after promising to stop by in the morning, Sydney said goodbye, her gaze traveling one last time to the machine pumping air into Kyra's lungs. Aware she would go through the entire process again in Chip's room, she tore off her gown and gloves and tossed them in the trash before leaving. Small price to pay for remaining virus-free.

One hallway over in the real ICU, she braced herself for Chip's mother's tears. Mrs. Reynolds had been by her son's side since the day he'd been admitted and, because of that, had been allowed to stay, especially now that her younger son was in the hospital too. In fact, she'd flat out refused to leave. "You think I'm going to let my babies die alone?" she'd screamed at Dr. Steinberg, who had been wise enough to back away. Now Chip's girlfriend was a patient too. Sydney wondered if he knew. She hoped he didn't.

Burdened by her mounting despondency, Sydney felt the urge to skip the visit and take cover at home, but she thought of Chip's mother, a woman who in all likelihood was about to lose both children, her husband already long gone. What was Sydney's discomfort compared to that?

She opened the door to the ICU. Commotion consumed the room, just as in the makeshift unit, but an area on the right seemed the most chaotic. Sydney turned toward the noise and, with an accelerating heart rate, realized the pandemonium was coming from Chip's room, the door flying open as staff buzzed in and out.

She hurried over and reached for a gown, but none remained. She crossed to the nearest bin, found one, and quickly pulled it on before donning a pair of gloves and a fresh mask. She shot into the room.

There, surrounding Chip's bed, she saw Dr. Yukato, one of the ICU attendings; Dr. Fish, an ICU fellow; and Crystal, along with several other gowned, masked, and gloved staff members. Dr. Yukato was holding defibrillator paddles in his hand, and soon Sydney heard him yell, "Clear!" as he shocked Chip's exposed chest for what appeared to be more than the first time, judging by the burn marks on the young man's chest. He shouted for more epinephrine, and in lightning speed, a burly male nurse injected the drug, while another nurse recorded it on the time sheet. Others drew up meds, an anesthesiologist and a respiratory therapist monitored Chip's airway, and Dr. Fish administered cardiac compressions while waiting for the next shock. More staff stood nearby in the event they might be needed, and Sydney recognized a medical student tucked away in the corner, her eyes wide at the plight of her colleague.

Some part of Sydney's mind realized the student probably shouldn't be there, learning experience or not, but Sydney was too caught up in the scene to hustle the young woman to emotional safety.

Sydney's gaze found Chip Reynolds's mother, huddled in the back of the room, a nurse's arm around her shoulder. As always, she wondered about the intelligence of allowing family members in the room of a coding loved one. Then again, she wasn't the one enduring the woman's hell. Maybe Mrs. Reynolds needed to see this. Maybe she needed to see everything possible being done for her son.

As Dr. Yukato shocked Chip's body yet again and screamed for more cardiac meds, Mrs. Reynolds seemed to lose her footing, and although Sydney couldn't hear her above the noise, she could see the woman's body heave into sobs. There was nothing Sydney could do for Chip—there were already more people crammed in the room than needed—but she could at least offer his mother another anchor, no matter how uncomfortable it made her personally. She crossed the room, squeezing around yellow-gowned staff members as she went. Mrs. Reynolds recognized her immediately—Sydney had been in Chip's room so often—and fell into Sydney's extended arms. Sydney pulled her close and squeezed, which was more intimacy than she had ever given a patient or a loved one before. If a hug was all she could offer, she would. With no husband or family beside her, Mrs. Reynolds would need the support.

Sydney hardened her jaw, holding back tears. She couldn't remember the last time she'd cried. She wondered why some people inherited so much grief. Why wasn't there a moratorium on the stuff? Lose a husband, that was it. All other family members would be spared future harm.

Christ, it isn't fair.

None of it was fair. Not the Lambs, not Chip, not Kyra, not Duncan nor the dozens of others in the hospital destined to die in mere days. Sydney didn't want to believe any of it. *Couldn't* believe any of it.

So instead, she hugged. Just hugged and hugged and hugged.

7

———————

"Sydney? It's Liz."

Sydney gripped the phone in her hand, still half-asleep, unable to lift her head off the pillow. Her mouth felt dry and furry, and her eyes refused to open.

"What time is it?" she mumbled.

"Six-thirty."

Sydney's eyelids snapped apart. She bolted up in bed and felt around the floor for her clothes. Starting three days ago, the ID fellows were allotted only eight hours away from the hospital. She had exceeded her limit by thirty minutes.

"Sorry. Slept in. I'll be there in a few minutes." Her voice remained garbled and thick.

"That's not why I called. Listen to me. Sit down and listen to me, okay? I have bad news."

Bad news? So what else is new?

In the ten days since the first infected patient had died, there had been nothing *but* bad news.

"Are you sitting?" Liz asked.

"Yes, yes, sitting." Sydney pulled her pants on with one hand.

"Kyra just died."

Sydney's hand froze midair. With only one pant leg on, the other dangled like a useless appendage by her side.

"I'm sorry, but I didn't want you to hear it from anyone else."

Sydney remained mute, forcing Liz to ask, "Are you there? You okay?"

Sydney nodded for a good five seconds before any words came out. "Yeah, fine. I'll be at the hospital soon. Thanks, Liz."

Sydney could still hear Liz talking when she hung up, but she had had no choice. She had to get off the line. If she didn't, the dam would break. She'd witnessed too much death, had too little sleep, and saw no end in sight for the past ten days.

And now Kyra was dead.

Oh my God, Kyra is dead.

No, she decided. It wasn't possible. It was a dream. She'd get dressed, go to the hospital, and see Kyra behind the counter, wearing white nursing pants and a neon pink scrub top, just like any other day. Had she told Kyra how much she'd admired her? Had she dived deeper than the occasional compliment on nursing skills or work habits? Sydney knew the answer was no.

Never let anyone get to close. Always look out for number one.

And now it was too late.

An uncharacteristic tear fell, and Sydney slapped it away. What a nightmare. What an impossible, unbelievable night-mare. When was her last full night of sleep? Not since Mrs. Lamb was alive, that was for sure. Sydney racked her brain and tried to think through the timeline. Mrs. Lamb died one week ago—last Friday it was—three days after her husband. Chip Reynolds went two days later, the same day Kyra was transferred to the ICU. In the five days since, numerous others had followed, including Duncan, and hundreds more had fallen ill. Sydney tried to remember the last count. When she left the hospital at midnight the night before, there were a reported twenty-four hundred cases in the area, and those were just the ones they knew about. Worse, three-fourths of the patients died, and not just babies or old people or those with poor immune systems, but young people, healthy people, people who'd never been ill a day in their life. It didn't seem to matter. The new influenza virus was indiscriminate, accepted any race, age, or sex.

Now Kyra was dead. Eight days ago she'd developed a cold, and now she was dead—and she'd lasted longer than most.

Jumping up from the bed, Sydney screamed and threw a pillow across the room, knocking over a plant in the process. Ignoring the dirt on the floor, she teetered to the bathroom and splashed cold water on her face. According to the mirror, she'd lived a lifetime in the past week and a half.

She sank down on the toilet seat and put her head in her hands. She couldn't believe Kyra was dead. Not the woman who once subdued a three-hundred and fifty-pound combative patient with nothing more than a verbal tongue-lashing. Not the woman who could perform chest compressions beyond the time any normal person would cry "uncle," their arms weary and wobbly from the exertion. Even with Kyra weak and unresponsive on the ventilator, Sydney was sure she'd be one of the few who survived.

Her lower lip quivered, and she bit down hard to stop it. Finally, with great effort, she forced herself to a standing position and went through the motions of getting ready, grateful she'd showered the night before. Pulling on a gray turtleneck to go with the black pants, she headed to the kitchen and grabbed a cinnamon bagel and a banana for the road.

As she drove, she ate mindlessly and marveled at how much things could change in such a short time. It had been barely two weeks since Mr. Lamb was first admitted, eleven days since Sydney had entered the picture, and now the country was in turmoil—not only the United States, but the world as well. It took Dr. Tillman and Dr. Mayfield from the CDC little time to discover that similar cases had mushroomed throughout the world, and in the previous week, thousands of people had contracted the virus in New York, Michigan, Illinois, Washington, California, and most of the New England states. Thousands more in Africa, Asia, North and South America, Australia, and Europe, and each day additional states and countries joined the list.

As Sydney's Jeep idled at a red light, she recalled her telephone conversation with Dr. Steinberg the night before. Likening it to the influenza pandemic of 1918, Dr. Steinberg had said, "Do you realize that not since 1918 have we seen a virus spread so quickly and virulently? Forty million people worldwide, maybe even more, died during the influenza pandemic of 1918-1919, hundreds of thousands of them Americans. In fact, in the month of October alone, almost two hundred thousand Americans died from the virus, the highest death rate in U.S. history." She'd let that sink in and then added, "But that's not what scares me the most."

"What does?" Sydney had asked, her anxiety growing.

"The fact that this thing is such an indiscriminate killer. In 1918 the virus had a mortality rate of two and a half percent, over twenty times the rate of previous years. That in itself was horrific. But this thing? This Seneca strain, as they're calling it, kills three of every four people infected. How is that possible? How can that be?"

Dr. Steinberg's voice had become shrill and tight over the telephone, like air escaping a pinched balloon, and Sydney's own gut swirled in dread.

When the epidemiologist had collected herself, she'd said, "In 1918-1919, twenty-five million Americans contracted influenza. That was twenty-five percent of the population at the time. If this Seneca strain turns out to be equally pandemic—and how could it not, given our ease of travel from one place to another?—and if the mortality rate is seventy-five percent…well…you do the math."

Sydney had closed her eyes, not wanting to do the math. "What if every country closed their airports?"

"That is a highly political and costly thing to do. For now, airports are responding the way they did with SARS, questioning passengers for signs and symptoms of the virus. Besides, thanks to Mr. Lamb's air travel and the multiethnicity of his fellow passengers, the international damage has already been done."

"But that seems so insufficient. People can be infectious up to a day before they show symptoms. Just because they answer no to a few screening questions doesn't mean they're not inoculating the guy down the aisle."

"People are wearing masks. Let's hope that will be enough."

Considering they had hospital staff falling ill, those supposedly well-trained in proper isolation techniques, Sydney had lacked the same optimism.

She tried to push yesterday's conversation from her mind and instead focus on driving, but her thoughts drifted back to Kyra.

Bad dream. Has to be.

When she arrived at the hospital, she parked in the employee parking ramp, finding only a crummy spot on the lower level, and dragged herself out of the Jeep. She felt at least three hundred pounds, ironic considering she'd hardly eaten anything over the past week. Swiping her ID badge through the door's reader, Sydney trudged up two flights of concrete stairs to the third-floor skywalk. She paused in the middle of the glass enclosure and looked out at the grayness before her. Although the sun had risen, a blanket of clouds obscured its offerings, and a dreary mist dampened people and cars below.

She peeled herself away from the window and continued

down the walkway, heading first to find Casper. As it was no longer feasible to hold the daily staff meetings Dr. Burke had initiated five days ago, the infectious disease fellows were to at least meet with their attendings at the beginning of each shift. Most other communication between attendings, fellows, and residents, other than what took place during rounds when and if they occurred in a group setting, happened by way of e-mails and memos, Dr. Burke striving to keep everyone current on the latest developments. Since Casper spent most of his time in the lab, Sydney started there.

So far he'd had little luck. While scientists at the CDC deciphered the virus's genome, Casper tried to learn what made it so deadly. By exposing healthy animal lungs to the virus, he hoped to unveil its mechanism of action, but so far, exposed mice, dogs, and cats had shown no signs of disease. His next participant would be a chimpanzee, the species sharing ninety-nine percent of a human's DNA. If that, too, failed, then biopsied lung samples from uninfected individuals would be desired, in order to study healthy human tissue, which proved an ethical dilemma in and of itself. But exhaustive analysis of infected lung tissue from deceased individuals had so far yielded no answers, either by Casper or any other scientists around the world, leaving potentially no other choice.

As for Sydney, she conducted no research at all, too busy caring for the endless stream of patients. Fellows and attendings worked sixteen-hour shifts, residents even more, and although they were supposed to take a two-hour break during that time, few of them did. The fellows were then granted an eight-hour reprieve at home as long as they weren't on call.

After stopping for her requisite giant-sized cup of coffee on the main floor, Sydney descended two more flights to the lab, where she wandered past several steel counters cluttered with microscopes, centrifuges, gas analyzers, and high-tech computer components. The scent of sulfur filled the air, making her nostalgic for the research she wasn't doing.

The lab was eerily empty, most of its researchers pulled to patient care, but Casper was in his usual place in the corner of the room, working, as he apparently preferred it, alone. Sydney was about to say hello, when she saw him tuck two small vials containing what appeared to be human tissue into a soft-sided briefcase. Then, still unaware of her presence, he emptied a beaker of clear solution into a long test tube. After capping the tube, he deposited that into the black bag as well.

"Up to your old tricks again?" Sydney wasn't entirely surprised by his actions. After nearly a month of the guy's uniqueness, it seemed a waste of energy to raise an eyebrow.

Casper jumped at the interruption. "Oh, hello." He glanced at his watch. "It's already seven-fifteen. I thought you'd be on the ward by now."

"Overslept." Her tone carried the emotional heft of a robot. "I'll stay past my shift so Liz can get her full respite."

Casper nodded and closed his briefcase. Over the past few days, his clothing had become less formal. Gone were the usual jacket and tie. His face bore more stubble, too, and dark circles under his eyes marred his usual flawless features.

He hesitated for a moment and then nodded his head toward the briefcase. "Just some leftover tissue, that's all. I think I've told you, I sometimes like to work at home."

"At home? No, you haven't told me that."

"Hmm…well, yes I do. More sophisticated equipment, less distractions, that sort of thing." He quickly slid a slide underneath the microscope and swiveled a stool up to the counter. After taking a sip of diet soda, he adjusted the magnification of the lens.

Sydney stared at him, trying to imagine what sort of equipment his apartment possessed that would be suitable for a Biosafety Level 3 virus. Then she shared with him the anchor on her chest. "Kyra's dead."

Casper's head shot up. "Oh, no, I'm sorry. I really am. I know she was a good friend."

Sydney swallowed her grief. "There are people who've got it worse."

"I'm sure there are, but that doesn't make it easier." Casper was still hunched over the microscope, but his gaze remained on her. Then he surprised her by wheeling the stool closer and putting a hand on her forearm.

"Are you taking care of yourself?" His forehead creased in concern.

"Me? Um, sure. As good as anyone else." Sydney slipped her arm out of Casper's grasp and adjusted her ponytail band. "Look, I need to get to the wards. I'm already late, and I hate to keep Liz any longer. Is there anything you want to review with me before I go?"

Casper acted like he hadn't heard her, and though Sydney had already freed her arm, his gaze pinned her down. "You need to be careful. You need to take your full respite, get your sleep, and treat everything—and I mean everything—as if it's teeming with virus. This thing will only get worse, and I… well…I'd hate to see anything happen to you."

Sydney didn't know what to say. His concern was unexpected—and uncomfortable. "Um, I will, but I really need to get to the wards. Maybe you could walk with me and we could do our 'Burke exchange' on the way."

Once again Sydney wasn't sure if he'd heard her, because he simply stared, first at her face, then her hair. Finally, he said, "Yes. Yes, of course."

He locked his leather briefcase inside a large drawer underneath the counter. Then he stood and headed out of the lab, his manner back to that of an attending, as if they had been discussing the latest design of otoscopes rather than Sydney's welfare. "So, what's your patient load today?"

"I don't know, but I'm sure the numbers are high. On the drive over, I heard that seven hundred people died yesterday.

Seven hundred. In Boston alone. Dr. Steinberg has already likened it to the influenza pandemic of 1918."

"If only it would…" Casper's voice trailed off. He punched the up button on the elevator. When it didn't come right away, he said, "Why don't we take the stairs? Better exercise."

Sydney followed him. "What were you saying? If only it would what?"

"Hmm?"

"Before. You said, 'If only it would…' What did you mean?"

"Oh, well, I meant, if only we could figure out why so many people die."

"Or why others survive." Sydney started on their second of five flights of stairs. "What makes them different? Why do a fourth of the victims catch merely a cold, but the other three-quarters die a horrible pulmonary death?"

Casper didn't answer, so Sydney continued, getting more winded with each passing step. "As you know, the CDC is close to identifying the exact strain. Maybe then we'll have some answers. Plus, the World Health Organization is investigating swine near Nairobi in case pigs were the source of Mr. Lamb's infection. Seems unlikely, but everyone is desperate for an explanation."

Casper shook his head. "Knowing the virus's genetic code won't prove helpful at all."

"What do you mean? Of course it will help. That's like saying maps don't show the way to Boston. Once scientists understand the virus, they can scramble to make a vaccine."

"Won't do any good."

"Why not?"

"This is more than a typical antigen-antibody disease. The blood tests and pathology reports confirm that. We can make all the antibodies against the virus we want, but it won't do any good."

"Do you think it's a host response then? Our immune systems wreak havoc on our own organs?" Two flights left.

When was the last time I exercised? Sydney wondered.

"No, not that either."

Sydney's irritation grew. "And what crystal ball have you consulted? What makes you so certain doom is inevitable?"

Casper continued climbing but said nothing.

"It seems you're convinced nothing's going to work. Like you know something the rest of us don't."

More silence.

"Dr. Jones, you're making me nervous."

Finally, on the last flight of stairs, he said, "I don't know anything. Your imagination is marching feral."

Before Sydney had a chance to comment, Casper whipped open the door to 3 West. "You better start your morning rounds. I'll wander through the ward, see if anyone needs me. Then I'll be back in the lab."

He started to walk away. Without thinking, Sydney grabbed his arm, her voice shaky. "Dr. Jones…Casper, I mean…if you knew something, you'd share it, right? I mean, you wouldn't let—"

Casper pulled his arm free. "What kind of question is that?" He turned around and headed to the front counter, as if his own question were answer enough.

Unfortunately, it wasn't, and everything else he'd left unanswered resurfaced in Sydney's brain, having been buried the past few days under the huge number of patients: odd speech and mannerisms, tissue vials in briefcases, research equipment at home, discrepancy behind his name.

What was Sydney to make of these things? She'd already approached Dr. Burke about Casper, and his response had stung. Liz, too, thought Sydney was crazy. Who else was there to talk to? Mitch?

Right.

She couldn't even break up with the guy, let alone interest

him in the odd behavior of a man he barely knew, especially when there were hundreds of patients dying.

Sydney was almost at the ward desk when Liz hurried over and gave her a hug. "Oh God, I can't believe it. I can't believe Kyra's gone."

"Me neither." Sydney pulled free, knowing one more second of contact would push her over the edge.

Liz wiped her eyes, her respiratory mask dampened with tears. "Sorry, it's just so hard, you know? I've been holding it in all night." She took a big breath and tried to smile.

"I know, and I'm sorry I'm late. I'll stay longer tonight so you can get the extra sleep."

Liz nodded. "That'd be great. I'll send flowers to Kyra's family. Sign both of our names."

"Why don't you throw in some balloons or cookies for the kids?" Sydney's chest cinched at the thought of Kyra's five-year-old twin daughters. "Or maybe some coloring books or games or something." Her voice caught, and she had to tighten her jaw. "Just give me checkout on the patients. I can't talk about Kyra right now."

"Sure," Liz said, and together they sat at the counter, where Liz proceeded to give Sydney news no better than what they'd just discussed. Sydney was to oversee the care of sixty patients—three residents covering twenty patients each. She thought of all the regowning, masking, and gloving. She thought of all the last breaths she would witness.

She thought about Kyra in the morgue.

Standing, she said goodbye to Liz and attempted to hunt down her residents, but before she could locate even one, Mitch found her instead.

"Boy, someone looks happy to see me," he said.

"Sorry. Just—"

"I know, I know, just tired and busy. I've heard it all before. Come on." Mitch led Sydney into a resident call room down the hallway where the bed looked as though it hadn't been touched in days. Once inside, he took her hands. "I miss you."

Sydney sighed. It was hard not to go there, hard to resist the familiar. But it wouldn't be fair to him, so she pulled her hands free and took a seat on the bed. "I have patients to see. I'm already late."

"You can give me two minutes, can't you?" Heat flashed in Mitch's eyes but quickly vanished as he joined her on the bed. "I heard about Kyra. I'm sorry."

"Thanks."

"This virus is getting out of hand."

"You could say that."

"I've examined the lung tissue. It's totally destroyed. I've never seen anything like it."

"Me either."

"One of my attendings thinks it's a destructive enzyme, one that's localized to the lungs, but he doesn't know how or why it would happen."

"No one does."

Mitch paused and pushed up his glasses. "What about the great Dr. Jones?"

"What do you mean?"

"Isn't he supposed to be the renowned virologist? Why hasn't he found the answer?"

"Jeez, it's only been two weeks. Everyone's scrambling for an explanation." Sydney rose from the bed and leaned against the wall.

"Yeah, I suppose you're right, but don't you think there's something weird about that guy?"

For a long moment, Sydney said nothing, startled not only by Mitch's vocalization of the very thought she'd harbored for the past few weeks, but also because she was suddenly not so eager to agree. "What do you mean?" She picked a piece of lint off her sweater. "You don't even know him."

"I've seen him around. Walked in on him in a patient's room. He acted surprised, almost nervous."

"Well, his bedside manner isn't the greatest."

Despite her defense of the man, Sydney wondered what Casper had been doing in a patient's room. She imagined he'd be more likely to swallow a flaming torch than willingly see a patient.

"And I caught him staring at you the other day," Mitch continued. "You were writing in a chart, didn't even notice him, but he apparently couldn't take his eyes off you."

"Oh, come off it, Mitch."

"Come off what? Look, I know it's been hell around here lately, and I *am* really sorry about Kyra, but you act like I'm the last person you want to see. Whenever I try to talk to you, you push me away. Am I cramping you, is that it? Do you need more space? Is seeing me a pathetic few times a month crimping your loner lifestyle?"

Sydney closed her eyes and exhaled. Breaking up with Mitch while sixty patients waited to be seen and a deadly virus circulated the air seemed both shallow and cruel, but she couldn't put it off any longer.

"Sydney?" Apprehension replaced Mitch's sarcasm.

"I'm sorry," she said. "You're right. I haven't exactly been trying too hard. Maybe it's best if we…well, maybe—"

"Oh, man, don't say it, Syd."

"I think we need to take a break."

Mitch wiped a hand over his mouth. "Temporary or permanent?"

Sydney hesitated and then said, "Permanent."

Mitch shot up off the bed. "Whoa, whoa, hold on there. Just tell me what you need. Tell me what I can do different."

"It's not you, it's—"

"Oh please, you're not going to give me a cliché, are you? What in the hell is going on? Three weeks ago, everything was fine. Then all of a sudden I'm some disgusting dog you don't want to be seen with."

Sydney gave him a hurt look. "That's not true. It's just that—"

"It's him, isn't it?"

"Who?"

"Dr. Jones."

Sydney barked out a laugh. "That's ridiculous. Come on, don't be an asshole."

"Oh, *I'm* the one being an asshole?"

"Right now? Yes."

"I saw you guys together."

Bewildered, Sydney said, "What are you talking about?"

"That night you went into the hospital even though you weren't on call. The night Mrs. Lamb and that medical student were admitted. I thought I'd stop by, see if you needed another opinion. When I couldn't find you on the wards, a nurse told me she'd seen you in the cafeteria. Imagine my surprise when I found you and Dr. Jones at a table, deep in conversation, his eyes stuck to you like flypaper."

Sydney shook her head, disgusted. "Oh, please. We were discussing the patients."

"Don't deny it. Ever since he came into the picture, you've cooled to me."

"That's crazy."

"At least have the guts to admit it."

At that moment, the volume of work ahead of her and the ludicrousness of his comments set Sydney off. She felt herself snap. "Look here, Mitch, did you ever think my 'cooling' might have to do with the fact that we're not right for each other? Or—here's a thought—that it might have to do with you? You *can* be a little self-absorbed sometimes."

"Me self-absorbed? Ha! That's a good one. Kind of like Pig Pen telling Charlie Brown *he's* the dirty one." Mitch started pacing the small room, the limp from his prosthetic more pronounced than usual.

Sydney's tone softened. "Look, I don't want to fight. I have a zillion patients to see. I just think we'd be better as…friends. And if not that, then at least civil co-workers."

Mitch stopped pacing. "You know, if you want to break up, then break up. Don't make some lame-ass excuse about us not being right for each other. Dr. Jones is a good-looking guy, you don't think I know that? Not to mention charming, brilliant, and published a hundred times over. I can't compete with that."

Mitch's voice rose with each sentence, and Sydney worried someone would hear.

"But the guy's playing you, Syd. He wants to hook up, that's all."

Sydney stared at him, muscles tense, she-devil stirring. "Listen to me, Dr. Mitchell Price, I don't get *played*. Not by patients, not by you, and not by some new virologist." She lowered her voice. "You're jealous, that's what's going on here. Not just of Casper, but of his research. You can't stand that he's made a name for himself, that he's been a success, something you've never been able to do. And that fact kills you. It twists your tight, competitive ass in knots. It—"

With that Mitch flew out of the room.

Sydney fell back against the wall, heart pounding, head about to explode. She was suddenly fourteen, screaming at her foster mother du jour, calling her a bitch.

Guess you haven't come such a long way after all, baby.

She took deep breaths, in and out, in and out, until some semblance of calm returned. What had she done? Mitch didn't deserve that. His preposterous accusation had simply pushed her too far.

Frustrated and embarrassed by her tirade, she bolted out of the call room. Forcing herself toward the ward, she wanted nothing but to flee in the opposite direction, her overheated and exhausted body desperate to run as fast and as far as it could away from the hospital.

Instead, she somehow made it to the ward. She went through the motions. She talked, walked, and thought, and the next fifteen hours passed by in a dense fog. It was countless lung exams, blood gases, and viral cultures. It was endless orders for antivirals, for steroids, for breathing treatments, none of which did any good. It was admitting new patients, pronouncing dead patients, and comforting tearful family members at their sides.

Sydney suppressed thoughts of Mitch only to conjure Kyra instead. Her friend's body, down in the morgue, covered by a white sheet, or maybe in a body fridge if she was lucky enough to find the space. Soon Sydney couldn't breathe. Soon she was worse than her patients on respirators. She had to get out. She had to smell the night air.

Is it even dark yet?

She tried to find a window to check for nightfall but couldn't, so instead she ran to the stairwell and charged upstairs, running until she couldn't go any higher. She knew the door would be unlocked. She'd made trips to the roof before, never this erratic, never this desperate, but she'd been there nonetheless.

Finally, she burst through the door and into the night, taking deep, sucking breaths like an air-starved asthmatic. The wind was sharp and cold, but she didn't care. She needed its bite, needed its reminder that she was still alive.

She took more deep breaths. Finally, her head cleared. She hugged her coatless body and stared eight stories below at the collection of cars, some stalled and honking, others passing freely. Pockets of pedestrians dotted the sidewalk. Life still existed. The world still revolved.

Good. Very good.

She stood there for a long time, wondering about Kyra's funeral, wondering about the patients downstairs who needed her, wondering about Mitch and the wisdom of breaking up with him at such a horrific time. What kind of a monster was she? Part of her wanted to go back and find him. Tell him she was sorry, tell him he was right: *she* was the self-absorbed loser.

As she tossed the idea around in her mind, a sudden sound startled her. Someone had just pushed open the door. Sydney heard voices and, for reasons she couldn't explain, she panicked and ran to the side of the roof to crouch behind a vent. The moment she got there, she realized her insanity— what did she care if someone discovered her? But just as she was about to make herself visible, she recognized one of the voices as Casper's. Creeping back into the shadows, she peered toward the ledge and saw him there, staring at the cars below. Next to him was Jackson, the elusive orderly, in his usual white scrubs.

Sydney remained still, not sure what to do. Though common sense told her to leave, curiosity won out. She crouched back down and listened, but the wind carried away most of the conversation. All she could catch were incoherent snippets.

"Have you…protective…"

"…think so."

"…not much…"

"I know, I know."

"…Burke found…can't risk…"

"You don't need to tell…"

"Don't mess…forget…woman…"

Frustrated, Sydney shifted her body closer. The move was unnecessary, because Casper's voice suddenly rose, and he took a step back.

"You think I don't know that? I'm doing the best I can. You manage your job, and I'll manage mine!"

Sydney saw Jackson put a hand on Casper's shoulder as if to subdue him. Their voices dropped back down to whispers, forcing Sydney to shift her position once again.

Unfortunately, that was a mistake.

In her effort to get close enough to hear, she accidentally kicked an aluminum can. Its clatter on the rooftop was so loud, it could have woken the comatose patients below.

She threw herself back against the vent, but other than the howling wind, sudden silence filled the air. She cringed and closed her eyes. When she opened them, she saw two genetically blessed faces peering back at her. She pretended to look startled.

"Sydney." Casper's face and voice were cautious. "I didn't know anyone else was up here."

"Well, that makes two of us." She clutched her chest as if dying from fright. "You scared the crap out of me."

Casper gave a tentative smile. Jackson didn't.

Sydney made a great effort at standing up. She squinted at her watch in the dark. "What time is it? God, I must've dozed off. I came up here for fresh air, you know?"

Casper nodded. Jackson frowned.

"I've gotta go. Liz will be here soon, and I have to give her checkout. Sorry if I disturbed you guys."

Sydney didn't wait for them to answer. Instead, she brushed past and hustled to the door, flying down the steps back to the ward at a pace shockingly fast for her worn-out body. Her heart pounded, and her breathing sped up, but she had no idea why she was so agitated. It wasn't like she'd heard them confess to murder. In fact, none of what they'd said made any sense.

By the time she reached the ward, she'd calmed down and began slowing her steps. The gay theory came back to her. Maybe Casper and Jackson were worried Sydney had overheard their conversation and was about to out them. Maybe that's why they had mentioned Dr. Burke. Sydney replayed the snippets of conversation and figured that guess was as likely as any.

But something inside her said there was more. Jackson's

presence didn't add up. Why did Sydney so seldom see him, and when she did, why was it always with Casper? Maybe she was focusing on the wrong person. Maybe she should be questioning Jackson's character. That was something she could take to Dr. Burke. Unlike with Casper, Burke wouldn't perceive her suspicions about an orderly as a threat.

That was what she would do. She would ask around about Jackson—tomorrow. For now, she needed to give checkout, go home, shower, and collapse into bed. Her lack of sleep probably fueled her paranoia. What did she care what two grown men did in their spare time?

When Sydney finally climbed into her car, only six and a half hours remained of her respite. She planned on spending every one of them in a sleep coma.

Unfortunately, the coma wouldn't start yet. Outside of her apartment door stood Mitch.

"What are you doing here?" Sydney couldn't conceal her surprise. "We just broke up. I figure I'm the last person you'd want to see." She let them into the apartment and tossed her jacket and purse on the couch.

"Yeah, you were a real witch today."

Sydney narrowed her eyes, about to attack, but decided Mitch had suffered enough. So had she. Her shoulders slumped, and she fell to the sofa. "You're right. I'm sorry. That was completely inappropriate, but so were your accusations."

"Were they?"

She rested her head against the couch. "Look, I'm really tired. I need to sleep."

"I don't want to break up, Syd."

"Well, I do," she said flatly.

Still standing, Mitch rubbed his eyes underneath his glasses. "If it's not Dr. Jones, what is it?"

"It's nothing specific. We don't fit, that's all. I thought I already explained it." Sydney regretted her apathy, but she had nothing left to give. She just wanted him gone.

"No, you didn't explain anything." Mitch paused for a moment. He looked down at his feet. "It's not…I mean…it's not because of my leg, is it?"

Sydney's body sagged deeper into the couch. "Of course not. What kind of person do you think I am?"

He shrugged. "Someone who apparently thinks I'm an idiot. Maybe I am. Hell, I'm here, aren't I? You call me a failure. You show a complete lack interest in me, and yet, here I am, ready and waiting for more." He grabbed Sydney's silk throw pillow and squished it in his hands.

"I never called you a failure," she said meekly. "Not in so many words, anyway."

Mitch continued, as if not hearing her. "I know you could have any man you wanted, but I wish you'd give me a chance. I always feel like you're working against me. Or worse, not working at all."

Sydney remained silent, watching him torture her pillow.

"Feel free to jump in anytime." Mitch's sarcasm was obvious.

Sydney exhaled. "I don't know what to say. I only have the energy to break up once tonight, you know?"

With great effort, she stood and walked to the lone window in her apartment, its blind still raised. Randomly lit rooms in the opposite building formed an almost perfect X, and she wondered if it was some sort of sign. "Come on, Mitch, you had to see this coming."

"I'll tell you what I saw. I saw someone who was suddenly repulsed at the sight of me, someone who couldn't even manage a hug without pulling away. At first, I was confused, wondered what went wrong, but then I understood. You'd met someone else. A faculty member no less. Good one, Syd. Better hope no one finds out."

"Is that a threat?"

"Why, does it feel like one?"

That was the final straw.

"Get out, Mitch." Sydney's she-devil was back full force. "Leave me alone. And for the record, I didn't suddenly lose interest in you. There wasn't much there to begin with."

Mitch's head jerked back as if she had struck him.

"Oh jeez, Mitch, I'm sorry. I didn't mean that. It's just been a long day, what with the virus and Kyra. I don't even know when her funeral is."

Sydney stepped forward, but Mitch was already wrestling with his coat, his face a combination of anger and hurt.

She tried again. "Really, I'm sorry. I'm my own worst enemy today, you know?"

Mitch glared at her, a fire in his eyes she'd never seen before.

"Save your apologies," he said. "They're probably as cold as your feelings. Nice knowing you though." He yanked open the door and stomped into the hallway. Before leaving, he turned to fling a few more parting words her way. "You might want me out of your life because I'm not the right *fit*, but don't call me when you wake up lonely and alone someday. At the rate you're going, that's exactly what you'll be." Then he slammed the door with enough vigor to summon the dead.

Sydney closed her eyes and sank once again onto the couch. Her hands trembled. She hardly recognized herself, at least not the self she'd become since her youth. Mitch deserved so much better. It wasn't his fault she was screwed up. She put her head in her hands, and her breaths started to hitch.

Not bothering to turn off the light or brush her teeth or do anything else she should do, she lay down on her squashed throw pillow and closed her eyes. She needed to rest, needed some time to erase the demon she had summoned. Nothing felt real anymore. Or maybe it was the opposite. Maybe life was becoming *more* real. She didn't know.

She just needed sleep, that was all. A good night's sleep.

Everything would be fine in the morning.

8

———————

Sydney's drive to the hospital passed in a drunken stupor, only she hadn't consumed any alcohol. No drugs either, although she sure could have used some, and the six hours she'd slept did little to quell her exhaustion. She decided she was either serving a lifetime sentence in jail or spending one very long day in hell. Nothing seemed real anymore. Not her fellowship, not her breakup with Mitch the night before, not even her drive to work.

She braked for a red light and glanced around the familiar route: Ed's Deli on the left, Rooms by Design on the right, Dr. Mason's Chiropractic straight ahead, the guy who claimed an ill-adjusted spine accounted for half the maladies of humankind.

Got anything for a killer influenza virus?

They all seemed like stage props to her, merely one-sided set decorations made of brick and green awning. It was hard to imagine people inside, employees going about their usual business, while every hour brought more death and disease in hospitals across the city. The country. The world.

Plus, some people weren't wearing masks. Sydney was surprised to see unprotected passersby, despite the CDC's recommendations. Didn't they watch the news, read the papers, search the internet? Luckily, most citizens understood the seriousness of the quarantines in place, the need to stay home unless absolutely necessary, and the need for strict compliance, making normally public venues less populated.

Sydney pulled into the employee parking ramp, spotting Mitch's Saturn on the way. She wondered if that was nature's way of reminding her of what a jerk she'd been. Mitch's words about Casper played back in stereo sound, and Sydney half-expected to find Dr. Burke in her office, waiting to accuse her of inappropriate conduct with an attending. Normally such fodder would probably excite Dr. Burke—one more thing to use against her—but given the current climate, Sydney doubted liaisons between faculty members and residents, whether real or imagined, were the most pressing issues on the department head's mind. Mitch would recognize that too. He was a decent guy. The female employees were probably already lined up and waiting their turn.

Sydney parked the Jeep and headed toward the connecting walkway. She wondered how many new influenza cases there'd be today. How many new deaths, how many new cities, how many new countries? She didn't have the energy to listen to the radio on the way to work. She knew she'd find out soon enough.

The moment she stepped into the richly decorated doctor's lounge, she did. CNN blared from the television, in front of which a cluster of nervous physicians chowed down on bagels, their masks temporarily lowered by the sheer need to eat. Sydney nodded to those who made eye contact and grabbed a banana and yogurt for herself before lowering her own mask. In the last few days, she had avoided unprotected bagels and pastries from the lavish assortment they had all come to expect for no other reason than their M.D. initials. Although the baked goods were hard to refuse, in her para-noid state, Sydney preferred to stick with peel-able fruit and closed containers. Who knew where a droplet of influenza might land?

As she chewed, she listened to the somber anchorwoman announce that eleven more states had reported the virus, bringing the grand total up to twenty-one. The rampant spread continued in pockets throughout the rest of the world as well, especially impoverished areas, where actual numbers were harder to confirm given the ease of contagion in close-quartered slums. The CDC and WHO were continuing the desperate search for an explanation of the unprecedented death rate, and there was talk of increasing the virus to a Biosafety Level 4, but so far, only a few researchers had fallen ill, and it was believed the usual precautions for inhalation viruses should be adequate. This would allow scientists from around the world to study the virus, rather than limiting its evaluation to one of the few Level 4 labs in the country. Besides, the people at greatest risk of infection were those performing patient care—as if Sydney wasn't already paranoid enough. Every time she sneezed, whether from the sun in her eyes or a noxious smell, she was convinced she'd acquired the virus. Every time her throat felt the least bit dry, she was sure she was on her way to the morgue. And fatigue and general malaise? Sydney had those every second of the day.

Once satiated by the banana and yogurt, she headed down to the lab, surprised, but also relieved, not to find Casper in his usual corner. She was still embarrassed by their encounter on the roof the night before and wasn't particularly eager to meet up with him. She then climbed the five flights to 3 West and took a seat behind the counter, joining a unit clerk and two medical students, both of whom were probably rethinking their career choice. Sydney smiled at them underneath her mask as she swiveled her chair to an open computer and clicked on the hospital census.

As was becoming the norm, it was full of new admissions, those with symptoms of the Seneca strain highlighted in red.

The scarlet names had quickly overtaken the white, and most non-virus patients had been turfed to small-town hospitals, while influenza patients were sent to Boston General. Every hospital in the state was running at full capacity, and primary care doctors did their best to manage non-influenza cases as outpatients, having little desire to expose the individuals to the even greater risks in the hospital. Despite the high number of negative-pressure isolation rooms at Boston General, there were still not enough to accommodate everyone, and smaller hospitals had even less availability. Thus, unlike what Sydney witnessed in the outside world, there were no unmasked people trolling the hospital. No one dared take the chance.

"Pretty damn scary, isn't it?"

Sydney turned to find Liz in the next seat, dressed in the same light blue scrubs as her, neither of them having the strength for fashion. Liz's short, curly hair was somehow pulled into two tiny pigtails, and her glasses were askew on her nose. All she needed now were some dimples and freckles.

Sydney frowned underneath her mask. "Coming from a Pollyanna like you, that's saying something."

"Well, have you heard the latest numbers? Nine thousand patients have now contracted the flu in Boston alone, and that's not counting the surrounding areas. We simply don't have the beds, even with the makeshift hospitals, and our supplies of PPE are running low."

"Did all the new beds get filled overnight?" Sydney was referring to the non-care areas that the hospital had converted into patient rooms: waiting rooms, empty offices, even supply closets.

Liz nodded but was unable to answer because of a pending sneeze. Lowering her mask, she lunged for a tissue just in time. Once she'd tossed it in the trash, she turned back to Sydney and said, "We're out of ventilators now too. As soon as one patient dies, it goes to the next in line."

"Some probably won't even get one." Sydney printed out her lengthy patient census. "Not like it matters."

"Hey, not everyone dies, you know. Some don't even need a ventilator. You've seen the patients who get booted out as soon as it becomes clear their course is milder. In fact, this guy in room 310?" Liz pointed a gloved finger to the name Macaby on Sydney's patient list. "He came in a few hours ago, and so far he's doing pretty well. Normal blood gases and everything."

"So why did he get admitted?"

"His wife is on a ventilator. It was assumed he'd be next, but if his numbers remain this good, we'll get him out by tonight."

"Is he getting the usual cocktail?"

"Oseltamivir, amantadine, steroids, albuterol—also ceftri-axone, in case there's a bacterial component. We've even added interferon."

"What about immunoglobulins?"

"Not enough to go around. Besides, there's no evidence the antibody infusions help."

"There's no evidence anything helps. Why some people survive when the majority die is a mystery." Sydney trudged to the printer to retrieve her census and the latest pile of lab results.

"Dr. Jones having any luck?"

"I don't think so. I haven't seen him today, though." Sydney leaned back against the counter and, after a brief hesi-tation, said, "Do you think it's strange he does research at home?"

"At home? What do you mean?"

"I don't really know. He told me yesterday he sometimes likes to work at home. I think that's a little weird."

"What's strange about looking for answers away from the lab? Doesn't mean he's concocting the latest version of Dr. Jekyll's transformation serum."

Sydney was about to tell Liz about the tissue samples Casper had tucked into his briefcase, when Liz continued. "You seem convinced there's something wrong with the guy, but most researchers are weird by nature. They don't relate well to people. That's why they choose research over a clinical tract." Liz finished a note in one chart and moved on to the next.

Although Sydney wasn't sure she agreed with her colleague's social analysis, she decided to change tactics. "Have you met the new orderly, Jackson Bryant?"

"Who?"

"Black, muscular, handsome. Looks kind of like Dr. Jones, actually."

Liz looked up at Sydney, her blank expression answer enough.

"I'll take that as a no."

"Why do you ask?"

"Well, it's just that I haven't really worked with him, seems strange that he…" Sydney's voice trailed off as she caught Liz's expression, one that said, *People are dying and you're worried about orderlies?* She stood up, feeling foolish. "Guess I better get to work."

She grabbed a stash of fresh gloves and stuffed them in her back scrub pocket. Then she paged each of her residents, hoping for a semblance of formal rounds. While she waited for their responses, Liz coughed, seized another tissue, and blew her nose.

Every one of Sydney's sphincters tightened.

She turned as Liz replaced her mask. "You okay?"

"Me? I'm fine. Just haven't had any sleep."

"You sure?" Sydney didn't dare articulate what surely both of them were thinking.

"I'm *fine*."

Sydney watched Liz toss the tissue into the trash and then grab a patient's chart.

"Um, maybe you should—"

Liz gave her an exasperated look. "You worry too much. About Dr. Jones, about new orderlies, about me. You know, sometimes a sneeze is just a sneeze."

Sydney nodded. She tried to smile.

It didn't come.

"How are you doing, Mr. Macaby?" Sydney's voice sounded light, but she was relieved he couldn't see her face behind the mask and goggles—the latest addition to her bedside armamentarium—because her expression was anything but.

"I've been better." His muscled chest tugged underneath the gray patterned gown.

She hesitated, not sure how to proceed. That morning Liz thought maybe Mr. Macaby would be one of the lucky ones, one of the few that made it out alive. Now, almost eight hours later, his blood gas showed signs of fatigue, something his labored breathing confirmed.

Sydney cleaned the stethoscope hanging near his bed and placed it on his chest, buying herself more time. His lungs were crackly, the same way hair would sound if rubbed together against one's ear, and on top of that, Sydney heard a tight expiratory wheeze. Frowning, she wrapped the stethoscope back over the rail and palpated Macaby's belly. Then she sat on the edge of the bed and faced him.

"Your blood gases are worsening."

"I don't need a lab test to tell me that. My chest feels like shit." He spoke bluntly, but his face cracked, and his voice shook. "How's my wife?"

Sydney didn't say anything at first, just sat there snapping one of the non-latex gloves melting her hands. The young man caught her gaze with a hard stare. "I need you to tell me.

I asked the nurse an hour ago, but she hasn't come back. Please. Tell me. She's not…I mean…she's not…"

Sydney shook her head. "No, but she's very sick."

The words were a copout. Macaby already knew his wife was sick. He kept his gaze on Sydney, tears welling in his eyes. "Come on, Doc, I need to know."

Sydney blinked a few times. "She's not good. I don't think she'll last the night."

"Oh, God." The patient's words were swallowed by a sob.

Sydney grabbed his left hand and pressed it between her own, surprised by her increasing comfort with non-medically related patient contact. Macaby's skin was hot, even through Sydney's gloves. "When did you last see her?"

"Not since early this morning, just before they admitted me. The nurse won't let me go to the ICU, said it's too much of a risk having me out in the halls." His voice caught again and was followed by more sobs, the deep, guttural kind that come from a man who hasn't cried in years.

Sydney patted his hand, her heart pounding somewhere inside her throat. "I'm so sorry."

He looked up, his blue eyes glistening. "Please, you have to take me there. She has no one. She can't die alone. Her parents died two days ago, and God knows where my family is."

Sydney's heart ached even more. To lose your parents was bad enough, but to die alone was unthinkable. She reached up and pushed a strand of blond hair from the patient's eyes. Such an intimate gesture, and yet she realized she didn't even know what he did for a living. Graduate student? Fitness trainer? Car salesman? Never before had she felt so enmeshed, yet at the same time, so distant from her patients.

"Please," the young man pleaded again. "She can't die alone. I don't care about myself, but I need to be with her."

"You're not supposed to leave your room. You're in strict respiratory isolation. We can't risk infecting hospital personnel or the few non-influenza patients." The words came out automatically, words Sydney had recited many times, but as she spoke them now, she knew they were full of crap. This man, probably three days away from death himself, was not about to let his wife die alone.

And neither was Sydney.

She glanced at the two other patients in the room, one lying on an authentic hospital bed, the other on a cot brought in to accommodate the extra body. One of the men was elderly, the other in his forties. Both appeared to be sleeping, and their labored breaths echoed in the room.

"Can you walk?" Sydney asked, returning her gaze to Mr. Macaby.

He started to sit up, paused, and flopped back down. He shook his head, his tear-streaked face pale from the effort.

Sydney put her gloved hand to Macaby's cheek. He was burning hot, the antipyretics no longer breaking his fever. She buzzed for the nurse. When there was no response, she walked to the door and peeked out. She weighed the danger of taking Macaby to see his wife. They would only be going to another influenza room, and the staff all wore PPE. It should be fine. Just as she decided to go for it, she saw Casper heading toward Macaby's room, gowned, gloved, and masked, as if coming to see the patient. They looked at each other in surprise.

After a brief hesitation, he said, "I wondered where you were."

Sydney had deliberately avoided him all day. A patient's room was the last place she'd expected to find him. "Will you bring me a wheelchair? Quick."

Casper furrowed his brow in confusion but then nodded and walked away. She turned to her patient. "It will just be a moment."

Macaby's mournful face crumpled even more, and in Sydney's mind he became Liz. She imagined Liz lying in his place, feverish, weak, breathless, her hair disheveled and her tiny pigtails unraveled. Her knees trembled at the thought, but before she had time to conjure more images, she heard a knock and was relieved to see Casper with her request. She pulled the wheelchair through and mumbled a thank you.

Before she could close the door again, Casper said, "What are you doing?"

Sydney hesitated. "His wife is dying in the ICU. I'm taking him to see her."

"That's against policy."

"Don't you remember? I'm the one willing to bend the rules if the cause is right. Your words, not mine. Besides, does it really matter at this point?"

Fellow and attending locked eyes. "I'll watch your neck."

Sydney closed the door and wheeled the chair to the bed.

"Let's go see your wife."

Like a thief pilfering top-secret cargo, Sydney pushed the young Mr. Macaby down the hallway, portable oxygen tank and all, while every second expecting someone to question her antics. But no one did, everybody too caught up in their own tasks to worry about hers. When Sydney and Macaby made it to the fourth-floor ICU, now packed with more bodies than it could comfortably hold, the overworked staff gave them little notice. Sydney paused in front of the counter, scanned the patient board (confidentiality was taking a back seat to chaos), and found the name *Macaby* scribbled in slot number twelve. Together they hurried into what was normally a private room, but now, given the need for extra space, had an additional bed crammed up against the window. Mrs. Macaby was closest to the door, while an older woman had the bed by the window.

Sydney's patient let out a sob when he saw his wife. Despite the ventilator pumping air into her lungs, Mrs. Macaby's oxygen saturation hovered dangerously low, only in the high seventies. Her heart tracing was also erratic, and Sydney realized she had overestimated her earlier calculation of the woman lasting into the night. Mrs. Macaby would be lucky to survive another hour.

"How is she?" her husband asked, oblivious to the ominous tracings coming from the machines.

Sydney squatted down next to him. "Not good."

"Is she dying?"

Sydney glanced once more at the woman's heart rhythm. "Yes."

Macaby's chest heaved even more. "Oh dear God, please, I have to hold her. She has to be in my arms when she dies."

Sydney glanced at the door. A doctor or nurse could come in at any moment. But there was nothing more to do for Mrs. Macaby, and given her husband's worsening symptoms, he would be next. What harm would letting him lie by her side do?

Sydney squeezed her eyes tightly together. She hated this. The young couple should be home watching TV or making babies or out shopping for furniture. Anywhere but here.

"Please," Macaby sobbed again.

Sydney nodded, and then stood and helped him onto the bed, careful not to dislodge the oxygen cannula underneath his blue mask. While she held Mrs. Macaby's own tangle of tubing out of the way, Mr. Macaby gently scooped his wife into his arms and together they sank into the bed. The pair made for unusual lovers, he with his mask and portable oxygen, and she with her tubing and machines. While Macaby stroked his wife's cheek, his tears dampened her brown hair, and though she remained unconscious, Sydney hoped some part of her knew he was there.

Sydney stepped back, trying to keep her own emotions at bay. She imagined herself as the woman in the bed. Alone. No one holding her. Mitch's words about her ending up alone and lonely replayed in her mind, and it was all she could do to keep from joining Macaby in what was now a soft steady weeping. The husband and wife remained that way for what seemed like forever, but after only ten minutes, Sydney noticed Mrs. Macaby's oxygen level drop even lower—sixty-three percent, sixty, fifty-seven—and her heart rate slow even more. Soon the tracing showed only an occasional erratic blip, and though the monitors would normally be wailing at these fatal numbers, their alarms had long since been silenced, no amount of shocking or medications or CPR useful now. At least this way she could die in silence.

When the heart tracing finally flat-lined, a nurse and ICU fellow quietly entered the room, the telemetry behind the counter no doubt alerting them to Mrs. Macaby's demise. They both looked startled to see Sydney and Mr. Macaby there, but other than an initial hesitation, they said nothing. Instead, the fellow placed his stethoscope on Mrs. Macaby's chest, listened for a full minute, looked at the clock with weary eyes, and pronounced her dead. The act intensified Mr. Macaby's sobbing, and after the nurse disconnected the wife's tubing, she looked uncomfortably at Sydney and the ICU fellow. Sydney mouthed "five minutes" to them. The young physician nodded, and together he and the nurse left the room.

Sydney leaned against the wall, exhaling for what felt like the first time since she had entered the unit. After five minutes, she coaxed Macaby away from his wife's side, despising herself as she pried the man's fingers from the woman's motionless body. But the bed and ventilator were needed. With effort, Sydney helped Macaby back into his chair, and as she wheeled him down to 3 West, his crying ceased, replaced by an eerie silence, almost more unbearable than the sobbing itself.

By the time she settled Macaby into his own bed, having to answer an inquiring nurse's question as to his whereabouts in the process, Sydney was emotionally exhausted and needed a moment away. She sought out one of her residents at the front counter and told the young woman she would be in her office for the next few minutes. Before the resident could respond, Sydney hurried away down the hallway, where to her surprise she saw Jackson leaning against the wall. He appeared to be loitering, harboring no real purpose other than to stare at her, and for a moment Sydney's step faltered.

She mumbled something in greeting, but he either didn't hear or preferred not to respond. Instead, he kept watching her. His odd behavior made her pick up her pace, and she felt a strange relief when she passed him, so much so that once inside the stairwell, she flew up three flights of stairs to her office on the sixth floor, throwing frequent glances over her shoulder along the way. Finally, she reached the partitioned maze that led to her desk, and within seconds she collapsed onto the desk chair. Just a few minutes. She just needed a few minutes away.

Sydney let her brain catch up to her emotions. Never before in her lengthy training had she been so disoriented and overwhelmed, not even during an oncology rotation when she had watched two of her patients, both parents of young children, die on Christmas day. Sydney thought that was the worst she would see. Figured she'd be spared daily death in an infectious disease fellowship, not to mention emotional entanglement.

She rested her head on the desk, grateful for the surrounding silence. The ID secretaries had left for the day. No beeping machines, no ventilator pops, no sobbing husbands or weeping mothers. Sydney squeezed her eyelids tightly together, so tight bursts of light sprang forth. Yet she still couldn't get the image of Macaby and his wife out of her mind, their intertwined bodies branded into her brain.

When she finally succeeded in pushing them away, she saw Jackson instead, staring at her in the hallway. Had he been lurking around waiting for her? Or was Liz right? Did Sydney love to create drama where there was none? It dawned on her that she hadn't told Liz about her breakup with Mitch.

Instead, she'd gone on about Casper and Jackson, as if there were some wild conspiracy between the two of them.

Maybe I'm crazy. Maybe I'm finally losing my marbles.

It was only a matter of time, right?

She sat up, and after a few moments of mindless blinking, she realized if she was going to take time away from the wards, she'd better make it productive. Waiting for her computer to boot, she reached into the top desk drawer and pulled out a power bar and some pretzels. Dinner.

A third of the way into the energy bar—a misnomer for sure because she still felt lifeless—the computer was ready, and Sydney clicked open the internet, where she entered her favorite medical chat room, knowing full well what the topic would be. After a quick scan, she found *gramstain3* discussing the lack of hospital space at his institution, while *poxmd* listed ways his own hospital had dealt with the bed shortage.

Looking for more, Sydney left the active chat room and entered the most recent message board. She scanned some of the entries and learned that a New York hospital had already lost a dozen employees, including two nurses and one physician. Sydney thought about Kyra, shivered, and moved down the list, where she found a message from *idman65* questioning if the virus's pulmonary destruction was a result of a strong host response. Sydney remembered Casper's dismissal of that theory and considered typing in a response when something farther down the screen caught her eye. It was a name. A name she had only recently learned, but one that stood out as clearly as her own.

Patrick Michael Jones.

Casper's birth name. His publishing name. The name whose initials were plastered at the bottom of all those articles he'd given her.

She clicked on the entry, posted by someone with the user name of *sedrate,* and started to read. Soon her mouth went dry, and the hair on the back of her neck prickled.

The good news, for those of you who know him, is that Dr. Patrick Michael Jones will be returning from China early. We were colleagues together at Johns Hopkins before he took a position at Mt. Sinai, and although he'd planned to spend the year in China, he's cutting his sabbatical short because of the epidemic. Wants to research it back in New York. If anyone can crack the Seneca strain, Patrick can. He's…

Sydney didn't read anymore. Couldn't. Surely there must be a mistake. Dr. Burke had mentioned Casper's sabbatical in China—that she knew—but according to this message, Casper was still there.

Impossible.

She checked the date the message was posted. Saturday, November 21st , 4:26 p.m.

That's today. A little over an hour ago.

Sydney swallowed and sank back against the chair. As always, her fingers found the mole on the back of her neck, and she started to rub, her mind searching for answers. There had to be two Patrick Michael Jones's, both virologists. That was the only explanation. And to distinguish himself, Dr. Jones used the "old family name" of Casper.

Sydney's hands flew back to the keyboard, and she googled the name Patrick Michael Jones. Soon a screenful of possibilities appeared. Plenty of Patrick Jones's and plenty of Michael Jones's. Even a Michael Patrick Jones. But only one *Patrick* Michael Jones. And certainly only one Patrick Michael Jones, M.D.

She clicked on the entry and found a West Nile virus article. Another entry promised the same thing, just a different publication. She kept clicking, all the while her heart rate soaring, but everything came up the same. A virologist specializing in West Nile virus, Johns Hopkins, Mt. Sinai, China—but no Boston General. Sydney even found one photograph, but it most definitely wasn't Casper. No smooth brown skin there. Only a pasty-looking man with a gaunt face, wire-rimmed glasses, and a head full of tousled hair.

Sydney's hands shook, and a copper taste filled her mouth. She googled another name—Casper Jones—and something came up, but unless Casper had suddenly become a musician, it wasn't him.

She sat back once again, stunned by the discovery, her whole body tense. While the real Patrick Michael Jones was in China, Casper was taking his place. Why or for what reason, Sydney had no idea, but for the first time since she'd met him, the uncertainty she'd felt in his presence seemed justified. Despite that small vindication, she felt hurt and betrayed, not to mention confused, because now that she had proof to show Dr. Burke, the thought of doing so filled her with anxiety.

Exhaling slowly, she clicked back to the message board and printed out the entry. After a long pause, she trudged out of her office toward Dr. Burke's. She didn't understand the hesitancy she was now feeling to show the department head the proof. Wasn't this what she'd wanted?

When she reached Dr. Burke's office, the door was wide open, but the room was empty. Strange for him to leave it unlocked.

Sydney picked up his phone and paged him. As she waited for her boss to respond, her reluctance grew. She pictured Casper yesterday morning, worrying about her welfare. She pictured the look on his face when he'd learned of Kyra's death. Or the way he squeezed his temples with his palms when he got news of another dead parent or child. Surely she hadn't imagined his sincerity?

She shook her head. It didn't matter. Casper was impersonating someone else, and she had no choice but to report it.

After four minutes, Sydney paged Burke again, wondering where he was. It dawned on her she hadn't seen him all day. She drummed her fingers on the fancy mahogany desk and for the first time noticed its clutter, a far cry from Dr. Burke's usual neatness and order. It looked as if a tornado had blown through the office, and although most of the papers appeared to be memos and correspondences from other department heads across the country, something poking out from beneath the mess caught Sydney's eye.

After closer scrutiny, she realized it was Casper's CV. Sydney eyed the door and, with a renewed energy, slipped the resume out from underneath the pile. Strange Burke still had it loose on his desk, but given the recent events, Sydney supposed many items had been left unfiled, his secretary overwhelmed with other matters.

The CV was long, with pages and pages of publications attached, P.M. Jones the lead author on most. Sydney studied the personal information. No spouse or children, which she had already known, not even a list of hobbies. She studied Casper's address and recognized the area from her wilder days. Not exactly nice digs for a virologist.

She returned the apparently fraudulent resume to the bottom of the pile. Her edginess deepened. Where was Dr. Burke?

She couldn't afford to waste any more time. She decided to search the wards, but before she got the chance, someone had entered the office suite and was coming down the hallway. Startled and not wanting to be accused of snooping, which of course she was, Sydney hustled away from Burke's desk and stepped out of the office. Instead of finding a department colleague like she had expected, Sydney came face to face with Jackson.

She stifled a cry and brought the hand still clutching the computer printout to her chest. "Jeez, you scared me. Is there something I can help you with?"

Jackson eyed the paper in Sydney's hand but said nothing. With shaky motions, she folded up the printed evidence of Casper's dishonesty and slipped it into her back pocket. "I'm sorry, but these are the infectious disease offices. No other staff should be up here after hours."

"I'm looking for Dr. Jones."

"He's not here. Probably in the lab." Sydney wanted to question the man further, find out exactly why he was there, but something in his manner warned against it. She decided it was time to leave.

Jackson decided otherwise. Planting his muscular body in Sydney's path, he said, "You and Dr. Jones are pretty good friends, isn't that so?"

"Dr. Jones and me? He's my attending."

"You sure about that?"

Sydney tried to still her heart, having no idea where this exchange was going. For a bizarre instant she imagined Mitch sharing his story with Jackson, the one where she and Casper were lovers, but the idea was preposterous. Mitch didn't even know Jackson. "I'm sorry, I don't know what you mean."

Jackson scrutinized Sydney. After a beat, he said, "You be sure to tell Dr. Jones I'm looking for him."

Sydney swallowed. "Um, yeah, sure. Now if you'll excuse me, I have work to do."

With that Jackson stepped aside, allowing Sydney to exit the office suite and return to the wards. She trotted at a brisk pace, pondering the unnerving encounter she'd just experienced. Was Jackson merely a jealous lover, deluded with the idea that somehow Casper and Sydney were involved? Seemed unlikely considering what Sydney had just dug up on Casper. There had to be more at play, yet she could think of no other explanation. She had no time to come up with ideas, either, because when she reached 3 North, one of the third-year residents awaited her.

"Hey, I've been looking for you. Another patient di—" Troy cut himself off. "You okay? You look like you've seen a ghost."

"Something like that." Sydney's breaths were still shallow. "Listen, have you seen Dr. Burke?"

"You mean you haven't heard?"

"Heard what?"

"He's missing."

"Missing! What do you mean, missing? I just saw him yesterday."

"Yeah, but no one's been able to reach him since."

"Well, that doesn't mean he's missing." Irritation crept into Sydney's voice. "What about Dr. DeWitt? I'm sure she's spoken to him."

"Not her either. She's been trying to call him all day. Even went to his house, but no one was there."

"What about his wife?" Sydney had no idea how to process this startling news.

"Can't find her either." Troy looked around and moved in closer, his deep-set eyes darting nervously above his mask. "People are saying they left, headed out of town to avoid getting sick."

"That's ridiculous. Burke would never do that. He's been trying to fight this thing as hard as anyone."

Troy shrugged. "He wouldn't be the first hospital employee to bolt. People are leaving in droves. Mostly—"

"Well, not Dr. Burke." Heat flashed in Sydney's eyes. "Think about what you're saying. Stop spreading malicious rumors." The idea of Burke running scared was too farfetched for Sydney to believe. Despite their differences, she still respected the man and wasn't about to have his name smeared. "Has anyone called the police?"

"Dr. DeWitt's going to if he hasn't returned her call by tonight." Troy's flippant tone had been replaced by a more cautious one after Sydney's tongue-lashing.

Sydney nodded. "Good. Sorry I snapped at you. I'm just tired and edgy. We all are."

She proceeded to hear Troy's update on his patients, and for the next four hours until her respite, she was forced to continue with patient-care duties, despite what she'd uncovered about Casper, despite her rattling encounter with Jackson, and despite the sudden disappearance of her boss. She felt suffocated, as if she were drowning in quicksand and couldn't come up for air. Although she wanted to pass on her discovery, wanted to make sure she hadn't completely lost her mind, there was no one to turn to. Liz had gone home for much-needed sleep. Mitch hated Sydney's guts. And the only attending around was Casper, whom Sydney still hadn't seen since their exchange outside Macaby's room hours earlier. She debated whether to call Dr. Steinberg or Dr. DeWitt, but whenever she reached for the phone, another patient issue would come up and she'd be pulled away. What would she say over the phone, anyway? That she had reason to believe Dr. Jones was impersonating another virologist? They'd think she was suffering from viral encephalitis and have her wheeled straight to neurology.

Finally, at 11:30 p.m., eyes blurry from studying chart after chart and hand aching from penning hundreds of notes, few of which held any optimism, Sydney decided it was time to go home, especially considering she was on call the next night. Although the incriminating paper still burned in her back pocket, she decided it would have to wait until morning.

She closed the chart in front of her and stood. Tomorrow she would put everything in Dr. DeWitt's hands. Let her figure it out. Sydney barely had time to piss let alone decipher a mysterious new attending. Not to mention an intimidating orderly. A lump rose in her throat, and she feared the onset of tears. She had never felt so out of control in her life.

Her loneliness made her think of Macaby and the young wife he'd lost. Swallowing her pity, she decided to check on him one more time before leaving. His most recent blood gas was dismal, his inability to oxygenate becoming more pronounced, and Sydney worried if he didn't get a ventilator soon, he'd join his wife more quickly than planned.

As she walked to Macaby's room, the smell of her own overtaxed body reached her. She thought about how nice a warm bath would feel. Soothing bubbles, lavender oil, burning candles. She had taken baths at one time, hadn't she?

After pulling on her personal protective equipment and reapplying her goggles, she pushed open Macaby's door.

She froze and blinked a few times.

What she'd just walked in on didn't make sense. Maybe her fatigue and protective eyewear were making her see things. She stood motionless, door still open, trying to formulate an explanation.

What was Casper doing in the room?

And what had he just injected into her patient?

Sensing someone's presence, Casper swung around to face her, a needle and syringe in his hand. "Oh, hi, Sydney, just checking on Mr. Macaby."

Sydney struggled to see Casper's expression in the darkened room, especially given the mask, but the way he darted to the sharps container and disposed of his evidence spoke volumes enough.

Sydney stood there, open-mouthed, not sure what to say. She looked at the sleeping patient, his chest heaving even more than an hour before. She glanced at Macaby's two roommates, also asleep—or unconscious.

Her gaze returned to Casper. "What in the world are you doing in here?"

"Like I said, checking our patient."

"But you're doing research, not patient care."

"I try to help out when I can."

"Since when? Most of your patient contact is through me." Sydney moved toward him. "What was that you gave him, anyway?" She nodded her head towards the sharps container.

"Oh that?" Casper shrugged, as if the topic wasn't worth discussing. "That was some dexamethasone."

Sydney frowned, thoroughly confused now. "I don't understand. The nurses dispense the medications, not us. Otherwise there'd be duplicates and other mistakes."

"I was helping Peg out. She's swamped like everyone else."

"Why…how…well, did you at least mark it on the med sheet so we'll know a dose was given?"

"Um, sure. Say, I have to go. I'm going to get some sleep in one of the call rooms. Then I have more work to do before I go home. I'll ramble with you later."

With that Casper started stripping off his gown, but before he could finish, Sydney's brain leaped into action, and she remembered the computer printout in her back pocket. Before she could change her mind, she rushed to the door.

"Wait, Casper, I need to talk to you." She realized it was the first time his name had flown so effortlessly off her tongue. Or at least the name he claimed was his.

"Yes?"

She faltered for a moment, wondering how to proceed.

"Is there something wrong?" he asked.

After another pause, Sydney reached into her back pocket and pulled out the printed message. She pushed her fear aside and handed it to him. "I think you need to explain this."

Casper gave her a strange look and then unfolded the paper and read. For a few moments he said nothing, but despite the shadowy room and the mask over his face, Sydney saw uncertainty in his eyes.

He refolded the paper and cleared his throat. "So?"

Sydney tore the paper from his hands and shook it in the air. "What do you mean, *so*? Explain to me how you can be in two places at one time?"

"I can't, of course. Obviously, this individual is confused. I'm no more in China now than I am in India."

Casper turned around as though about to leave, but Sydney rushed forward and slammed her back against the door, relieved to have her fighting spirit back. "Something is going on. I don't know who you really are or what you're doing here, but something doesn't make sense."

Casper refitted his mask. "Listen to yourself. I think your lack of sleep is taking a toll on you. The guy who wrote that doesn't realize I took the job at Boston General early, that's all." Casper tried to pull Sydney from the door, but she wouldn't budge.

"What did you give my patient?" she demanded.

"I told you. Steroids."

"I don't believe you."

"Sydney, please, I have work to do." This time Casper's grasp was less gentle, and he succeeded in plucking her away. He turned and opened the door.

"I'm going to pass this message on," Sydney said, making Casper freeze. "Maybe not to Burke, since apparently God only knows where he is, but to someone else on staff. I think they'll find it interesting. A simple phone call should—"

Casper spun around and grabbed Sydney's arms, an intensity in his eyes she'd never seen before. He closed the door with his foot. "Listen to me. Not everything is as it seems."

His sudden fervor shot dread down Sydney's spine.

"You have to trust me," he said. "Can you do that? Can you trust me for a little bit longer?"

She stammered, not knowing what to say, his grip still tight on her arms.

He must have sensed he was scaring her, because he lowered his voice and loosened his hold. "Despite what you might think, I'm not a bad man. I am who I say I am. It's just...well..."

"It's just what?" Sydney's question was barely a whisper.

Casper rubbed the skin under his goggles and then put his palms over his temples and squeezed. Sydney worried he might scream—that was how anguished he seemed.

His reaction frightened her. "Dr. Jones?"

"Look." Casper's hands remained on his scalp. "I may have a theory, okay?"

"A theory? About the virus?" Sydney was incredulous.

Casper nodded and eyed the door. His expression was nothing short of torture. "But you can't tell anyone yet, okay?"

"What's going on? If you have something that can help, that's good, right? You have to tell people." Sydney's voice sped up. "I mean, you can't keep it a secret. You have to——"

"Please," Casper pleaded. "Just give me twenty-four hours, that's all I ask. Then you can do as you please, but until then, you have to trust me." More anguish in his eyes. "I'd feel terrible if something happened to you."

Sydney stepped back, fear prickling her spine all over again.

"Can you trust me, Sydney? Can you?"

Another step back.

"Please. It's more important than you realize."

Before she could answer, before she could do anything to make her mouth move or her legs bolt, the door popped open. Mitch stood in its frame.

In obvious surprise, his gaze darted from Sydney to Casper and then back to Sydney. "Syd? You okay?" When she didn't answer, he said, "The nurse saw you come in here ten minutes ago. She thought she heard arguing." Mitch—fully gowned, masked, and gloved—stepped all the way into the room and let the door shut behind him. Eyeing Casper with anger and suspicion, he asked Sydney once again if she was okay.

At the same time, Casper's expression remained pleading.

Sydney's heart pounded, and her hands burned inside her gloves. She didn't know what to do. She was completely torn, and the fact that she was made no sense at all. Here was her chance to tell someone about Casper. Wasn't that what she had been waiting for? Mitch would believe her. She knew he would.

But then there was Casper, the look in his eyes so tortured, she barely dared glance away. What if what he'd said was true? What if he had a theory? Some sort of answer to this impossible, horrible nightmare. What could twenty-four hours more of her silence hurt?

"Syd?" Mitch's concern intensified.

She remained frozen, still staring at Casper.

"Sydney, please, what's wrong?"

With a jolt, instinct took over, and Sydney came to her senses, but her answer surprised her. "I'm fine, Mitch. Everything's fine. Dr. Jones and I were just discussing the patient."

Throwing one last glance at Casper, his body sagging in relief and his expression displaying a gratitude Sydney felt reluctant to take, she tore off her gown and stepped out of the room.

What was another twenty-four hours?

9

———————

Sydney gripped the steering wheel. What in God's name was she about to do? What had seemed like a reasonable —necessary even—idea at the time now seemed crazy. Breaking and entering at the age of thirty-one was a different story from breaking and entering as a juvenile, and unlike now, that ugly tidbit from Sydney's past was the result of a coercive boyfriend.

No one was forcing her now.

But Casper was still at the hospital, and one look was all Sydney would need. One quick peek to tell her what was going on. At this point, she was willing to do anything to get the image of Macaby and his wife out of her mind. And the Lambs. And Duncan and his wife's beef stew that Sydney would never get to try. And Kyra.

And, dear God, Liz.

That was the deal breaker. The thought of Liz getting sick. The thought of Casper having something that might help Sydney's best friend and realizing that twenty-four hours could be too late, promise or no promise.

Sydney shut off the engine. She could do this. It wouldn't take long.

Shivering, she stepped out of the Jeep. Wishing she'd worn more than a fleece jacket, she crossed over a darkened basketball court adjacent to the apartment building Casper had listed as home on his resume. Who knew if the address was real?

With pepper spray clutched in one hand and keys splayed between her fingers in the other, Sydney maintained a brisk walk until she reached the front of the building, which was poorly lit by a streetlamp. Its own entrance light was burnt out. She tried not to think of how late it was. Tried not to think of who might be lurking nearby. Instead, she opened the building's main door and was unsurprised to find it unlocked. Although an old keypad hung on the brick wall adjacent to the door, the loose wires suspended from its base suggested there'd been no need for a security code for quite some time.

Once inside the building, she blinked at the sudden brightness and was relieved to find the hallway empty. The interior was more promising than the outside, and although the walls were scuffed and bare, the carpet was clean and the air well-scented. Once she realized no one was going to jump her, she relaxed enough to tuck her keys into her purse but kept the pepper spray accessible. She climbed one flight of stairs to where she estimated apartment twelve would be. She didn't have to go far. Number twelve was two units down.

Heart pounding and stomach swirling, she paused in front of its warped door and glanced both ways down the hall. Then she inspected the lock and was grateful to find no dead-bolt. Although lock picking was another fine trade bestowed upon her by that same delinquent boyfriend—from group home number one or two, she couldn't remember—it had been years since Sydney had practiced the skill, not since medical school when she'd locked herself out of her own place. She'd be rusty. Then again, judging by the pathetic lock in front of her, the effort required would be minimal.

She glanced down the hall one more time, blood pulsing

in her temples, and dug around the bottom of her purse for two bobby pins. She came up with three and released the extra. Rolling the remaining two between her fingers, she questioned again what she was about to do, but the longer she hesitated, the more suspicious she'd look. It was past midnight, and tenants might be returning home soon after a Saturday night out. For all she knew, the neighbors across the hall already had their eyes jammed against the peephole.

"Who's the tall blonde?" the husband would ask.

"That's for the police to decide," his wife would rattle back, her hand on the phone.

Just do it.

Sydney licked her lips and steeled her nerves, reminding herself of what she might find, of the questions she would finally get answered. The world no longer made sense. Death lurked everywhere. She hadn't had a full night's sleep or an acceptable meal or a breath of fresh air in days. If Casper had an answer, Sydney was determined to find it. Desperate even.

She took a big breath and tapped on the door. She hated drawing attention to herself, but she also feared finding someone on the other side.

No response. She tried again, daring to knock a little louder.

Still nothing.

She scanned the hallway one last time. Then, steadying the doorknob with her left hand and slipping one of the bobby pins through the hole with her right, she jimmied the lock. It didn't take but three seconds.

Jeez, Casper.

With a dry mouth, Sydney opened the door and hurried inside. She pressed her back against the wall and let her eyes adjust to the darkened room. The place was quiet. If someone was there, he or she was sleeping and obviously didn't snore.

From her purse, she pulled the flashlight she'd retrieved from the Jeep's glove compartment and, with suspended breath, swept the light around a living room that contained nothing but a couch, a chair, and a lamp. Shining the light in the opposite direction, she found the kitchen. She pointed the shaky beam towards a small hallway, where an open door suggested a bathroom. Walking a little closer, she saw there was one more room, presumably the bedroom, but the door was closed, nothing but silence behind it.

Sydney's heart drummed so loudly she worried it could be heard into the next apartment, where the neighbor's wife was probably chatting with the police already, hands on hips and eyes throwing "I told you so" glances to her husband. Sydney could already see the headline: *Local Doctor Arrested for Breaking and Entering.*

Lovely.

She looked at the closed door. What if someone was sleeping behind it? Though she heard nothing, she couldn't be sure.

She reached for the doorknob, its metal cool in her sweaty palm, and again questioned her antics. Yet she forged on, turning the knob and slowly opening the door. With a shaky hand, she aimed the light at the bed.

Empty.

Exhaling in relief, Sydney swept the flashlight around the rest of the room. Once convinced it was vacant, she returned to the living room and switched on the lamp. She flipped on the kitchen light as well.

The sudden illumination confirmed what the flashlight had initially suggested—the place was sparsely furnished with nothing adorning the walls. A small television set Sydney had missed on first inspection sat in the corner of the room, and a few empty soda cans lay scattered on the carpet.

The kitchen revealed nothing more than the expected appliances, a phone, and a few more empty soda cans on top of a *USA Today* newspaper that was spread out on a small island bar with a chipped Formica countertop. Stepping farther into the kitchen, Sydney found a few dishes in the sink, but they appeared well-rinsed, and the faucet, too, was wiped clean. Other than the smattering of empty soda cans, Casper seemed to be a tidy guy.

Sydney's gaze traveled to the fridge. She knew she needed to hurry, but her heart rate had slowed to a more manageable level, and she was curious to know what the mysterious Dr. Jones ate. One could learn a lot about a person from their refrigerator. Health nut? Dairy freak? Alcoholic—or in Casper's case—sodaholic?

After a glance over her shoulder, Sydney opened the fridge. Just as she'd suspected, there appeared to be a life-time supply of soda, all of it diet. There were diet versions of root beer, Mountain Dew, Coke, Pepsi, Sunkist, 7-Up— the guy definitely didn't discriminate when it came to sodas. Sydney couldn't help but smile. What was up with that? Next to the soda stood beers, mostly Samuel Adams and Budweiser.

Aside from the stockpiled beverages, Casper appeared to be a healthy eater. Plenty of fruits and vegetables and a huge leafy-green salad. Some milk, yogurt, and left over chicken breasts completed the picture.

Sydney closed the fridge and started to walk away, but then she frowned and reopened its door. Something was miss- ing. Casper was diabetic. Where was the insulin? She dug around the various food items but found none.

Odd.

Maybe he had run out? If so, that wouldn't be good.

She told herself to forget the medicine and get on with the task at hand. Moving on to the bathroom, she discovered another unadorned space. In fact, no personal touches enlivened any of the rooms—save the empty soda cans—not even a picture on the wall or a plant in the corner or a mirror in the living room in which to admire his gifted perfection. The shower curtain proved boring as well, just a clear plastic lining, and not even the single white towel could be relied upon for a splash of color.

She was about to exit the bathroom, resisting the urge to raid the medicine cabinet, when something on the vanity caught her attention. It was a brown bottle, about the size of a vitamin container, and through the thick glass, Sydney discerned what looked like pills, only about a fourth left.

She leaned in for a closer look. It appeared to be a prescription, but from no pharmacy Sydney had ever heard of.

BennitWorld Pharmaceuticals?

She picked up the bottle, interested in knowing what Casper took, but when she read the label, she inhaled sharply. In her surprise, the bottle dropped from her hand and clattered on the countertop.

Sydney froze, worried she'd be exposed by the noise. When nothing untoward happened, she picked the bottle back up. Surely, she'd read it wrong. It must have said *Inderal* or *Iodine* or *Ippity Dippity Doo.* Anything other than what it did.

She rechecked the label and tightened her grip.

Insulin.

In a pill form.

Impossible.

Filled with shock and disbelief, Sydney untwisted the lid and looked inside. It was a joke, that was all, someone playing a gag.

She tried to dump one of the pills into her palm, but her hands shook too much, and a bunch of mini M&M-sized tablets scattered into the sink. In her panic, she went to collect them but instead managed to knock most of them down the drain.

Shit!

She rescued what she could and stuffed the remaining pills back into the bottle, but there couldn't be more than ten left, and she was horrified by her clumsiness. Then she remembered what the pills claimed to be, knew that was nothing short of impossible, and at most, she had just plugged the drain with a handful of phony pills.

Sydney cupped the bottle in her hand and studied it a little longer. She carefully retrieved a pill, this time reaching in a finger instead of dumping the bottle. She brought the tablet close to her eyes. The word *Insulin* was imprinted in the center, the number twenty-five underneath.

She reached out and found the toilet lid. Lowering it, she sank down.

Insulin didn't come in a pill. Hopefully it would someday, but as of now it sure didn't. Oral forms had proved too unstable, their ineffectiveness condemning many diabetics to a lifetime of shots. Or maybe the pump. But not a pill. Never a pill.

Sydney remained glued to the toilet seat, staring at the pill, the pill that couldn't be, and for once in her life she had no opinion, no speculation, no words of wisdom. She couldn't have felt more jittery than if she'd just won a hundred-million-dollar jackpot.

It was a joke, a gag gift, that was all. Maybe from Jackson, he with the enormous sense of humor.

Sydney kept studying the pill, shocked and enthralled, but finally, after what seemed like forever, she realized she better get moving. She tucked the tablet into her purse, figuring one less pill wouldn't matter since she'd managed to spill most of the bottle. Her gaze went back to the label. She'd never heard of the pharmacy, didn't believe its contents, and couldn't find the fill-date, only some eight-digit serial number on top.

She replaced the bottle on the cabinet and backed out of the room. If a mind could be speechless, hers most certainly was.

She started towards the bedroom, unaware of how long she'd been in the apartment, but incapable of aborting her search now. The insulin discovery, whether real or fake, had once again fueled her curiosity.

When she turned on the light, she found the bed smaller than she'd first appreciated with the flashlight, simply a double-sized mattress shoved up in the corner, no box spring or headboard. There was also no dresser, just a closet near the bed with two neatly hung suits, a pair of jeans, two pairs of slacks, and a small collection of shirts and ties. On the floor rested new sneakers and a pair of casual shoes, next to which a box containing neatly folded underwear, socks, and a handful of T-shirts sat. The amount of clothes seemed more suitable for a long trip rather than a home residence.

The rest of the space was more laboratory than bedroom. On the wall across from the bed sat a long table littered with journal articles, two lamps, several legal pads, and a slew of pens and highlighters. Gone was the neatness Sydney had seen in the kitchen. In the center of the table sat a black, oval object, measuring the size of a large makeup compact. Sydney figured it was a calculator of some sort. To the left was another wall with two more rectangular tables pushed up against it, both holding expensive-looking equipment, only a few pieces of which looked even vaguely familiar. Was this the "sophisticated equipment" Casper preferred to keep at home?

Sydney approached the tables and started with what appeared to be a microscope, although it was the most unusual microscope she'd ever seen, made of shiny chrome and possessing vertically angled eyepieces like those of an optometrist. The lenses were attached to the base by a thin, diagonal rod that bifurcated near the bottom into an inverted V, and on the plate sat a circular slide, rather than the more traditional rectangular shape.

Sydney picked up the unit in her hand. It couldn't have weighed more than a pound.

Wow. High tech, Dr. Casper Jones.

The other pieces of equipment on the tables were equally impressive, and while Sydney recognized the names, their structures were hardly recognizable. At the end sat a white machine labeled *Scanning Electron Microscope*, but its size was no larger than a toaster and Sydney doubted its authenticity. Scanning electron microscopes required stable environments with no interference—not likely in a bedroom. It was attached to a thin computer screen, and next to that was what appeared to be an incubator, complete with carbon dioxide control and temperature reading, but again, much smaller than anything Sydney had seen in the lab.

The table also held what seemed to be a small laminar flow hood but with no place to vent, a centrifuge, and two other shiny chromed machines, one labeled DNA sequencer—impossible, considering it was barely the size of Sydney's palm—and the other a strange triangular contraption that resembled an odd-shaped waffle maker. God only knew what that was for. Underneath the table, Sydney spotted a small refrigerator—*that* at least she recognized—and next to it was a plastic bin holding various sized beakers and test tubes as well as forceps, probes, and other handheld tools.

Intrigued, Sydney bent down and opened the fridge, all the while wondering where Casper had procured such unusual equipment and why he seemed so reluctant to share it. Inside the refrigerator were small glass containers not unlike the one Sydney had seen in Casper's office, the one that held a sample of Mr. Lamb's lungs. That sample was still there, and next to it was another bottle labeled *Healthy Tissue* in poorly scrawled penmanship. Not exactly precise labeling techniques, but Sydney supposed when conducting research at home, amid equipment worth thousands and thousands of dollars, one could do whatever one wanted.

She poked around at some of the other vials. They were labeled *Virus Sample 1—Protein (+)*, *Virus Sample 2—Protein (-)*, and so on, but Sydney had no idea what they meant.

Frowning, she closed the fridge and stood up, trying to take it all in, but once again she was dumbstruck. She, who could justify anything. She, who could come up with an explanation for why people shrank with age, or why bad things came in threes, or why, no matter what, she always picked the slowest moving line in the checkout lanes. But this? For this Sydney had no words.

She looked back over the equipment. The fact Casper kept it at home was strange enough. The fact it looked like nothing Sydney had ever seen before was downright creepy. Was he some sort of inventor? Or maybe an affiliate of an ultra-modern research society?

She stood there a few moments longer, hands on her hips, trying to connect the bizarre equipment with the equally bizarre information she'd found on the internet earlier that day. She couldn't. She glanced at her watch. She'd been in the apartment for fifteen minutes, and while the surprises on the table had temporarily calmed her nerves and distracted her mind from the possibility she might get caught, the implication of what she was doing suddenly hit her full force. Unease swirled in her belly, and despite the fact Casper claimed he was staying at the hospital, Sydney knew she better get moving.

But she still hadn't found any answers.

Only more questions.

She walked to the other table, the one with all the papers scattered on top. She studied the black, oval object in the middle and bent down for a closer look. The item was shiny and smooth, and, out of curiosity, Sydney rubbed her hand on the top. To her surprise, the piece opened.

Startled, she jumped back. She was even more horrified when a glamorous woman materialized in front of her. In a seductive voice, the apparition said, *"Hello, Casper. I trust things are going well."*

Sydney stood there—frozen, shocked, confused. The blonde-haired beauty remained before her, a transparent body shimmering in the air above the table, like a translucent fairy conjured on command. The woman measured about two feet tall, and though Sydney could have passed her hand right through the vision, she hardly dared try. It was unlike anything she'd ever seen before, and she worried if she didn't sit down soon, her knees would give out.

But then she noticed something else, something that made it difficult to breathe. The see-through woman was her. In Sydney's shock, she hadn't recognized it at first, but the flickering hologram was indeed a mirror image: straight blonde hair, large eyes that were too widely spaced apart, thinnish nose. But unlike Sydney, the woman's face was adorned with makeup, and her strapless red gown outfoxed Sydney's pungent blue scrubs.

Sydney stepped back, mouth wide, mind devoid of reason. *What…how…*

Before she could formulate any rational thought, the woman who was her spoke again. *"I'm waiting, Casper."*

Sydney shuddered. Even though the vision's voice wasn't her own, the resemblance between them disturbed her greatly.

Finally, she tore her gaze away from the creepy apparition and took a tentative step forward to better view the black object underneath the image. What Sydney had thought looked like a compact or a calculator was apparently no such thing. Stepping even closer and trying to ignore the glamorous figure shimmering in the air, Sydney peered down at the dark, oval object, its cover now raised and its base revealing what appeared to be a tiny computer screen with a collection of colorful icons. The icons were unrecognizable, made up of three-lettered acronyms and weird symbols. Sydney focused on a green one labeled *MLB*. After a brief hesitation, she lifted a shaky finger and pressed the small icon. A keyboard materialized in the air above the black case, replacing the sultry woman.

"Holy crap," Sydney said aloud.

She nearly passed out when the computer—*is that what it is?*— answered back, using the same seductive voice as before, but this time without the accompanying woman. *"Command and voice not recognized. Prompt required to bypass voice-activation."*

Mesmerized, Sydney stared at the shimmering air in front of her, the air that had suddenly become a keyboard, full of color and definition but also see-through and non-physical. Swallowing, she pushed her finger through the letter *H* on the air-suspended keyboard. Nothing happened. She tried once more but snatched her hand away when the computer spoke again. *"Password required to access letterboard."*

Sydney paused, eyes wide, breaths shallow. Her gaze flew back to the black object on the table, and she scanned its collection of icons. Holding her breath, she pressed a blue one labeled *FLC*. The computer seemed displeased with the choice, because the keyboard dissolved, and Sydney's smaller, sexier, translucent counterpart rematerialized.

"Password or voice recognition required to access files."

The woman seemed to stare right through Sydney, lips slightly parted, hands waving gently by her side. Sydney clasped her own hands together, unsure what to do next. Didn't matter. The sultry computer maiden decided for her.

"Computer shutting down. Access not authorized."

Within seconds the image in front of Sydney dissolved, and she was left staring at the wall instead. Meanwhile, the compact laptop on the table closed, retreating into its silent shell.

Exhaling slowly, Sydney folded her hands and brought them to her lips. She couldn't move. Couldn't think. She'd never witnessed anything so strange in her life. Not the computer, not the equipment, not the secretive research.

And certainly not the insulin pills.

She took a few more deep breaths, and although it was difficult to move past the oddity she'd just witnessed, she turned to the papers on the table. She still hadn't found evidence Casper had discovered something—anything—to stop the viral killer, and although tempted to bolt, Sydney reminded herself that the whole reason she had put herself through this ridiculous stunt in the first place was to find out exactly what Casper knew. Maybe these papers held the answer.

She ran a hand over the dozens of journal articles littering the table and picked one at random: *Influenza, A Review.* She tossed it aside and chose another, the word *Seneca* catching her eye: *The Seneca Scourge, Learning from History.*

Seneca Scourge? Sydney looked at the lower right corner to find the journal that published the article. *Microbiology Medicine.* Even though she didn't understand the title, her gut tensed and her mouth tasted coppery.

She released the paper and picked up another one. *Prions: The Real Cause of the Great Seneca Scourge?*

Sydney's hands shook, and her gaze once again fell to the lower right corner, but this time it wasn't the journal's name that caught her eye. This time it was the date.

Sydney dropped the article as if it had burst into flames.

No. Not possible.

She swallowed, blinked a few times, and then swallowed again. It was a trick, that was all. Casper was a sadistic bastard creating a sick, twisted farce.

With twitching fingers, she put her hands to her face. Her flesh felt warm and tingly. Retrieving the paper, she dangled the corner between her thumb and index finger like a soiled tissue. She reread the journal name and date.

Microbiology Medicine Vol. 112, No. 4 October, 2189.

Sydney's whole body trembled, and blood rushed in her ears. She tossed the article aside and grabbed another. This one was titled: *Dismantling Prions, Use of a Viral Transposon.*

It was dated December 2205.

Head spinning, Sydney dropped the paper to the desk. She groped for the chair and sank down.

This was all a trick. It had to be. Casper was probably a

weird space trekkie who got his kicks from manufacturing fake futuristic materials.

She leaned forward and put her head between her knees, trying to ward off the vertigo. She thought about what she'd read, not just the date—that was too incomprehensible, too creepy—but the content. The Seneca Scourge? Was that referring to the influenza pandemic? Was Casper's handiwork implying the current outbreak would become the next global scourge, akin to the horrible black plague?

And what was that suggestion of a prion? Prions caused mad cow disease, not influenza. What in the world did prions have to do with the illness?

Sydney lifted her head, grabbed the third article, and tried to read its abstract, something about prions and their likely association, but her mind refused to work, refused to connect the words with their meanings. She couldn't think, couldn't speculate. It was all too bizarre.

She needed to get out. Needed to get out and clear her head. Take time to figure out what kind of freak Casper really was.

Slowly, she stood, wanting to avoid another woozy rush. She was about to leave, when something else caught her eye. Another article. One that socked her in the gut like a sledgehammer.

Sydney's blood ran cold. It wasn't possible.

A Review of the Great Seneca Scourge: What Was the Real Microbial Agent Behind Two Billion Deaths? Sydney looked at the lower right corner. *Journal of Medical History, 2nd Quarter, 2201.*

She lowered the paper and took a step back. Her heart thundered in her chest. Two billion deaths? That was almost one-third of the world's population.

Sydney thought of the inexplicable virus that had killed Mr. and Mrs. Lamb. And young Mrs. Macaby…and Duncan and his wife…and Kyra…and countless others so far. She thought of its vicious attack rate, its unfamiliar MO, its seventy-five percent mortality rate.

No. Impossible. Casper was playing a joke, a cruel, twisted joke.

On shaky legs, Sydney hurried out of the room. The papers were a forgery. She didn't know how, didn't know why, but they were.

She reached the front door, eager to escape, but then she stopped short. The insulin. What about the insulin?

She ran back to the bathroom and picked up the bottle. Her hand was shaking so bad, the jar fell once again to the sink. It bounced and clattered inside the white basin but luckily didn't break. Trembling and panting, she retrieved it, all the while terrified she was about to be discovered. She looked once again at the serial number, or what she had presumed to be a serial number.

"Oh, God," Sydney said, her voice unsteady. Inside the jacket and scrubs, sweat pooled and rolled down her skin.

10152209 wasn't a serial number.

It was a date. It was October 15, 2209.

She jumped back, shaking her head, her throat making a weird gurgling noise. In her haste to get out of the bathroom, she rammed her shoulder against the doorframe, sending shards of pain down her deltoid. She cried out and rubbed the muscle, but she still couldn't take her eyes off the bottle. She continued retreating backwards, facing the pills, the pills that couldn't be.

Have to get out. Have to think this through.

She picked up the pace, eyes and brain still trying to comprehend the pills. It was a trick. She'd figure it out.

Finally, Sydney spun around and lunged for the door. She turned the knob and ran out.

And dived right into his arms.

10

———————

They stared at each other, Sydney clutched in Casper's arms. Her heart galloped, and sweat broke out on her forehead. She wondered if this was what the first few seconds of a cardiac arrest felt like. Casper, on the other hand, seemed more resigned than surprised, an oddity Sydney didn't have time to ponder.

"I knew it would be you," he said. "You shouldn't have come."

His calm only unsettled Sydney more. She tried to pull free, but Casper squeezed more tightly, and she was afraid of what he might do.

He must have sensed it, because he looked wounded and said, "I'm not going to hurt you. Let's go inside."

Although Sydney wanted to trust him, her brain said hit the pavement.

"Please, come inside. Let's get out of the hallway."

Casper released Sydney from the bear hug and grabbed her hand. He pushed open the apartment door and motioned her inside, but instead she yanked her hand free and started to run. Casper caught her from behind before she made it two feet. Putting both arms around Sydney's waist, Casper buried his face in the back of her hair. If someone had stumbled upon the two, they'd think they were merely two lovers in a passionate embrace.

"Please, come in. I'm not going to hurt you. I'd never hurt you. We just need to talk."

Sydney turned around, and though Casper's hands still clutched her sides, he had loosened his grip. Their faces almost touched, and his eyes were as pleading as his voice. Certainly didn't look like a psycho about to kill. Then again, weren't most psychopaths charming and believable?

"What did you mean when you said, 'I knew it would be you'?" Sydney's voice shook, and her body perspired inside the fleece jacket.

Casper hesitated for a moment, and then removed his hands from Sydney's waist and lifted them to her face. With his thumbs, he stroked her cheeks. "Just come inside. Please?"

His fingertips felt like silk against her skin, and she was startled by the intimate gesture, but his touch yielded the desired response. Her muscles relaxed, and her breathing slowed.

Would he really harm me?

Another moment passed, and a door opened one floor below. Casper put two fingers over Sydney's unmasked lips and mouthed the word *please*, his eyes wider than her own.

She wanted to trust him, wanted to hear his explanation for the things she'd discovered. She'd come too far to chicken out now. She thought about the pepper spray in her purse. Thought about her two years of Karate. Would either of them help if Casper turned violent?

Footsteps mounted the stairs. Sydney searched Casper's eyes but saw no threat. After another moment's hesitation, she nodded, at which time he lowered his hands from her face and guided her into the apartment. Once inside, he shut the door, leaned up against it, and closed his eyes.

Sydney stood there, unsure what to do next. She alternated between shoving her hands in her coat pockets and hanging them by her side. Casper's eyes remained closed.

Sydney cleared her throat and repeated her earlier question. "How did you know it was me? You couldn't have possibly known I was going to break into your apartment. I didn't even know until right before I did it."

Casper shook his head. "I wish you hadn't. I really wish you hadn't."

"Yeah, me neither."

"Why'd you do it?" He looked more like a child whose sandcastle had been crushed than a man whose home had been invaded.

"Why did I do it?" Sydney's voice rose. "You don't think you've given me ample incentive? Especially after injecting my patient with God knows what? If you've found a treatment, I have to know."

"But I asked for twenty-four hours. You couldn't give me that?"

"Twenty-four hours could be too late for thousands of people."

Casper didn't respond, just stared at Sydney with those sad eyes. He sighed and removed his jacket, his white shirt pulling tight across his shoulders as he hung the coat on a hook in the closet. Apparently no longer worried Sydney would run, he made his way to the couch. He patted the cushion, suggesting she join him.

Ignoring the invitation, Sydney asked once again, "How did you know it was me?"

Casper leaned back and raised an arm. "I knew it was you because I have a security sensor. If someone breaks into my place, an alarm on my watch goes off." He pointed to a red dot above the door without looking in its direction, as if everyone in the world had special spy sensors and watches to signal a security breach in his or her apartment.

Sydney peered at the red dot and then Casper's watch.

She started to speak but stopped. There were so many questions, she didn't know where to begin.

"Although my watch told me someone broke in, it didn't tell me who. That part was a scholarly guess."

Sydney inched over to the couch and sat down, keeping her purse with its pepper spray close to her side. Once again, the reality of what she'd done hit her like a Mack truck. "Are you going to report me?"

Casper exhaled slowly. "My reporting you should be the least of your qualms."

Sydney's stomach tensed, and she worried she might have made a mistake in trusting him. "What exactly is that supposed to mean?"

"It means we need to talk about what you saw."

"I didn't see anything. Just came in, felt guilty, then left."

Casper waved his wrist in the air. "Nice try, but I have a timeline remember?"

More silence between them. Sydney sat on the end of the couch, daring a look in his direction. He seemed weary and worn out, as if her breaking in was another burdensome event in his day. Certainly not the reaction she had expected. She smoothed her scrub bottoms over her thighs and redirected her gaze to the curtainless window, waiting for Casper to speak.

Finally, he did. "What would you say if I told you I liked to create things? That everything in here is merely an interesting hobby?"

"I'd say I wanted to believe you."

Casper shifted his body toward her. "You *can* believe me. You can walk out that door and believe me. I'm an inventor, that's all. And we'll never have to talk about this again—providing you keep everything to yourself."

"Probably won't work." Sydney picked at her scrubs.

"Why not?"

"Because I've never been good at taking a backseat."

"I don't understand."

She frowned at him. "The reason I'm here in the first place is that I couldn't look the other way. You expect me to do that now?" She thought back to the things she had found and shivered.

"But there's nothing here for you."

"I disagree."

"You need to forget about it."

Sydney barked a sharp laugh. "Forget about it? How do I forget about a talking computer, or inexplicable medical equipment, or papers dated two hundred years in the future?" She stood up and started pacing the room. "I think you owe me an explanation."

"I owe *you* an explanation? You're the one who broke into my apartment, remember? You should never have come here."

Sydney kept moving, her face flushed. "What did you inject into my patient?"

"I already told you. Dexamethasone."

"Bullshit. We both know steroids don't help fight the virus." Somewhere in the back of her mind, Sydney realized she'd sworn at her attending, but the fact hardly seemed relevant now.

"It was worth another try."

"Dr. Jones, please, what's going on?" Her eyes implored him, and she wasn't sure how much more she could take.

Casper avoided Sydney's gaze and sank even deeper into the cushion. He rubbed his hands over his dark moss of hair. "Please. Let it go."

Sydney's agitation rose, matched by a new dizziness. "I'll tell you what I think. I think you've come up with a cure, or a treatment, or maybe even a vaccine. Only thing is, I think you scaled unconventional channels to get there, and that's why you're keeping it hush hush. That's why you do your research here."

"Sydney, please—"

"And I also know you're not who you say you are. The real Dr. Jones is still in China, apparently oblivious to the fact someone has stolen his identity."

"Sydney—"

"But that's where I draw a blank. I mean, all this other stuff?" Sydney pointed to the direction of the bedroom, her voice climbing higher. "I don't know what's up with that. I don't understand, don't know how it's possible, don't know how you—"

"Please don't get involved."

"Get involved with what?"

"I…it's…." Casper's words trailed off.

Sydney stopped pacing, her dizziness heightened. Sweat flowed in a steady stream down her back, and she wanted to tear off the jacket, but instead she darted to the couch and knelt before Casper. "Maybe I can help you. Maybe we can work on this treatment together." She knew she sounded desperate.

"There's nothing to help with. I haven't discovered any cure for the virus, and the stuff in my bedroom is just a hobby."

"Yeah, well, what about this?" Sydney reached into her purse and pulled out the insulin tablet. "This a hobby too?"

Casper blinked at the pill.

"You know, Casper, for someone with so much to hide, you do a lousy job."

Sydney waited for Casper to explain, expecting another excuse, but instead he closed his eyes and squeezed his temples with his palms, his face wearing the same tortured expression Sydney had seen in Macaby's room. "This wasn't supposed to happen. You weren't supposed to get involved. Everyone warned me to be careful, warned me I wouldn't be able to handle this."

"Handle what?"

"But I was the best choice. I was the one with all the research. I was the one with the knowledge of medical history."

Sydney felt sick to her stomach. She hadn't expected Casper to confess. She felt like a little girl who'd begged and begged to stay up for a scary movie, but now, in the middle of the terrifying film, wished she hadn't.

Casper grabbed her shoulders and locked his dark eyes onto hers. "I'm giving you one last chance. Forget about this. Pretend you saw nothing. Sometimes it's best not to know."

His words sparked a chill in her, and she wondered if maybe he was right. Maybe it was time to get the hell out of Dodge. Otherwise, she might end up like that imaginary little girl and witness something she wished she hadn't.

He gripped her shoulders tighter. "Once you know about me, there's no backing out. You can't undo it."

Sydney swallowed.

"And you can't tell anyone. No one. Can you do that? Can you keep a secret? A huge, gigantic, show-me-some-goddamn-proof secret?"

Suddenly, Sydney was in first grade, explaining away a black eye and fat lip to an inquiring teacher. Then she was twelve years old, terrified that Lonny, her second foster father, would keep his word and kill her pet hamster, Sprinkles, if she told anyone he'd touched her "down there."

Sydney shook away the ugly vision. "I've been keeping secrets all my life. Tonight will be no different."

"How do I know I can trust you?"

"I didn't tell Mitch, did I? I could've blown your cover right then."

Casper's face softened, and he reached for a lock of Sydney's hair. He rolled it through his fingers. "No, you didn't, and I thank you for that. But this knowledge could put you in danger, and I'd feel forever responsible if something happened to you."

"Seems I'm already in danger." Sydney was once again nonplussed by his intimate gesture.

Casper let go of her hair and wiped the back of his hand across his mouth. He stood and took over her role of pacing the room. "Jackson can't find out. He'd kill us both if he knew I told you."

Sydney's voice barely registered. "So, I take it the guy's no orderly?"

Casper looked at her, a fear in his eyes that only intensified Sydney's own. He once again put his head in his hands. "I don't even know where to begin."

Sydney held up the insulin tablet. "How about we start with this?"

Casper glanced at the pill but said nothing.

"Come on, insulin doesn't come in a pill," she said.

He reached out and took the tablet. "It does where I come from."

11

———————

S ydney took a deep breath. "Okay, let's see if I have this. You're from the future—the year 2209 to be exact—and you've been sent back in time to study a virus, a virus that will ultimately wipe out almost one-third of the world's population and cause the greatest scourge humanity has ever known."

Casper raised a hand. "Please, this is too much for you. I shouldn't—"

"And they've chosen you, not only because you're a virologist, but because you are a historical microbiologist. Did I get that term right?"

"Yes."

"And you've studied the Seneca strain in detail, or at least have read all about it, and think you know why it's so deadly."

"There's a working theory that's been passed along through the years, but no one's been able to prove it."

"Why not?"

"Because there are no virus samples available. They, along with all other potential biological warfare agents, were destroyed under the International Coalition of Peace and Humanity Act in the year 2099."

"Oh, of course, silly me." Sydney, who had gone back to

pacing, halted her steps and allowed her brain to catch up with his words.

She studied him, unaccustomed to seeing him so disheveled. His dress shirt was untucked on one side and hung limply over his slacks, which were now wrinkled and worn and had a stain on the thigh. His cell phone jutted from the front pocket. Stubble dotted his face, and he wore a pinched and weary expression.

"But why now?" she asked. "Why would anyone care about a viral outbreak that happened two hundred years ago? Assuming you are, as you say, from the year 2209."

"Because we think the same virus has reemerged, or at least a similar strain."

"You mean you're experiencing another outbreak?"

"No, not yet, but an unusual swine strain has infected hundreds of pigs throughout the country, and based on historical records, DNA analysis suggests it's similar to the Seneca strain. But my treatment has no effect on pigs. Nor on chimps or dogs or any other animal I studied. So I needed human subjects on which to study my theory, and since I can't ethically expose human beings, I was sent here, back to the year 2009, to test my treatment on infected patients."

Dreaming. I must be dreaming.

"Although this swine strain hasn't infected people in the year 2209 yet," Casper continued, as if expecting Sydney to easily follow along, needing no time at all to absorb his words, "that doesn't mean it won't. We need to be absolutely prepared. We can't risk having another worldwide scourge."

Sydney stood firm, hands on hips, mouth open, so many questions to ask, but no words coming. It was too unbelievable, too entirely fantastic, and as she listened to his words in his sparsely furnished apartment, she wondered what would make him sprout such a story. Maybe he was a delusional schizophrenic, fresh off the psych ward. Maybe he'd happened to come across Dr. Patrick Michael Jones's name on the internet and assumed his identity. She was sure it wouldn't be the first time such a thing had occurred, and it made more sense than his explanation.

But what about all that equipment? And those papers? And the insulin?

Suddenly, she couldn't take any more, not an hour, not a minute, not a second more. She was tired and dizzy, and long overdue for a shower and sleep.

She darted for her purse and coat.

Casper shot up from the edge of the couch. "You're leaving? What about all I've told you?"

Sydney scooted backwards. "It's just…well…it's a little too farfetched for this girl."

"You think I'm crazy, don't you? You think I've made this all up."

Sydney shrugged, trying for a sympathetic smile, all the while creeping backward toward the door.

Casper rushed in front of her. "It's the truth, I promise you. How else can you explain everything you saw?"

She shook her head and reached for the doorknob. Casper's arm shot out to stop her. "I didn't want to tell you, but I had no choice. You should never have come here."

"You're right." Sydney sounded like a squeaky mouse. "You're absolutely right."

She tried again to open the door, but Casper's outstretched arm pushed firmly against it. "I can't let you leave."

Sydney's earlier fear returned. "Why not?"

"You have no idea what you've gotten us into. I can't let you go."

"I won't tell anyone." Sydney knew that probably wasn't true.

"It's not just that. I…have to think this through. If Jackson finds out I've told you, he'll…well…"

"He'll what? Kill me? Yeah, I think you mentioned that."

"Just please, stay here tonight. You can take the couch or

the bed. You need your sleep. You have to be back at the hospital in less than six hours."

Sydney was well aware of that fact but said nothing.

"Then we can go to the hospital together in the morning, and you'll see I'm telling the truth. You'll see Mr. Macaby is improving. Well, at least I hope he is."

"Oh, and then what? You go back home on your little spaceship and leave the rest of us to die?" Sydney shook her head at the absurdity. She pulled open the door with a grunt and managed to wedge in a foot before Casper could close it again. "I'm leaving."

"Please, you have to stay. There's more to explain. There are things you don't know."

Sydney strained and pulled the door open a little wider, at least enough to squeeze part of her body through.

"You have to listen to me." Casper's voice grew even more desperate.

Sydney ignored him and finally pushed all the way through, but just as she was about to bolt down the stairs, he said something that stopped her in her tracks.

"He's got Dr. Burke."

Sydney turned around, her legs wobbly. "What did you say?"

"Please come back inside."

"Who's got Dr. Burke?"

Casper leaned his head against the doorframe. "Jackson. And if you threaten to tell anyone what I've told you, he'll kill him."

That last comment was uttered softly, but its meaning came out loud and clear.

"Please come back inside. At least in here, I know you'll be safe."

Dazed and overwhelmed, Sydney cupped her ears. She didn't know who or what to believe. None of this made sense. It was all so impossible. But Burke *was* supposedly missing. Did

Casper know that? Was he using it as a ploy? Seemed possible, but then again, was Sydney willing to risk Burke's life for what may or may not be a bluff?

She raised her head and looked hard into Casper's eyes. As usual, his gaze appeared sincere.

"Come back inside," he said. "In twenty-four hours this will all be over, and if you keep quiet, no one will get hurt."

Twenty-four hours? Didn't seem like a long time, and yet in the last sixty minutes, Sydney's whole universe had shifted.

Casper held the door open, his gaze beseeching her.

"Is Dr. Burke really in danger?" she asked, not yet taking a step.

Casper nodded.

"Why?"

Casper hesitated. "Because he discovered the same thing as you."

The phone. Somewhere a phone rang. No, not a phone. A pager. Was that her pager? Automatically, Sydney's hand flew to her waistband and groped for the pager as she lay supine.

No, the noise wasn't that. It was an alarm. Somewhere an alarm clock chimed. She reached out an arm to silence it but met nothing but air. Then she remembered where she was—on Casper's couch.

Her eyes fluttered open, and she shot up to a seated position, taking in the empty walls around her, nothing but a streetlamp outside the window to see by in the still-dark morning. She flung her legs over the side and leaned back against the cushion, the sofa creaking beneath her.

So it was all true. It wasn't a bad dream. Sydney blinked and focused on the fluorescent hands on her watch, trying to convince herself the five hours she'd slept were enough. Last night she thought it would be impossible to sleep on Casper's couch, considering everything he'd told her, but within a few minutes, she had fallen into a deep and dreamless slumber.

She stretched her arms above her head, wondering what to do next. What did one do after learning her attending was from the future and her boss had been kidnapped? Go to the hospital and pretend it wasn't true? That was apparently what Casper wanted her to do.

Sydney rolled the stiffness out of her neck and got an unpleasant whiff of herself in the process. The alarm clock she'd heard had since been shut off, and before she could rise from the couch, Casper entered the room. He turned on the kitchen light, and for a moment the silence between them was heavy and uncomfortable.

Casper cleared his throat. "We need to be at the hospital soon." Dressed in dark slacks and a clean shirt, he appeared to have recently shaved. He must've read Sydney's mind, because he added, "I showered last night so you could use it this morning."

She nodded, rubbed her eyes, and yawned. Leaning over, she grabbed her purse from the floor and plucked out her car keys. She tossed them to Casper and, in a garbled voice, said, "Black Jeep. Outside by the basketball court. Clean pair of scrubs in the back."

Ignoring the pain in her neck, she stood and ambled to the bathroom, still clutching her purse. She was desperate for a shower to wake her up. Maybe then she could clear some of the debris clunking around in her brain.

Lingering in the shower longer than she should have, she hoped that in addition to the dirt and grime, the hot water would wash away everything she'd experienced in the last eight hours. When she finished, she grabbed the clean towel on the vanity, wrapped it around herself, and dug in her purse for her comb and the travel toothbrush she carried for the nights she was on call.

After brushing her teeth, she opened the bathroom door a

crack and found the fresh pair of scrubs on the floor. She put them on, grateful she ignored the hospital's policy of not removing scrubs from the premises. *Who didn't?*

When she finished, she rolled up the used scrubs and stepped into the kitchen. Casper sat at the island bar drinking coffee, an empty plate with toast crumbs in front of him. He jumped up when he saw her.

"Coffee?" His tone sounded anxious.

Sydney nodded.

"Do you want toast? Or I have some cereal or—"

"Just coffee." Sydney sat on one of the rickety bar stools. Truth be told, she was a little hungry, but sharing breakfast with him seemed too strange.

Casper brought Sydney the cup, along with some milk and sweetener, both of which she accepted. She clutched the warm mug in her hands and took a sip. The silence around the them was palpable.

Sydney cleared her throat. "Okay, look, we need to start over. I need you to tell me the truth, and this time tell me everything." She glanced at her watch. "And you have only twenty minutes to do it."

Casper paused and then sat back down on the stool next to her, a wonderful scent of…what?—cinnamon and vanilla?—coming from him.

"I told you the truth."

"Then I need more of it, because what you told me last night is a little hard to swallow."

"Just tell me where you want to start," Casper said, relenting.

"Who is Jackson? Not an orderly, I take it."

"He's an NIU agent. We falsified an ID badge for him so he has access to the hospital, but he never sticks around long."

"NIU?"

"The National Investigative Unit. I suppose you could

compare them to your FBI but with a different type of power. They work directly for the Presidential Body."

"The Presidential who?"

"It's our five-person, multi-partisan governing body. The traditional president-vice-president system you're familiar with was abolished in the year 2050, triggered by too many unilateral decisions from misguided presidents."

"Oh." Sydney sipped her coffee but failed to be warmed.

"Jackson works for the NIU and was assigned to accompany me on this mission. Make sure I followed procedure."

"Why him?"

"He's also a microbiologist. Used to work with me at the Klier Institute of Microbiology until he joined the NIU and became a travologist."

"A travologist," Sydney said flatly, wondering why she was listening to such delusional dribble.

"Someone who goes back—and forward—in time."

"Oh, of course."

"The ability to cross time is a new phenomenon, one that's highly secretive. That's why all movements are controlled by the NIU. Jackson had a contact there, and when he learned of the possibility of time travel, he made a career change. Crossing time has always been his passion. Well, that and other people's wives." Casper got up to refill his coffee, leaving an awkward silence.

Sydney smoothed her scrubs. "So, you and Jackson used to be friends?"

"Co-workers, not friends." Casper's jaw tightened. "I was happy to see him go. He never was a very nice sam, kind of a sadistic side to him."

"I take it yours was the wife in question?"

Casper said nothing, but the look on his face was answer enough.

"So where does Jackson live? Why isn't he here?"

Casper gave Sydney a stern look. "You're lucky he isn't. That couch you slept on is frequently his."

Sydney swallowed, the coffee burning her throat, and she realized how easily she could have been caught the night before.

If she believed all this, that was.

Feeling a little less glib, she asked, "Where is he?"

"He's traveled back with…well…"

"Traveled back with what?" After a moment's hesitation, she added, "Or whom?"

"With Dr. Burke. He's taken Dr. Burke to keep him from talking."

Despite the hot coffee, a chill ran through Sydney. "Why?"

"Because Dr. Burke discovered the same thing you did. That the real Patrick Michael Jones was coming back from China early. Unfortunately, he wasn't as lucky as you."

"Dr. Burke isn't going to be…I mean…he's not going to get…" It was all too outrageous for Sydney to believe.

"Killed? Hopefully not. Kind of depends on you at this point. If all goes as planned, Jackson will bring Dr. Burke back tonight before we leave for good in the morning."

"Well, Burke won't remain silent." Sydney brought the mug down hard, spilling coffee on the counter. "And what about his wife? She'll get suspicious."

Casper gave Sydney a sad smile. "First of all, I'm from two hundred years in the future. We have medicines that can wipe out short-term memory quite nicely, but we need some time for it to work. Besides, even if we couldn't, who would believe him? He'd have no proof. People would think he's a fool. As for his wife, he'd already sent her away to be with relatives. Didn't want to expose her to the virus. The poor woman probably doesn't even know he's gone."

"But…well…" It occurred to Sydney that she, too, would be called a fool if she started flapping her lips.

Casper leaned toward her and put a hand on her forearm,

the concern back in his eyes. "I'm only telling you all this because I don't want the same thing to happen to you. I might not have been able to do anything about Dr. Burke, but I refuse to let anything happen to you."

Casper's intensity embarrassed Sydney, not to mention his hand on her arm, and she found herself thinking of his computer. She debated whether to ask. Finally, she did. "Why does your computer image look like me?"

Casper removed his hand, returned to the other side of the kitchen, and leaned against the stove. His head remained lowered, and just when Sydney thought he wouldn't answer, he said, "You can make *your* computer screen display what you want, right?"

She nodded.

"Well…so can I."

Another awkward silence. Casper ran his fingers over the coils of the burner, while Sydney tucked her still-wet hair behind her ears.

She took another sip of coffee and changed the subject. "What did you give my patient last night?"

Casper straightened, seemingly relieved for the new line of questioning. "It's all very complicated."

"I'm a doctor, remember?"

"Fair enough. Look, I don't know how many of those papers you read in my bedroom, but so—"

"You mean those journal articles you drafted for the next *Star Trek* convention?"

"They're not fake, if that's what you mean."

Sydney shrugged.

"Anyway, last night I told you there was a theory about the Seneca Scourge but no formal proof."

Sydney's mind flashed back to one of Casper's papers. "Are you referring to the one about prions causing the 'Great Seneca Scourge'?"

"That's the one."

"Prions cause mad cow disease, not influenza."

"I know. That's why it took so many years to discover. Scientists always connected prions to slowly progressive central nervous system disease, not to rapidly fatal respiratory viruses."

"But a prion is a protein, one that's changed its molecular configuration to form a more unstable compound. It has nothing to do with influenza."

Casper looked impressed by Sydney's medical school retention, but it wasn't exactly the time for kudos. "Now you understand why it took years to discover."

Sydney shook her head. She didn't understand anything.

"Don't you see? This particular viral strain has mystified microbiologists for two hundred years. In fact, its obscurity is what spawned historical microbiologists like myself in the first place."

"Why's that?"

Casper looked at Sydney as if she were joking. "Because it killed off almost one-third of the world's population, that's why. Can't you imagine how much chaos that caused? It took decades to re-stabilize the world."

Sydney sighed. She didn't know how much more she could take. "So how does this prion thing work?"

"When a person becomes infected with this particular influenza C strain, the virus binds itself onto the respiratory cell epithelium."

"So? That's what all respiratory viruses do."

"Yes, but this one's different. It takes it a step further. Instead of just inflicting the usual cell damage and local immune response, it causes a cell membrane protein—and all the other proteins like it—to become unstable and change its molecular configuration, thereby becoming a prion."

Casper paused to make sure Sydney was following. She nodded.

"Once the abnormal proteins—or prions—are present,

the cell membrane can no longer maintain its shape. It, along with all the other cell membranes in the respiratory tissue, breaks down, causing massive alveolar destruction. Clinically, this leads to cough, fever, difficulty breathing—all the symptoms of influenza. Only with a prion, the body can't repair itself, and soon the pulmonary destruction is so vast, the patient loses the ability to effectively oxygenate, and, as you've seen, the lungs become like soup from all the tissue damage."

"But I don't understand. Why do some people live? Sure, the fatality rate is astounding, but twenty-five percent survive."

"Once again, that's remained one of the great mysteries. It was believed the individuals who survived had a mutation, a mutation that coded for a respiratory protein immune to the effects of a prion. Their cell membrane protein was probably very similar, maybe only one amino acid difference, but that difference was enough to keep it from folding into a prion. Therefore, the patient merely suffered a cold, like with any other influenza C strain. Many probably showed no symptoms at all."

"And this prion is found only in the respiratory tract?"

"It appears to be, since all the other organs are normal other than damage from lack of oxygen."

Sydney put her head in her hands. "So, what's your treatment?"

"Well, first of all, the theory needed to be proven, at least in humans, anyway. That's why I'm here."

"And did you prove it?"

"Yes."

"That quickly? My, you must be a magician." Sydney's voice was flat.

"You have to understand, I come from a time when molecular genetics are as easily studied as Cliff Notes. You saw my equipment."

Sydney waved a hand his way, her head still buried in the other one. "Go on."

"My theory was, if I could take a simple virus—just the everyday, common cold—and make it code for a 'mutant' protein, one that couldn't be converted to a prion, then the cell membrane would be protected from destruction. No prion, no widespread cell death."

"And how would you do that?"

"With a transposon."

Sydney looked up with a blank stare.

"It's really quite simple. You take a mild respiratory virus, alter it with a transposon—a small section of DNA that can jump into the patient's own respiratory DNA—and then inject it into a patient with the Seneca strain. Once the patient's respiratory cells take up this mild virus, the small piece of programmed DNA can then code for a new cell membrane protein, one that won't fold into a prion, and the patient is thereby protected."

"But won't the patient still have existing prions present?"

"Yes, but the hope is the transposon will code for enough protective protein to overpower the prion." Casper stepped forward, the excitement in his voice rising. "Pretend the prions are an army of soldiers. We're just sending in another army, only this army is hopefully bigger and stronger and can effectively hold the little army at bay."

"And this genetically altered virus is what you gave Mr. Macaby? The common cold complete with its own battalion of microscopic soldiers?"

"Yes. I call it my protective factor."

"And now he's better."

"I hope so. I got unexpectedly called away last night, so I didn't get a chance to find out." Casper gave Sydney a small smile.

"Sorry," she said.

"I need at least twenty-four hours to be sure. I wanted to observe him longer, but Jackson's arranged for us to return tomorrow, says we can't afford to take any more time."

"So, if it proves successful, your job is done."

"Yes."

"And you'll return to wherever the hell it is you're from."

"Yes," Casper answered more slowly.

"And leave millions of people to die."

Casper returned to the stool next to Sydney and sat down, his knee touching her own. "I'm not here to save your world. I'm here to save mine. I'm sorry, but that's the way it is. You can't alter the future."

"You treated Macaby. That's altering the future."

"That was a risk we decided to take. I needed a young subject, and Macaby was a good choice. His old charts show he had testicular cancer as a teenager and, as a result, he's now sterile. No sperm was frozen. If he can't produce any offspring, we hopefully haven't altered history too greatly."

Sydney looked at Casper. Studied him good and hard. Then she burst out laughing. She couldn't help it. This was all so absurd, so absolutely ridiculous. When had she stepped out of her life and into an H. G. Wells novel?

"What's so funny?" Casper asked, startled.

"You. You're what's so funny. How in the world do you expect me to believe all this? You might as well tell me you're the Messiah and you're here to take back the kingdom of God."

"Isn't Mr. Macaby proof enough?"

Sydney's laughter stopped. He had her there.

Casper hesitated and then rested a hand on Sydney's knee. "Look, I know this seems unimaginable, but you have to quit fighting me. You have to quit implying I'm making this up. I'd never hurt you like that. In fact, I'm the worst liar there is. That's why you're here right now. I obviously failed to blend in and keep my mission secret. They all worried I'd do just that."

"Who are 'they'? Jackson?"

"Him. Others."

Sydney pivoted on the stool to face him. "Okay, if you're

from the future—two hundred years in the future to be exact —why do you speak like us? I mean, sure, you have a few flub ups, but I couldn't imagine myself pulling off a similar stint in the year 1800, what with all those 'tis thees and thous."

Casper's smile was back. "True, but I had the luxury of studying recording disks from the past—movies you called them. I'm a historian, that's what I do."

"I thought you were a virologist."

"That too," Casper said, Sydney's sarcasm apparently lost on him.

"Why are those articles I found printed on paper then? Surely you must have some fancy electronic journal keeping?"

"Of course we do, but nothing that's compatible here."

He acted like it all made perfect sense. Sydney tried a different tactic. "How did you get here? Hop on a spaceship that surpasses the speed of light? Last I heard, that wasn't possible."

"It's not."

"What did you use then? A nifty little machine? A time portal? A wormhole?"

"Something like that."

A jolt shot through Sydney. "What do you mean?"

"Look, one thing at a time. I couldn't tell you the specifics if I wanted to. The ability to cross time is a new phenomenon. The Presidential Body and the National Investigative Unit wouldn't entrust the mechanics to me. Look how badly I messed this up. I obviously wasn't convincing, at least not enough to make you suspect I was…well…normal."

"You mean like hoarding up on soft drinks? What's with that, anyway? No soda in the year 2209?"

"No."

Casper's quick and matter-of-fact response halted Sydney's obstinacy. One day she would look back at their conversation and realize that was when she first believed him. *Really* believed him. Stupid, of course. Stupid that such a simple little response could convince her of something so unimaginable, so inconceivable. But there was so much honesty, so little thought packed into that one word, that it seemed only natural to believe him.

At the current time, however, Sydney only knew that her hands trembled and her mind spun. She felt like she was floating, completely dissociated from her surroundings, as if she'd stepped off a cloud onto another planet, one where she could walk upside down and breathe underwater.

She also had no idea what to say next. So instead, she just stared off at Casper's bare wall, listening to him ask if she was all right.

Finally, after what seemed like a century, another one hundred years to add to their two-hundred-year age difference, she spoke. It was nothing intelligent, nothing earth shattering or monumental.

She simply said, "There's really no soda in the future?"

12

S till rooted to the barstool, Sydney started on her second
cup of coffee. "Tell me about the insulin pill."

Although she was due at the hospital in less than five
minutes, the need for promptness seemed a bit ridiculous in
her current situation. She had already paged one of her residents to tell him she'd be a few minutes late, and considering
the ominous nature of the virus, there was little harm either
he or any of the others could do in Sydney's absence.

"We should leave." Casper glanced at his watch—the
same watch that had sealed Sydney's fate—and grabbed a
Diet Pepsi from the fridge.

"Just a few more questions. I think you owe me that."

Casper raised his eyebrows as if to argue the point but
leaned back against the stove. "Okay. Insulin. What's to tell?"

"I can't believe a stable oral form was discovered. It
must've revolutionalized the disease."

"I'm sure it did, but that was way before my time."

Sydney eyed him with suspicion. "So why don't you have a
cure for diabetes then?"

"Even with gene modification, it's tricky. Insulin-depen-
dent diabetes is a heterogenous disease with multiple genetic

and environmental triggers. No definitive cure for cancer either, although tremendous strides have been made, what with gene therapy and all. On the other hand, insulin resistance has almost been eliminated, or what you know as Type II diabetes."

"What do you mean? How? When?" Millions of questions ricocheted in Sydney's mind.

"Obesity no longer exists, or at least not to the extent your time tolerated it."

"Tolerated—that's an interesting choice of words."

"Obesity was a huge drain on healthcare resources. It smokes my mind to think of how many preventable diseases your people accepted. Obesity alone wasted billions of healthcare dollars on hypertension, cardiac disease, insulin resistance, arthritis, depression, cancer, sleep apnea…the list goes on. And let's not even mention tobacco."

"Let me guess, no smoking in the year 2209."

"Definitely not. Cigarettes have been banned for over a hundred years. And those—what are they called again—fast food places? Long gone."

"Along with soft drinks." Sydney folded her arms, surprised to find herself on the defensive.

"Absolutely." Casper took a swig of Diet Pepsi.

"Your words seem a little self-righteous for someone who's been guzzling soda pop like it's the greatest invention since the insulin pill."

"I'm sorry, I didn't mean to sound pompous. Everything's easier in retrospect, I guess. And don't get me wrong. I've enjoyed my time here. It's kind of like being a kid in a giant amusement park with no parent to dictate my actions. You have so many liberties you're not even aware of."

Sydney was surprised by the sadness in his voice. "I would've thought our freedoms would be less, not more," she said.

"In some ways they are, but in others, we're much more restricted."

"How so?"

Casper paused. "It's hard to explain. Take obesity, for example. Our weight is regulated."

"You've got to be kidding."

"No, it's true. Unlike you, we have free health care, but it's a very comprehensive system, intertwined through all facets of life. It's called the Health and Reproduction Maintenance and Stabilization Association, or HARMSA.

"Sounds like Big Brother."

"Big who?"

Sydney ignored the question. "What exactly does HARMSA do?"

"It's really not so bad. It's all based on prevention. Not counting inflation, we spend much less on health care than your time does."

"But you have to weigh in? Like cattle or something?"

"We're expected to maintain a healthful weight, which is easy given we take a 'food to live' not a 'live for food' mentality. Plus, unlike your world, we're not bombarded by unhealthy foods every second of the day."

"And what's the reproduction part, or don't I want to know?"

Casper smiled and slipped his hands in his pockets. It was the most relaxed Sydney had seen him in days, and she imagined in a less stressful venue, he'd be pretty cool to hang with.

"You know what, this might be too much," he said. "Maybe we better focus on the present. *Your* present."

"No, really. I want to know."

"Well…reproduction is regulated. It's not so easy for us to have kids. Probably a good thing. The amount of unwanted and neglected children in your time is heartbreaking."

Sydney had no argument for that.

"We're given birth control at the onset of reproductive age

—both males and females. The right to have a child must be applied for through HARMSA."

Sydney frowned. "What kind of birth control?"

"An implantable hormonal device."

"For men too?"

"For us it's more of a spermatogenesis inhibitor, but I'm trying to keep it simple."

"Well, some people must slip through the cracks."

"Some do, but mothers who have children outside of a monogamous relationship tend to get ostracized. Guess some things never change."

Sipping coffee, Sydney gave thanks for her own place in the evolutionary timeline.

Casper crossed the room and joined her at the counter. "Having children is very different from how you know it. We can…choose things."

"What kind of things?" Sydney asked warily.

"All sorts of characteristics: tall, short, smart, athletic, disease-free. Well, certain diseases, anyway. Of course, I'm simplifying, but that's the short version."

Sydney raised her eyebrows. "So, everyone is as perfect and beautiful as you?"

Casper laughed. "Oh, I don't know about that. I'm a pretty average Sam."

A feeling of dissociation came over Sydney, and the dream-like sensation returned. Maybe she was in a coma, practically brain dead from a terrible accident. There was no Seneca strain, no global scourge, no Casper. Just her own malfunctioning, coma-induced imagination.

"Well, if you're pretty average," she finally managed to say, "I must be dog food."

"Oh no, you're perfect." Casper studied Sydney's hair. "We have so little variety among us. Most of the races have fused, at least in America. A good thing in terms of racial intolerance, but it's also washed out that beautiful spectrum of colors, especially in the extreme ranges."

Before Sydney could comment, Casper added, "To be perfectly honest, I find you fascinating and fresh, so different from the numbness of my own world. I've always felt I was born at the wrong time, came a couple hundred years too late."

Sydney shifted positions on the stool.

"They were right. I wasn't cut out for this mission. Everyone said I'd get sidetracked, said I was too much of a pacifist, too much of an idealist. They were justified in their comments. I did get sidetracked. Sidetracked by dying patients, sidetracked by your culture, and sidetracked by… well…you get the picture."

"Of course you'd get sidetracked! Who wouldn't? Casper, you have the chance to make all of this go away. No scourge. No billions of deaths. Maybe not even a HARMSA. I don't understand how you can just up and leave."

Casper's smile was sad. He lifted a hand, as if about to touch Sydney's hair, but whatever his intention, he never got the chance. A sudden noise made both of them nearly leap off their chairs.

A key was turning in the door.

Sydney spun around on the stool, eyes wide. Casper's expression was equally alarmed. Before Sydney knew what was happening, he whisked her off the barstool, hustled her into the bedroom, and practically threw her into the closet. He held a finger to his pursed lips, but the gesture was hardly needed. Except for the pounding of her heart, she intended to be as quiet as a corpse.

With the door closed, she tucked herself into a dark corner and tried to hide behind Casper's clothes. The attempt was laughable given the limited wardrobe, and Sydney knew she stood out like a giant blow-up doll. If the key in the door was Jackson's—and who else's could it have been?—and if Jackson opened the closet, Sydney was doomed.

She willed herself to calm down. There was no reason for Jackson to open the closet. No reason at all.

Unless he figured out Sydney was there.

That's when she remembered her scrubs and her purse. She'd left them by the kitchen island. Had Jackson seen the items? Had Casper had time to remove all traces of her presence?

Sydney's hands shook, and the coffee she'd drunk began its acidic ascent. She tried to steady her breathing and focus on the men's voices, but their words were muffled through the bedroom and closet doors. After a few minutes, the voices stopped, and Sydney sighed in relief, thinking the worst was over. But then the bedroom door burst open, and her panic returned full force.

"But I still don't understand. Why did you come back early?" It was Casper's voice, the strain in it betraying his attempt to act casual.

"I told you, I don't trust you. The NIU doesn't trust you. Nobody trusts you."

Definitely Jackson, and he didn't sound pleased. Sydney tried to keep her breaths quiet, but it was difficult considering she sounded like Darth Vader inside her own head.

"It's taking too much time. We've already had one person discover your deceit. We can't afford another. Besides, every second here is a chance to get sick. Now where—"

"What about Dr. Burke? If you're staying here until scheduled navigation tomorrow, how will he get back?" Casper sounded nervous, and Sydney prayed Jackson wouldn't catch on.

"Agent Mann will navigate back with him tonight. She traveled with me this morning and has since returned with the GTD. That way there'll be two of us to escort you home. We need to keep an eye on you, make sure you don't execute your pathetic compassion and treat anyone else but Macaby. That is, if you haven't already."

"I'm surprised the NIU approved an additional navigation."

"It's not additional. We'll leave tonight instead of in the morning."

"But that's too soon! I need at least twenty-four hours to observe Macaby. I still don't know if the treatment will take, and your constant pressuring is doing little to speed things along."

"Clamp down and just show me what you've got."

Silence filled the room, and Sydney could hear someone opening the small refrigerator underneath Casper's in-home lab table.

"Here, these two vials. That's all there is, but they need to stay in the fridge."

"Oh, they'll stay in the fridge all right, because I'll be watching you. Just in case you're thinking of leaving a little sample behind."

"Watch me all you want." Casper sounded angry now. "But you'll have to do it at the hospital. I need to follow Mr. Macaby closely. I could really use more time."

"You've had plenty of time. I would've thought you'd be glued to Macaby's side, so imagine my surprise when I went to the hospital this morning and found no Casper. And..." Jackson paused, perhaps for emphasis, "no Dr. McKnight."

At the sound of her name, Sydney's knees buckled, and she nearly dropped to the ground. Jackson's voice had moved closer, and although Sydney couldn't see through the solid door, she suspected he was sitting on the bed, close enough to hear her breathing.

"Where is she?" Jackson demanded.

"Where's who?"

Sydney's body felt as tense as an over-wound guitar string.

She thought again about her purse and rolled-up scrubs and prayed they wouldn't be seen.

"You know very well who. The flaxen-haired maiden, the one you can't keep your eyes off of. The one you've immortalized forever as your sexy computer prompt." The words came out as a sneer, each syllable making Sydney's heart beat faster.

"How should I know where she is? For someone in such a hurry, you've done nothing but slow me down." Casper's speech grew more distant, and Sydney imagined him backing out of the room, trying to lure Jackson out.

Jackson seemed to be following. "I'll be watching you. Just because your tracking device has proved worthless here doesn't mean I won't be watching you. I'll be watching her, too, and if I discover you've leaked even the tiniest bit of information, a computer memory will be all that's left of your fair-skinned predecessor."

After that, Sydney heard only silence, followed by a slamming of the door, probably Casper's way of telling her they were gone.

She leaned back against the wall, her body sagging in relief. It was another few seconds before she dared move. Finally, she peeked at the fluorescent hands on her watch. Casper walked to the hospital—he lived only six blocks away —and Sydney knew if she wanted to stay in her own century, she'd better beat both Casper and Jackson to Boston General.

She cracked open the closet door and scanned the room. Then she exited the small space, pausing before she went any farther. When she didn't hear anything, she tiptoed down the short hallway, all the while terrified Jackson would jump out at her like some evil Jack-in-the-Box dressed in white scrubs.

Her worries were unfounded. When she stepped into the kitchen, the place was deserted. She scanned for her purse and scrubs, panicking for a moment when she didn't see them. Then she spotted blue fabric behind the island and sighed in relief. Casper must've kicked them back there. Good thing Jackson hadn't wanted a soda.

She scooped up her belongings, grabbed her fleece coat from the front closet, and darted out of the apartment. She probably looked like a maniac running out of the building and across the basketball court, but she didn't care. It wasn't until she was locked inside her Jeep that she started to feel even the semblance of safety.

Allowing herself a few seconds, she leaned her head back and took some deep breaths. Then, with shaky hands, she started the engine and pulled out, praying she'd get to the hospital in time.

13

———————

"Eight more states in the last couple of days?"

"Yep, including Alaska. Probably spread up from Canada."

Sitting at the front counter, collecting her census for the day, nervous system still not recovered from the early morning scare, Sydney listened to the two medical students exchange the latest influenza factoids, their respiratory masks shifting over their lips as they talked.

"How can the thing spread so fast?" the blond, spiky-haired student asked.

His dread-locked counterpart returned a chart to its designated slot in the rack. "Typical flu can reach all fifty states within a month or so, can't it? It's bad in Europe and Asia too. Africa as well, although the more remote villages seem less affected. At this point, they think the Seneca strain's going to exceed the overall mortality count of the influenza outbreak of 1918. Man, did you ever think you'd be caught up in something so big?"

Although not directed at Sydney, his words cut like a scalpel.

No, Sydney certainly didn't think she'd ever be caught up

in something so big. Didn't think she'd ever be cowering in a closet while two men from the future discussed her fate either. She was lucky she'd beaten them to the hospital, and although she'd crossed their paths once already, Casper avoiding eye contact while Jackson looked with suspicion back and forth between the two of them, Sydney wasn't eager to do it again. In fact, unknown to the two students, both of whom were now walking away headed to more death and disease, they'd only skimmed the surface of the irrationality that had become Sydney's life.

She gathered her notes and cleared the computer screen. Her hands still trembled, and she wasn't sure how she'd survive the day. Wasn't even sure what she should do. Every time she thought about telling someone, she struggled to find credible words. Even if she were to be believed, what good would speaking up do? Casper and Jackson would take off, back to their own messed-up century, and Sydney would be left looking like a fool. And what about Dr. Burke? He might be left forever trapped in the future if she interfered.

There was also the enormity of the virus itself, the part Sydney hadn't had time to ponder. Two billion deaths? Was it truly possible? If it was, why was she wasting her time in the hospital, pretending her actions made a difference? All their efforts would be futile. Pointless. How could Casper leave? Jackson, she could understand, but Casper?

"Sydney?"

Sydney jumped at the sound of her name. She hadn't even seen Crystal sit down at the counter.

"Are you okay?" the resident asked, worry in her eyes. "You look as pale as a marshmallow."

Sydney tried to smile underneath her mask, but the swirling in her gut made the attempt difficult. "I'm fine. Just zoning out. What's up?"

Crystal paused for a moment, scrutinizing Sydney, but then her eyes lit up. "I asked if you've heard the good news."

"What good news?"

"Macaby, our patient in room 310. Have you seen his chart?"

"Not yet. Why?" The cramping in Sydney's abdomen intensified, and she worried she'd need to race to the bathroom.

"Someone's finally improving! It's a miracle." Excitement sparked in Crystal's eyes.

Sydney tried to feign ignorance. "How so? The last I saw of the guy, he was in need of a ventilator and still far down on the list."

"Well, yesterday it was almost a given he'd die, just like everyone else that ill, but during the night, his blood gases improved. They're still not normal, but they're close. He's conscious and talking, and his oxygen requirement is down. It's a miracle," the resident repeated.

Sydney's whole body trembled, and she had to work to keep her voice steady. "What's the reason for this sudden resurrection?"

"Nobody knows. Dr. DeWitt was here last night and she's as flabbergasted as everyone else. She's probably still in her office poring over his treatment course to see what, if anything, was different. If only Dr. Burke was here to see it. Rumor has it he's flown the coop."

At the mention of Burke's name, Sydney felt nauseated.

"You okay?" Crystal's enthusiasm diminished. "Maybe you should go lie down."

"No, I'm fine. Really. That's great news about Macaby. Let me know what they find."

"Dr. DeWitt asked me to consult pulmonology. Their docs have been using heliox as well as nebulized magnesium, and Dr. DeWitt wants to know if these were used on Macaby. If so, she wants the pulmonologists to draft a treatment protocol for all patients."

Heliox. Magnesium. Unknown substance from time-traveling virologist. Sydney knew where her chips were stacked.

"In fact, I paged Dr. Price. He should be here any minute."

Sydney pulled back in surprise. "Mitch?" She felt like she'd been floating in a surreal bubble that had suddenly been popped.

"Yeah, he's on call today and tonight. Why?" Crystal stared at her for a moment and then comprehension set in. She put a hand to her mask-covered mouth. "Oh my God, I forgot you two broke up."

Jeez, am I back in high school? How did word travel so fast?

Crystal looked mortified. Sydney tossed a chart her way. "Relax. I'm a big girl."

Crystal nodded, but before she could say anything else, the pulmonologist in question sauntered up to the counter. His pace slowed when he saw Sydney.

Mitch greeted her with a faint but discernable degree of contempt. Sydney could hardly blame him.

"Here's Macaby's chart." Crystal handed Mitch the one he needed, but his eyes remained focused on Sydney.

She swallowed and only half-listened as Crystal told Mitch about Mr. Macaby, the resident fluffing her auburn ponytail and smoothing her white coat as she spoke. Then she hurried off in response to a page, leaving Sydney and Mitch alone. Even the ward clerk was absent at the moment.

Mitch leaned against the counter. "You okay? You don't look so good."

Sydney took a deep breath. God, how she wanted to tell him, but what would be her fate if she did? What would be Burke's?

"I'm fine," she said.

"You didn't seem fine last night."

"I was tired."

Mitch leaned in closer, his elbows resting on the counter.

"What exactly was going on between you and Dr. Jones inside Macaby's room?"

"Nothing."

"Didn't look that way to me. What were you arguing about? A lover's quarrel, perhaps?"

"We disagreed on a treatment plan."

"I'll bet."

Sydney ignored his sarcasm and nervously scanned the hallway. "Mitch?"

"Yes?"

Sydney hesitated. "If I told you something, something unbelievable, would you—"

That's as far as she got. Jackson had just stepped out of the stairwell. He was writing something on a clipboard as if he were actually working. He was too far away to have heard what Sydney said, but her heart jumped to her throat nonetheless. His gaze met hers, and although she tried to act casual, her trembling was hard to subdue. Was he aware of how much she knew?

"What were you saying?"

Sydney turned back to Mitch and worked hard to keep the panic out of her voice. "Um nothing, really."

Mitch crossed his arms, his blue scrub top puckering inside his lab coat. "What's going on?"

"Nothing, okay? I was going to tell you Macaby is better. A lot better. It's really unbelievable."

"I know that. That's why I'm here." Mitch narrowed his eyes, his expression suggesting he hadn't bought Sydney's response.

"Excuse me, I've got a lot of work to do." Sydney stood, avoiding Jackson's gaze from across the hallway.

Mitch shook his head. "Whatever. Hey, how nice of you to even give me these few minutes. I know how 'uninteresting' I can be." With more force than necessary, he closed the chart in front of him and started to walk away. Before he got far, he turned around and leaned over the counter one last time.

"You know, Syd, you might find Dr. Jones irresistibly fascinating, but remember something: Exciting isn't always better." Mitch raised his eyebrows, blew Sydney a masked kiss, and walked away, heading to Mr. Macaby's room.

The day didn't improve much after that. While everyone else rejoiced in the miracle that was Ted Macaby, Sydney felt more uneasy by the second. She'd spotted Casper outside Macaby's room a few times but didn't dare speak to him in case Jackson was lurking nearby, waiting to beam Sydney up to the future as he'd done with Dr. Burke. On two of those occasions, Casper had caught her eye, but they didn't let their gazes linger. Dumb really, considering their lack of interaction was probably more suspicious than if they had carried on as normal.

Sydney had seen Jackson several times as well, and although his scrubs and respiratory mask allowed him to blend in with the rest of the hospital personnel, his only real work seemed to be keeping an eye on her and Casper. Sydney wondered how he had managed to escape patient care duties for so long. Surely a nurse must've grabbed him for help at some point. Then again, Jackson's past visits were brief and usually spent in the stairwell with Casper. Plus, the hospital was overfilled and understaffed. Who had time to pay attention to a wayward orderly? And what did he care if someone realized he wasn't actually an employee? He had a nice warm wormhole waiting for him.

Despite Jackson's foreboding presence, Sydney's ongoing silence grew more difficult. She was desperate to see Liz, but her friend didn't arrive until four. Should Sydney tell her?

Could Liz keep it secret? More importantly, was Sydney willing to put Liz in danger?

Trying to bury her dilemma, she spent the next several hours seeing patients and pretending to recreate the miracle concoction that had rejuvenated Mr. Macaby, who, for the record, didn't appear too thrilled with his reincarnation. Nothing like a young wife in the morgue to dampen one's healing spirit.

"Wow, look at you," Sydney said when she went back to check on him in the afternoon.

He was sitting up in bed, oxygen prongs in his nose, the flow rate down to two liters. Jeans and a T-shirt had replaced the flimsy hospital gown, which was now tossed in a heap on the floor. "Fully dressed too. I'm impressed."

Ted Macaby shrugged. "The gown was crap. I felt better the minute I put on real clothes."

Sydney nodded. It wasn't the first time a patient had told her that. She forced a smile and sat on the end of his bed. "You know, you're causing quite a stir around the hospital. Once you're off oxygen, you'll be able to go home."

"Go home to what?"

Sydney's smile faded. "I'm truly sorry about your wife. She was a nice woman."

"Did you know she was getting her PhD in mathematics?" Macaby wore a sad, but at the same time proud, expression on his face.

"Really?"

"Yeah, it was pretty funny. She was one of the few women in the program, this fashionable girl surrounded by a bunch of nerdy guys." Macaby was smiling now.

"She must've been really smart."

"Oh, she is." His face crumpled. "*Was*, I mean. She was off the charts smart."

Sydney reached for the stethoscope but paused when Macaby continued.

"I used to call her the chic geek." He hung his head. "Kind of stupid, I guess."

"No. Not stupid at all."

Macaby was silent after that, allowing Sydney to conduct her exam, but although his lungs were almost clear and his pulse strong, her own heart felt on the verge of breaking.

She saw several more patients on the fourth floor (none as fortunate as Mr. Macaby) and then made her way back to 3 West and 3 North where the bulk of her patients resided. A precise ICU no longer existed. Ventilators were used wherever they became available, which was easier than transferring patients back and forth. The hospital administration had even created a family wing on 3 North and 5 South, where some families were fortunate enough to be admitted together so they wouldn't have to spend their last few days apart.

Sydney entered the stairwell and descended a flight, studying her census as she went. With a pen, she checked off the patients she had seen. For the last hour or so, work had allowed a mental escape, and she circled the names of patients she still needed to visit.

Footsteps tapped behind her.

She spun around. Jackson was only a few steps back.

Fear churned in Sydney's gut, but to her surprise, anger wormed its way in too. "I'm sorry, do you need something?"

Jackson remained mute, but his dark eyes narrowed above his mask, and his jugular veins, enormous really, pulsed in time to Sydney's own thudding heart.

"Well, with a hospital this packed with patients, I'm sure you can find something to do." Despite Sydney's anxiety, she held Jackson's gaze.

He waited a few moments and then turned around and left. Whether that meant he was convinced of her innocence, Sydney didn't know, but she wasn't about to hang around to find out. She picked up her pace and whipped open the door.

By the time she made it to 3 North, her breathing had

slowed. Maybe Jackson didn't suspect anything after all. Maybe he was merely ensuring Casper kept his distance from her.

Sydney rounded up a few of her residents for the latest update and tried once again for distraction. That proved fairly easy, because the first room she entered, room 334 at the end of the hallway, was occupied by a round-cheeked baby lying in a crib, her body hooked up to a ventilator bigger than the infant herself.

After a startled pause, Sydney spotted the two other beds, one occupied by a boy with a short afro, probably about seven years old, still alert and not yet on a ventilator like his sister, and the other filled by an adult male, presumably their dad, Sydney's patient. Clinically, he looked somewhere in between his daughter and son, not yet on a ventilator, but also not up and alert like his son.

The man's level of exertion suggested he'd need a vent soon, but whether it would come in time, Sydney didn't know. Additionally, a petite woman sat in a chair, the mask on her face doing little to conceal her grief, she apparently the only family member not yet infected. Her presence surprised Sydney, given the woman's chance of contracting the virus was higher in the hospital than at home, but try telling that to a mother whose entire family was about to die.

Sydney, meet the Hortons.

Sydney introduced herself, the lump in her throat the size of a golf ball. Though she was only responsible for the care of the father, her thoughts and eyes kept wandering to the children, and she wasn't sure how she'd handle this family-unit concept. After glancing back at Mrs. Horton—the woman's expression blank and her eyes rimmed with dark circles—Sydney realized her own discomfort was a teardrop in the ocean next to the young mother's.

On it went, patient after patient, family after family, protective gear after protective gear. Over and over again.

After a while Sydney felt herself deaden. Deaden to Jackson, deaden to Casper, and deaden to the patients. Sleep deprivation and stress tended to do that to a person, and pretty soon nothing seemed real. Everything became dissociated, as if life happened around a person rather than to him or her.

Sydney exited a patient's room and ambled down the hallway toward the bathroom, in desperate need of a break. Standing in front of the mirror, she splashed cold water on her face and let the cool drops flow down her skin and onto her scrub top. Blinking, she tried to reconnect with reality, but what reality was that? The reality where she spent hours helping people she wasn't really helping? The reality where an epidemic of such improbable and unfathomable proportions would soon change the whole world as they knew it?

The futility of it all hit her once again, and she squeezed the edges of the sink until her knuckles whitened. She rested her forehead against the mirror. She felt nothing but darkness and surrender, but before she could sink further into defeat, her brain fought back. Anger resurfaced. Fury, even. How could Casper leave? How could he treat the patients as if they were nothing more than an experiment? That couldn't be his intention, not after seeing all this.

Sydney lifted her head and checked her watch. Almost four. Liz would be there soon.

She would tell her. She would take the risk and tell Liz. Then maybe together they could convince Casper to stay. Or at least leave behind what he knew.

She waited for four o'clock.

It came. Liz didn't.

Swallowing apprehension, Sydney went to see her next patient, a thirty-two-year-old woman whose daughter had already died. As she told Sydney her story, Sydney placed a radial art line into the woman's wrist, a procedure that up until one week ago she hadn't performed since residency. Child's play now.

The woman, tears pooling in her eyes, plucked a photo of her daughter from her wallet: a preteen girl sporting braided hair and a baseball uniform, a bat in her hands, arms ready to swing. She wore a huge smile on her gawky face, and a large gap separated her two front teeth.

Sydney looked away and put all her energy into taping the radial line in place. What was happening to her? She'd always prided herself in her ability to detach. Shouldn't she be immune to this? How many deaths did it take to harden a heart? Maybe she should ask Casper.

An arm's reach away, an elderly woman moaned something about needing more oxygen. Sydney glanced at the clock above the woman's head. Four-thirty. Liz should be at the hospital by now.

Sydney changed her gloves and reached out to the old woman, who looked all of about eighty pounds. She took care not to squeeze the patient's hand too tightly, worried the bony fingers would crumble, like those of a long-entombed skeleton. The woman's ribs jutted out of her hospital gown with each air-sucking breath, and her body perspired from fever. Sydney knew the woman was in dire need of a ventilator but also knew she'd never get one.

"What can I do for you, Mrs. Edwards?" Sydney asked softly, even though the word *nothing* came to mind. Other than calling in a self-purported historical microbiologist from the year 2209, she had zilch to offer.

"I need…more…oxygen," the old woman managed between struggling breaths.

In the guise of doing something, Sydney pretended to crank the control dial higher, the frail woman apparently unaware she was already receiving the highest dose her oxygen mask would allow.

"There, let's try that." Sydney made her voice as soothing and reassuring as she could.

Sydney could tell by the woman's eyes she wasn't fooled.

She knew Sydney was as scared and unsure as everyone else. She knew Sydney was as hopeless and helpless as every other one of the so-called medical experts pacing the corridors in their long white coats.

Sydney adjusted the elderly patient's pillows, checked her IV sites, and listened to her heart and lungs, again under the guise she was doing something. She attempted a smile underneath her mask and told the woman the nurse would check on her soon. As she headed toward the door, she could feel the woman's frightened gaze on her, and the weight of that unseen stare almost cannonballed Sydney into tears.

She took a deep breath and stepped out. Then she lumbered to the nurses' station to clean her goggles and sterilize her hands—which were by now red and painfully raw—before donning fresh gloves. How long before they ran out of PPE?

Four forty-five. Still no Liz.

Sydney walked to the front desk, jaw clenched and stomach knotted. With one of the hospital phones, she dialed Liz's number. If Liz didn't answer, she would try her pager.

On the fifth ring, Liz's faint voice came on the line. "Hello?"

"Liz, what's wrong?"

Liz tried to speak but coughed instead, and Sydney's stomach twisted even more.

"Liz?"

"I'm fine," her friend said when the cough subsided.

"You don't sound fine."

"I'm worn out, that's all. Got a cold. I thought I'd get a little more sleep before coming in."

Sydney squeezed her eyelids shut.

Liz must have imagined Sydney's response, because she said, "Come on, you always think the worst. Isn't it possible I just caught a cold? I mean, we still have plenty of *those* viruses around—"

"Do you have a fever?"

"Not really."

"What do you mean, 'not really'?"

"I'm a little warm, that's all. Nothing to break out the cooling blankets for."

"But you're only twenty-four hours into the virus. You could spike any time."

"Gee, thanks for your vote of confidence."

"Liz, this is serious."

"You don't think I know that?" Liz's response was the closest to a snap Sydney had ever heard from her.

"I'm sorry. I didn't mean to patronize you, but I'm worried."

"Me too," Liz whispered.

Sydney swallowed, not sure what to say. She teared up and blinked the moisture away. "Have you called your mother?"

"No."

"What about Larry?" Larry was Liz's on-again, off-again tax-accountant boyfriend.

"No."

"Why not? You shouldn't be alone."

There was a long pause before Liz said, "I think we both know it's probably best I am." As was her nature, she added, "I'm sure it's just a cold though."

"Cold or not, you need to come in."

Silence from the other end.

"Liz, you have to come in."

"There's nothing anyone can do for me there. You know that."

"Well, you have a better chance here than at home."

"How can you be sure they'll admit me to Boston General? I could get turfed to one of the makeshift hospitals instead. Maybe a school or community center."

"Between Dr. DeWitt and me, we'll make sure you get a bed. You work here for Christ's sake."

Liz finally agreed to come in, and though Sydney knew her friend was right, knew there was little more they could do for her in the hospital, at least Liz would be within reach. At least she wouldn't be alone.

After hanging up the phone, Sydney rested her head in her hands, once again nauseated. She wanted to throw up. Wanted to puke and puke until all of this purged away. She struggled for air underneath her blue mask, its stuffy occlusion growing tired and tedious. She tugged wildly at the straps, trying to loosen their hold as they dug into her flesh.

Someone tapped her shoulder, and she jerked her head up in surprise.

Casper was standing in front of her. Sydney scanned the area around him. No Jackson.

"Are you all right?" he asked.

Sydney didn't answer, just stared at him.

"Sydney?"

Her breaths were short and choppy inside her mask, and the lightheadedness intensified. Casper had to stay. She had to get him to stay. Or at least to share his treatment. What had he called it? His "protective factor"? Well, that factor had worked on Macaby, the man suddenly as revered as a stigmata-pocked saint.

And now it would work on Liz.

Sydney bolted up from her seat, her sudden movement startling Casper, as well as a few other hospital personnel her behavior had managed to attract. She grabbed Casper's arm and pulled him down the hallway, wanting to act before Jackson returned from eating or peeing or whatever he was doing in this rare lapse of guardianship. Perhaps a nurse had enlisted his help after all.

Sydney's jaw was set in determination. "I need to show you something."

Casper followed along, struggling to keep up, mumbling something about whether being seen together was wise.

She dragged him to the end of 3 North.

"Where are we going?"

Sydney stopped in front of room 334 and grabbed two protective gowns from the bin. "Do you know what this wing's been converted to?"

"It's the…temporary family ward."

"That's right, and I want you to meet some of my new friends. You've told me about your world; now I want to *show* you mine, the part you've chosen to ignore."

No sooner had Sydney spoken the words than they were greeted by the high-pitched wailing of a gowned and masked woman being led down the hallway, no doubt another mother whose child had died. That was followed by a baby's cry and the harsh, croupy cough of a toddler somewhere down the corridor. Sydney tried to catch Casper's eyes, but his pained expression was focused on an orderly wheeling a stretcher to the elevator, a body half the size of his own underneath the white sheet. Sydney and Casper watched until the elevator doors closed, and Sydney knew without looking what button the orderly had pressed. LL. Lower level. The yellow-bricked road to the morgue.

She glanced at Casper. His complexion appeared clammy under the heavy fluorescent lights, and his hands fidgeted inside his gloves.

Before he could regain his senses and protest Sydney's intention, she opened the Hortons' door and practically dragged him inside. She thrust one of the gowns at him.

His gaze went to the crib, and he took a step back to leave, but before he got the chance Sydney introduced him to Mrs. Horton, who, despite Casper's obviously uncomfortable behavior and Sydney's almost frenzied determination, still managed to look nearly catatonic.

Sydney walked to the woman and knelt. "How is your family doing? Any change since I was last here?"

Although Mrs. Horton stirred to the question, she merely shook her head in response.

"Has the pediatrician been by for Jessica and Elijah?"

"Yes. He said Elijah is stable for now but may need a ventilator by tomorrow. As for Jessica…well, she…so young and all." Mrs. Horton raised a tissue to her eyes, and a small sob escaped her lips.

Sydney's chest tightened, and she placed a gloved hand on the mother's forearm and squeezed. Then she stood and put an arm around the woman's stooped shoulders. Little comfort, Sydney knew, but the power of human touch was all she had left, and it was becoming increasingly easy to give. Nothing else in her black bag seemed to be working.

She glanced at Jessica, then Casper, his expression still wan. Sydney told Mrs. Horton she wanted to examine Mr. Horton once again, and as she walked past Elijah to get to his father, she tried to smile reassuringly. She doubted it worked but thought she got a smile in return. Hard to tell under the child's big oxygen mask. His dark eyes were wide and his breaths harsh, and when he asked if his daddy would be okay, Sydney wanted nothing more than to tell him a big, fat lie. Instead, she paused and glanced at Elijah's father. No, Daddy would not be okay. Daddy was already unresponsive, and if he didn't get a ventilator soon, he would die before his infant daughter. In fact, Daddy would soon be transferred to another room so that his oldest child wouldn't witness his demise.

"Your daddy is very sick, but I'll do my best to make him comfortable, okay?"

The little boy nodded, but Sydney could see the fear in his eyes.

She grabbed Mr. Horton's stethoscope and started her ritualistic exam. When she moved on to his abdomen, Elijah's small, muffled voice asked Casper, "Are you a kid doctor or a big people doctor?"

Casper threw Sydney a pleading look, his hand still on the

door. Sydney ignored him and went on with her exam. Casper cleared his throat and approached the boy. "I'm a big people doctor."

"You look like my uncle, only he's shorter, and he has more hair."

"Is that so?" Casper shifted his feet.

"Are you her boss?" Elijah pointed his finger Sydney's way.

Casper laughed a little at that. "Yes, I guess you could say that." Although still shaky, his voice gathered strength. Elijah's, on the other hand, rushed out between labored breaths.

"Is she a good worker?"

Sydney turned toward the child and smiled. "Hey, what are you implying?"

"Nothing." The boy grinned underneath his mask.

His smile moved Sydney, and she wished with all her might he could be out of this sickening infirmary, doing all the things little boys his age were supposed to be doing, like going swimming, walking their dogs, playing catch.

As if reading her mind, Elijah asked Casper, "Do you play football?"

"Um, no, not really."

"What do you do, then?" Elijah asked, as if all men must of course play some sport.

"I box."

Sydney looked at Casper in surprise. She hadn't expected that. How did he stay so pretty?

Elijah raised a fist. "Cool."

"And I play, well, I guess you'd call it soccer."

"Do you play for a team?"

"I used to."

"Which one?"

"Oh, you wouldn't have heard of them."

Sydney noticed Casper had moved closer to the child's bed, and he seemed to be smiling underneath his mask.

Elijah sat up straighter. "I play soccer too. In fact, this spring we're going to have an even better team."

Silence from the big people.

"I can't wait. I hope I get a new soccer ball for Christmas."

Just then Sydney's pager went off. She lifted her gown and saw the number for 3 West. "I gotta get this," she said to Casper. "You coming?"

"In a second." He turned back to Elijah.

For a moment, Sydney felt a ray of hope. She returned to Mrs. Horton. "Someone will come later to transfer your husband. I think it will be for the best."

Mrs. Horton nodded, and her eyes filled again. Sydney gave the woman one last hug, glanced at Casper, who was still deep in conversation with Elijah, and then tore off her gloves and gown, washed her hands, and left the room.

Once outside, she put on new gloves and walked to the counter to answer the page. By the time she hung up, Casper was out of the Hortons' room and waiting for her. He looked each way down the corridor, no doubt scouring for Jackson. Once Sydney was free, Casper led her down the hallway past a collection of nurses and students who'd gathered. He didn't stop until they were in front of a patient's room in one of the back pods. It was as alone as the two were going to get.

"That wasn't fair," Casper said.

"Fair? You're telling me about fair?"

"It just wasn't…necessary, that's all. I was about to…"

"About to what? About to leave?"

Casper nodded.

Sydney looked at him, surprised to be surprised by his words. "Oh my God, you're really going to do it, aren't you?"

Casper sighed. "Ted Macaby is better. He's off oxygen now, and though I'd like to observe him longer to make sure he doesn't rebound—still a strong possibility—I don't have that luxury."

"Luxury. Ha. By all means, you should have luxury."

Casper looked pained by Sydney's anger. "There's nothing I can do. I'm—"

"Bull. There's plenty you can do."

"I'm leaving tonight."

"Beautiful. Well, if your work here is done, why not leave now? Why not leave this very second? Why take even the tiniest risk that I might spill the beans?"

"I wouldn't advise that." Casper sounded more sad than angry. "You know, it's not as if I can come and go as I please. Launching the GTD is a scheduled event. It takes significant preparation. I can't just snap my fingers and take off."

"Too bad, huh?"

Sydney knew she was acting belligerent. A baby, really. She also knew that if she didn't get a grip, her behavior would induce the exact opposite response of what she wanted.

"Look." She softened her voice. "Liz is sick."

Casper rubbed his temples but said nothing.

"My best friend—my only family, really—is sick. She's coming here to be admitted, where you and I both know she will die." The words cut like knife blades in Sydney's throat.

Casper squeezed his scalp.

"Please, you can help her."

He shook his head.

"I know you don't really want to leave all these people to die. That's not you. That's not your character."

"You don't know my character."

"I think I do."

"You don't know what you're asking." Casper's expression was anguished. "We can't change the order of things. Who knows what might happen?"

"I know Liz wouldn't die. I know millions of other people wouldn't die. I know I wouldn't have to spend every second of the day terrified *I'm* going to die."

"Please don't say that."

"Well, it's true. Whether I want to face it or not, it's only a matter of time before I get sick." Once again Sydney saw herself lying in a hospital bed. Alone.

"Please, I have to go. Jackson could be here any second. I hate to leave you. It's not… I'm going to…"

For a moment Sydney thought Casper might cry, but he straightened and, after a deep breath, said, "I'm sorry. I have to go."

He started to walk away, but Sydney reached for his arm, her eyes wide and begging. "Please, at least give me something for Liz. One little shot for my best friend." She turned toward room 334. "And maybe the Hortons. Come on, Casper, think about Elijah. Think about—"

Casper freed his arm and, with one last glance Sydney's way, mumbled, "I'm so sorry." Then he took off.

Sydney thought about running after him. Thought about chasing him down and screaming and kicking until she finally made him see things her way. With a little more time she was sure she could. Just a few more children. Maybe a visit with Liz.

She hurried after him, watching as he turned toward the stairwell, but then she stopped. Jackson had just exited the same stairwell Casper was about to enter. The two men looked at each other and, after a hesitation, Casper nodded. They headed back through the door, Casper first, followed by Jackson, both pausing long enough to throw Sydney a final glance, one menacing, the other tortured.

Then they were gone. Nothing left of them but the memories they would leave in Sydney's brain, and even those she would surely question with time.

14

———

"Now get some rest." Sydney tucked an extra pillow underneath Liz's head. Liz, like Kyra, had insisted on her own pajamas: blue ones with dancing lambs that juxtaposed with the hospital's death theme.

"How'd you manage to score me a bed?"

"I have my ways." Sydney didn't mention the elderly woman who had died in the bed one hour earlier.

"Oh, come on. Don't look so glum." Liz held up her hand and wiggled the oxygen saturation probe on her index finger. "See? My sats are above ninety percent. Just a little cold I tell you."

Sydney replaced the bedside stethoscope. Based on her exam, Liz's lungs were a far cry from "a little cold."

"Have you called your mom?" At that moment, Sydney's pager went off, but she ignored it.

Liz nodded. "I'm sure she's raising all sorts of hell trying to get in here. Only daughter and all."

"If anyone can do it, your mom can."

Liz blinked a few times and gazed toward the window, the blind already drawn. "I'm scared. Scared for myself, scared for my mom, scared for the country."

"Me too." Sydney grabbed Liz's hand and squeezed. Her friend's uncharacteristic display of fear only worsened Sydney's own, and when she tried to pull away, Liz wouldn't let go, her face still turned toward the window.

How could Casper just leave?

In her mind, Sydney saw Casper's apartment along with the small refrigerator in the bedroom, the one tucked underneath his makeshift desk and filled with poorly marked containers and test tubes. She wondered about the solutions inside, wondered if a dose of the factor remained in the cooler for Liz. According to Sydney's watch, it was half past seven in the evening. Were Casper and Jackson still in this century?

A restless energy consumed her, and it was at that moment, standing at Liz's bedside, both of them staring at the covered window, Sydney knew she needed to do something. Anything. Even if it meant leaving her patients unattended at the hospital. The situation with Casper was too dire. She had to at least try one more time.

Her brain whirled. She could break into his apartment. She'd done it before. This time she would call the police—leaving out the part about the future; no need to have them question her mental competence—and tell them a scientist had made a discovery and refused to share.

Oh yeah, that sounds believable.

Okay, maybe she would report the address and tell the cops she was being attacked. Anything to get them there. She had no choice. Liz was squeezing her hand as if she'd never let go, and Sydney refused to watch Liz die without knowing she did everything she possibly could. She would have to desert the already overwhelmed staff on her call night, but again, she had no choice. She was the only one who knew the truth, however delusional and unbelievable it seemed. To hell with changing the future. Let Liz live. Let her mess up the rest of eternity. Let her have dozens of children, scores of grandchildren, hundreds of great-grandchildren to carry on her genes, her beautiful, optimistic, and cheerful genes.

Sydney put a gloved hand on Liz's cheek. Warm with fever, its rosy glow gave the false impression of health. "I have to go, Liz. There's something I need to do."

"Okay, but come back and check on me."

"I will, and I'm going to make you better. You'll see."

Sydney gave Liz's hand a final squeeze before leaving the room. Out at the ward counter, she paged one of the residents. While waiting for his response, she jotted a quick note in Liz's chart. When the senior resident finally returned the page, Sydney told him she needed to leave for an hour or two, family emergency. He didn't know her only "family" was lying in a hospital bed across the hall. She asked him to page Dr. DeWitt directly with any concerns.

Sydney would have to account for her AWOL status later, but that seemed a trivial point at the present time. Then, before the resident could ask any questions and before Sydney could change her mind, she hung up the phone and ascended three flights of stairs to her office. After grabbing her purse from the desk drawer, which, to her surprise, she'd forgotten to lock, Sydney darted downstairs once again, but this time she exited toward the skywalk that led to the parking ramp.

She tried not to think about the residents and nurses she was deserting. Or the patients. She had to do this. She had to try. Although she might end up alongside Dr. Burke in some sort of George Orwellian nightmare, it was a risk she had to take.

Where was Burke now, anyway? Had they really brought him back? Would Sydney's interference risk his life?

Her pager went off again as she entered the skywalk, but like before, she ignored it, not wanting to get caught up in something and lose the nerve she'd found. Instead, she pulled her cell phone from her purse and planned to call the police once she reached the car. She knew she risked looking like a fool, but she still possessed the knowledge that Casper was impersonating someone else. She at least had that to save face, even if he was long gone.

Still, a nagging intrusion nudged its way into her brain: her last conversation with Casper, the one where he said the order of things couldn't be changed without expecting ramifications. Dozens of faces Sydney didn't recognize flooded her mind, faces of people who might never exist because of her meddling. But what about all those who would? Wasn't that equally important?

Once in the ramp, Sydney took the stairs to the lower level to her car. Her pager went off yet again, and for the third time she silenced it without checking the number. Cell phone clutched in one hand, she approached the Jeep and dug in her purse for the keys. Not there. She dug deeper, scratching at the bottom, all the while looking around the uninhabited parking lot, nerves jittery.

Still no keys.

She pulled the purse open wide and looked inside, her nose near the leather fabric. Where in the hell were her keys?

With heart rate rising and hand thrust in the bag, Sydney again scanned the darkening lot. Thinking maybe she'd left the keys in the car—unlikely—she pulled on the door handle. To her surprise it opened. Bewildered but relieved, she sank down into the front seat and scanned the ignition for keys.

Nothing.

She licked her lips, her mouth too dry to do much good, and on the inside her stomach flipped. Something wasn't right.

She raised her cell phone. If she couldn't get to Casper's, at least the police could. With a shaky hand, she started to dial 911, but before she got past the 9, something shuffled in the back seat.

Sydney spun around, and to her horror a masked figure popped up from the floorboard. Just as she was about to scream, a hand clamped over her mouth. Despite her fear and her own respiratory mask, she started to bite.

She heard a cry of pain, and then, "It's me! It's Casper!"

Casper whipped his hand away, the action sending a familiar scent of vanilla and cinnamon into the air. He pushed up against the backseat and rubbed his hand across his chest.

"Casper! What are you doing? You scared the crap out of me." In her panic, Sydney had pulled the pepper spray from her purse, and although she had a moment of uncertainty as to whether she would need to use it, the look in Casper's eyes suggested she wouldn't.

He lowered his injured right hand, but his left remained oddly pressed against his neck, and Sydney realized it clutched a cell phone.

"I'm sorry, I didn't mean to scare you, but I couldn't afford to be seen."

"How did you get…" Sydney glanced at her purse, and her eyes widened. "Did you take my keys?"

Casper nodded.

"Why?" she asked, breathless with anticipation as she realized what this might mean.

Casper craned his neck, cell phone still pressed against his skin, and searched the parking lot. "We need to get out of here. Can you drive somewhere?"

"Does this mean…are you going to…" Sydney could barely form the words.

Casper looked her in the eyes but said nothing. He didn't have to. She inhaled sharply, hardly believing the moment was real, and in an odd way—though maybe not so odd considering their circumstances and what they were about to do—she felt more connected to him than any other human being. Ever. In fact, she hardly dared move, frightened she would disturb his image and find an empty backseat instead.

"If you had answered your page, I wouldn't have had to hide so long on the floor of this ancient relic, sweating missiles." Casper handed her the keys. "Let's go."

Sydney turned around and started the car, at which time Casper slunk back down on the floorboard. She longed to get started, to get right back inside and treat Liz, but Casper apparently had other plans.

As if reading her mind, he said, "The hospital will be the first place Jackson will look for me. He might not know what kind of car you drive, but I don't want him spotting me none-theless."

"Where should we go?"

"Anywhere. I just need to talk to you without worrying about being seen."

They both fell silent as Sydney backed out, drove down one level, and scanned her security badge at the unattended gate to exit the lot and pull onto the street. A few back streets led her to Cambridge, and after two blocks, Casper sat up. In the rearview mirror Sydney could see the cell phone still pressed against his neck.

"What's with the phone?"

"I'll explain later. Why don't you go to a hotel? Nothing too close to here. I'm going to need a place to wait for a while."

"Wait for what?"

Casper didn't answer, and in the mirror, Sydney could see him scanning the street, his gaze darting back and forth, as if Jackson would run up to the car any second.

Sydney worked her way toward Longfellow Bridge. "How about the Ralston? It's far enough out of our way and big enough to hide in."

"Fine."

Although Sydney longed to know what Casper had planned, he didn't offer anything else, and the way he kept surveying both sides of the street made it difficult to gauge his thoughts.

"How did you get away from Jackson?" she finally dared to ask.

"I fled the apartment. Waited for him to use the bathroom, cracked two bottles over his head, and secured him as best I could with sealant. Guess he didn't figure me as a flight risk." Casper let out a weird laugh and added, "He does now."

Sydney wondered what in the world *sealant* was but didn't feel it was her most pressing question. "So, he's looking for you at the hospital?"

"Assuming he's conscious and free from the glue, yes. I nailed him pretty hard."

"Why my car?"

"I had to enter the building to get your keys from your desk—you're not the only one who can break into locks—but I felt it was too risky to stick around and find you. Instead, I scoured the parking lot for your Jeep and paged you to my cell phone."

Sydney's heart sank. "Which I didn't answer. It would've been my fault if he'd found you."

"It's not only myself I'm worried about."

Sydney gripped the steering wheel more tightly and worked her way towards Boylston Street. "Is he aware of how much I know?"

"No, but if he doesn't find you at the hospital, he'll get suspicious. What made you come out to your Jeep, anyway? It was quite a shock when instead of answering my call, you showed up in person."

Sydney hesitated. "I was on my way to your apartment. I was going to call the police for help."

Casper looked up at the rearview mirror.

"I couldn't let Liz die. I just couldn't. Not without a fight, anyway."

They drove in silence for the next several minutes, lost in

troubling thoughts, but as Sydney pulled into the hotel entrance, something horrible occurred to her. "What about Dr. Burke? Will our actions affect him?"

Casper looked somber, and it was a long moment before he spoke. "Probably. Another agent is supposedly bringing him back tonight on the scheduled navigation. The idea was to drop him off and then the three of us would leave. Now I imagine Jackson will use him as leverage."

Sydney felt sick. "Oh God, what if he dies because of me?"

Casper sat forward and put a hand on her shoulder. "If we're going to do this, we have to stay focused, have to think about all the people we can save rather than the few lives that might get lost."

Few lives? The enormity of what she was getting into hit her full force. She turned around to face Casper, but before she could say anything a valet attendant opened the car door.

"Checking in ma'am?" the polite kid asked.

It took Sydney a moment to register. "Um, yes, yes I am."

Getting out, she realized she didn't have enough cash for a room. To Casper, she said, "All I have is a credit card. I can't use that. Jackson could find us."

To Sydney's relief and surprise, Casper pulled a wad of bills from his front pocket. "Glad my paycheck will come in handy." He gave Sydney a small grin, the phone still pressed oddly against his neck. "I'll wait in here."

Sydney allowed the attendant to close the door and then stepped into the lobby to check-in, as if she were merely another out-of-town guest ready for a restful sojourn.

Using the name of one of her old foster mothers, Isabel Parker, the only one who had actually seemed more interested in Sydney than the stipend Sydney's care had ensured, she booked a room on the eighth floor. She ignored the clerk's scrutiny of her scrubs and general state of dishevelment and assured him she could carry in her own bags, which of course, there were none.

When she returned to the car, Casper stepped out, more appropriately attired in dark slacks and a button-down shirt that was open at the collar, leaving room for the mysterious cell phone of which he seemed not the least bit embarrassed. In his free hand he carried his soft-sided briefcase. Sydney handed her keys and a five to the attendant who promptly drove the Jeep away.

Using the elevator, Casper and Sydney made their way to the eighth floor, surrounded by other sharply dressed individuals, most of whom wore respiratory masks and all of whom had the decency not to stare at the slovenly girl in scrubs. At least Sydney's fleece jacket added some class. Not.

Once inside the room, which was a richly decorated space with two double beds, dark cherry furniture, and a huge bathroom, Casper took a seat on the bed, his leather bag next to him. Unsure what to do, Sydney slipped off her jacket and stood by the door, hoping to not look as awkward as she felt. Casper indicated she join him.

She took a cautious seat on the edge of the duvet and wondered what he had planned. He started to speak but stopped when something on Sydney's body caught his attention.

"Hand me your scrub tie," he said.

"I'm sorry?"

"The tie from your waistband." Casper used his free hand to tug on the strip of fabric holding up Sydney's scrubs.

She gave him an odd look, but when he motioned with his hand again, she stood, untied the drawstring, and pulled it free from her scrubs. She almost lost the pants in the process and had to yank them up and tuck them inside her underwear so they wouldn't fall down.

Casper thanked her and brought the drawstring close to

his collar. "Here. Tie it around my neck to secure the cell phone."

"What? I don't under—"

"Just do it. I'll explain in a second."

Sydney took the string and tied it around Casper's neck, leaving enough slack to slip the cell phone underneath so that it remained pressed against the left side of his neck.

"Wondering what I'm doing, right?" he said in response to Sydney's bewildered expression.

She nodded.

Casper leaned forward and pulled open his collar even more, both hands now free thanks to the scrub tie. He pushed the cell phone an inch to the left, and then took Sydney's hand and rested her index finger on his neck, not far from his carotid artery. "Right there. Feel that?"

Sydney shook her head, mouth slightly agape. All she could feel was warm skin and a strong pulse.

"Push harder. There, that little knot. Feel it now? It's like a BB."

Sydney felt it. Underneath her fingertip was indeed a firm nodule. She nodded, experiencing another rare moment of speechlessness.

"That's my Destination Tracking Device."

"You're, um, what?"

"Destination Tracking Device. We all get one, soon as we're born. For the most part it serves a good purpose—an abducted child, a runaway teen, an elder with dementia. It also contains our medical records. With it, a person can always be located, including a criminal. Or," he added, his expression grim, "a weak virologist who disobeys the NIU and fails to return to the future."

"Helping people isn't weak." Sydney's finger still rolled over the spot on Casper's neck. Then she yanked her hand away as the significance of what he'd just said hit her. "Can they track you here? In this…time period?"

"At first, no. To do so requires a radio navigation system using a series of satellites, but your satellite systems are extremely primitive compared to ours."

"So?"

"So, Jackson traveled back with a special receiver."

"And?"

"And he was able to track me. Until…"

"Until what?" Sydney sat on the edge of the bed, spine straight, body tense.

"Until I realized my cell phone caused interference."

Sydney's attention went back to the phone strapped to Casper's neck. "But…how…"

"The other day I left my phone in my front shirt pocket. Jackson later complained he couldn't track me all day. He said that except for a few scattered seconds here and there, all he got was interference in the signal. Same thing happened the next day, so I put two and two together. Fortunately, he didn't. He figured there was either something wrong with your satellite system or our receiver. Since then I've made sure I keep the phone turned on and near my neck. It won't work forever. Jackson will figure it out. But all I need is a few hours." Casper patted the phone. "Best thing your department gave me— even if they were linked to brain cancer in the year 2050."

Cancer?

Sydney couldn't dwell on that bombshell right now. Instead, she flashed back to Casper's disheveled appearance the night before, and she remembered seeing the phone in his pocket. "Why doesn't a person just remove their tracking device?"

His eyebrows shot up. "Did you feel where it was located? Right next to the carotid artery. Makes it a little difficult for your average Sam to remove."

"Some criminals must have tried."

"Of course they have, but they need to find an unscrupulous surgeon to do it, and even then removal is nearly impossible and the majority of them die. The implant is made of Ucillinite, a modern material that molds itself to the environment. The BB you feel is only a portion of the implant. The rest spreads out in the tissue, forming a nice little nest around the artery, like dozens of tiny little arms. Combine that with the invoked scar tissue, and unless you want to exsanguinate, you best leave it alone."

"Holy shit," was all Sydney could think of to say.

"Holy shit, indeed."

They stared at each other, neither saying a word, and it occurred to Sydney how way in over her head she was. Even worse, it occurred to her how dangerously far she had pushed Casper.

She exhaled loudly and rested against the headboard, its wood boring into her back. "Oh, Casper, I had no idea. I guess I never really thought this through. I didn't…I mean…"

"Some things shouldn't be thought through. Sometimes you just have to act."

"But—"

"Listen to me." He leaned toward her, pumped-up energy in his tone. "Once I start, there's no turning back, no changing my mind. I'm going to set off a chain of events bigger than you can possibly imagine."

Sydney remained motionless, mouth open, unsure how to respond. She'd spent so much time hoping for this moment, she'd done nothing to prepare for its reality.

"What we do now could change the future forever, but how and to what extent no one knows. This is uncharted territory we're crossing, and I'm not afraid to admit I'm terrified. Absolutely terrified."

By the look in his eye, she knew he meant it.

"But," Casper continued, his voice softer now, "I also know I can't return to the future knowing I left millions of people to die. Liz, Elijah…perhaps, you. They were right, every last one of them, I was entirely too weak for this job."

Sydney cleared her throat, longing for a glass of water. "What do you want me to do?"

"You? Oh, no, no, no. There's no need to involve you anymore. I'll take full risk. I'll treat a few people and get the word out as quickly as I can. All you'll need to do is carry on with the research and production of more protective factor once I'm gone."

"But what about Jackson? If you go to the hospital, he'll find you."

"Then I'll go somewhere else. There are plenty of other hospitals."

"What, you're just going to walk in somewhere and inject a patient? They'll think you're crazy, probably lock you away. And what about your tracking device? You said yourself Jackson will figure out how to bypass the interference. He'll eventually find you."

Casper shook his head and frowned with his eyes, as if speaking to a simplistic child. "I knew when I made the decision to go ahead with this, I wasn't about to get away. My job is to just get it started." He pointed to his neck and added, "If I stay here, I'll eventually be found, and if I go back to my time, they'll…well… justice will be swift and final."

"What do you mean? They'll send you to prison?"

The frown deepened. "That would be the happy ending. No, we don't really do the prison thing as you know it. Proof of guilt is much easier in my time—DNA maps of every individual, security cameras at every turn, Destination Tracking Devices—and with so few false arrests, the serious offenders are dealt harsh punishment. Despite all the goodwill and peace we've managed to achieve in the last century, that 'celebrate life' mentality doesn't extend to criminals."

"But—"

"Look, don't worry about me. Besides, who knows, maybe the NIU won't even exist after all this. Maybe *I* won't exist after all this."

Sydney blinked a few times, trying to process his words. Thinking back to an astronomy class she had taken in her sophomore year of college, she said, "What about the idea of parallel universes, the notion that you can't change the future because simultaneous worlds exist, each with its own predestined path."

Casper raised his eyebrows. "That's never been proven."

"Well, what about cosmic sensor?"

"Sydney."

"The idea that you can't alter your own personal hist—"

Casper silenced her by reaching out a hand and cupping her chin. "Stop, okay? As usual, your knowledge impresses me, but theories are irrelevant. All we have is the here and now. Nothing else."

Guilt flooded Sydney. "I'm sorry. I never meant for you… I never wanted…"

"Stop," Casper said again, this time more firmly, yet his hand was gentle on her face. "It wasn't my intent to make you feel culpable. I was only telling you what I'm up against. You didn't talk me into anything. You can't take the blame. It was my own decision. It all came down to one thing: Could I live with myself knowing I had walked away? The answer proved to be no. An unequivocal, big obese no."

"Big *fat* no," Sydney whispered.

"Okay, so my vernacular's not perfect. I'll work on it."

"But you can't go home again. In fact, you don't even know if you'll still *have* a home." Sydney marveled at how he so readily accepted his fate, as if second thoughts weren't an option. When had she ever done something similar? Put others' needs before her own? A lifetime of looking out for number one made her a shallow and thoughtless comparison.

Casper pulled his hand away. "I can deal with that. You know, my life in the future was far from perfect. I worked too much. My wife cheated on me, and when she left, she made me ineligible for the child we'd applied for."

"You *applied* for a child?"

Casper's somber expression brightened. "Yes. We had everything picked out: a boy, tall, athletic, knack for technology. Of course, there's never any guarantees, but I didn't care. I was really excited. We'd waited so long to have kids. It was her idea to wait until our careers were settled. Then we compiled Zion, and it was the best day of my life. I was already planning the next one. But two weeks before Zion's implantation, Alegela's plans changed."

Casper's face darkened again, and Sydney had no idea how to respond. She opted for, "I'm sorry."

He shrugged. "So you see, there's not much to return home to. Besides, I've told you all the bad things. Now let me tell you the good things." He smiled underneath his mask and starting ticking off fingers. "I get to save Liz. And my new child friend, Elijah. And millions more people. And, in the small chance I can somehow remain here without getting caught—you know, maybe have a phone permanently stitched into my neck—I get to drink as much soda as I want, and no one can regulate my weight. I get to remove this birth control implant from my forearm and father a child whenever I please. And well, if I'm lucky enough, maybe I'll even get to be with you." As he said this, Casper looked down and fiddled with the cell phone on his neck.

"You predicting the future? Thought you only wanted to deal with the here and now." They both fell silent long enough for the moment to get awkward. Then Sydney said, "By the way, is your name really Casper Jones?"

"Yes. I didn't even have to change my last name when I stumbled across Dr. Patrick Michael Jones in my research. His sabbatical in China gave me the perfect window. Some might even say it was fate."

"I don't believe in fate."

"Really? Even now?"

Sydney didn't answer, just closed her eyes and wondered how she'd gotten to this point.

Casper tugged on the knee of her scrub pants. "You better go now. Not to your house. Go somewhere safe. Somewhere where Jackson won't find you."

Sydney sat up straighter. "Why would Jackson come after me? Especially if you're the one dispensing the treatment."

"Because he knows that's the one thing that'll summon me. As much as leaving millions of people to die would weigh heavily on me, leaving you with him would weigh more."

"But you can't do this without me. You could get caught before you even begin." She pointed to his cell phone. "For all you know, the agent returning with Burke might have something to unscramble the interference. In fact, they might know where you are right now."

"I don't want you involved any further."

"Too late for that, don't you think? Besides the fact that I got you into this—"

"It was my choice. No one else's."

"Even if it was, I can't afford to have you get caught before we get started. Before we can save Liz. One of us has to go to the hospital, and my chances are better than yours."

"I don't think you realize the significance of what you're saying."

Sydney looked past Casper and saw her career—her hard work, her education, her reputation—spiraling down the drain. She saw herself and Casper on the run, fugitives against the law, the law from two hundred years in the future.

Then Sydney saw Liz, dead. And her own self on a ventilator in the hospital, or maybe in an old school gym, alone. An isolated death to cap off an even more isolated life.

"I'm as much a part of this as you." She shifted her weight on the bed, making the choice that wasn't. "And you're a sitting duck who needs a decoy."

Casper frowned. "Kind of like being stuck between cement and a hard space, isn't it?"

Sydney looked at him, her throat tight with worry but his misspoken cliché oddly warming her heart.

With a shaky hand, she tucked a few strands of escaped hair behind her ears. Then, pushing her fear aside, she stood. "Tell me what you want me to do."

15
____

Stop number one was the hospital pharmacy. Thanks to Sydney's unsteady hand in Casper's apartment the night before, she'd emptied almost his entire bottle of insulin tablets into the sink. As a result, Casper had informed her, rather nervously, that he'd need some of the old-fashioned type of insulin to get him by.

Get him by for what, neither of them knew.

Sydney had tried to assure Casper they would find the right dose—too much insulin would nosedive a person's blood sugar to dangerously low levels and put him or her into hypoglycemic la-la land—but in her mind, she prayed the injectable form of today was equivalent to the ingestible form of tomorrow.

Shifting her weight from one foot to the other, she waited for the pharmacist to complete the prescription she'd called in from Casper's hotel room. Three people stood in line behind her, and with every passing tick of the clock hanging above the pick-up window, Sydney grew more and more convinced each of them knew what she was up to. Or worse, Jackson did. She also worried the pharmacist would call hospital security and tattle on the disheveled doctor seeking a new prescription for insulin. As she pondered bolting, the pharmacist reappeared, his masked and tired face suggesting he had more pressing issues on his mind than Sydney's need for medication.

"Any questions on the insulin?" He barely looked up from the form he was completing.

"No, my uncle is very comfortable with the drug. I'm just picking it up for him. He's—"

"Sign here then."

Sydney signed and took the bag the pharmacist offered. "Did you include the syringes?"

"They're there."

Before Sydney could thank him, he'd already called out, "Next!"

Moving aside, she slipped the insulin into Casper's leather bag and exited the pharmacy's glass doors. Walking at a brisk pace, she headed to the nearest set of elevators, pushed the up button with one hand, and gripped the waistband of her scrubs with the other.

Which led Sydney to stop number two, her office, where a pair of chinos and a turtleneck sweater filled a desk drawer in case she ever needed a change of clothes. Every doctor and nurse had a horror story of an encounter with bodily fluids. It was an extra stop and would consume precious minutes, but unless Sydney wanted to wander the hospital with her scrub pants around her ankles, the detour was necessary. She thought about Casper with the cell phone tied to his neck. She thought about the thing buried *in* his neck. She thought about Jackson tracking him down like a dog.

And she thought about reaching her office in record speed.

Reminding herself that Jackson would have no reason to be on the sixth floor, she exited the elevator and hurried through the busy south wing and then the orthopedic recovery ward on which Sydney had no patient duties other than an occasional consult. The north wing housed the infectious disease office suite, and as Sydney neared its

closed and presumably locked doors—it was after nine p.m.
—the hallway became increasingly deserted and quiet. She
paused long enough to grab the keys from her purse, which,
along with the insulin, her fleece jacket, and a sealed envelope, was in Casper's leather case. With a final look over her
shoulder, she unlocked one of the double doors and pushed
it open.

Inside, the office suite was empty and dark. Sydney
fumbled along the wall until she found the switch for the over-
head fluorescent lights, blinking at the sudden brightness. She
listened for signs of occupancy. Nothing. Clutching the bag
against her side, she strode through the partitioned maze,
forcing herself to relax. No one was around. She would
change and then move on to stop number three. Thirty
seconds max.

Once inside the cubicle, Sydney dropped Casper's briefcase onto the desk chair and opened the bottom drawer
housing her clothes. She yanked off her shoes and then her
scrub bottoms, but her movements were frenzied and rushed,
and she almost toppled over. Slowing down, she pulled on the
chinos, peeled off her scrub top, and slipped the turtleneck
over her head.

She had barely gotten the sweater in place when the
double doors clicked open.

She froze.

Footsteps started down the hallway. Slowly. As if the
person was in no rush at all.

Springing to life, Sydney thrust her feet back into her Doc
Martens and grabbed Casper's bag. She kicked the worn
scrubs into a corner. Looking both ways down the corridor,
she racked her brain for the floor plan. Was there a back exit?
Another way to the stairwell? She'd always used the front.

The footsteps kept coming.

She decided to head toward the back and, with the help of
adrenaline, crossed quickly through more partitioned mazes,

past the secretaries' desks, past Dr. DeWitt's office, past the teaching and conference rooms.

Then she could go no farther. Nothing but wall.

There must be another exit. Why have I never checked before?

Panicked, she looked in both directions, but there was nowhere to go. To the right were more offices. To the left would just lead her back to her own cubicle.

But still the footsteps.

Sydney's breaths grew shallow and her mouth dry. Jackson had found her. She hadn't even accomplished the most important tasks, and yet he'd already found her.

"Hello? Anybody in here?" The male voice that spoke was aged and tremulous and most certainly not Jackson's.

Sydney sagged in relief. Gus, the overnight housekeeper. Sydney had spoken to him several times and had even baked him Christmas cookies the year before. Within seconds, he rounded the corner and came into view, his cleaning cart rolling behind him. He looked surprised to see her.

"Why, Dr. McKnight, what are you doing back here? Are you okay?"

"I'm fine. Just a little preoccupied, went the wrong way." Sydney tried to smile, but her anxiety made the gesture difficult.

"Poor girl. You must be exhausted. This virus is terrifying." Gus shook his head and put a shaky hand to his mask.

"Yes, it is."

"The good Lord has blessed me though. None of my family's taken ill. You doctors got your work cut out for you."

"We do." Sydney clutched the bag tighter and took a step forward. "Nice seeing you, Gus."

"You too, Doc. Make sure you take care of yourself now, you hear?"

"Thank you, I will." Sydney feigned another smile and resumed a brisk walk down the hallway. She made it only a few yards before Gus stopped her again.

"Say, Doc, I almost forgot. I was up here cleaning about twenty minutes ago—just came back to get the sweeper I left behind—and a nice gentleman was outside the door asking for you."

Sydney's breath caught. "Oh?" She turned around, a flood of possibilities racing through her mind.

Mitch? A resident? Jackson? Although the words *nice* and *gentleman* couldn't possibly coexist in the same sentence with Jackson.

"A darker-skinned fellow. Think he was an orderly. He was wondering if you'd been by, but I said I didn't know. He didn't leave no message or anything, but I thought you should know."

Sydney tried to swallow. Couldn't. "Thank you, Gus."

She turned and backtracked through the maze toward the double doors ahead, her limbs rubbery like Gumby's.

So, Jackson had been there.

And he'd been looking for her.

Stop number three—the lab—wasn't so bad, even though Sydney worried she'd self-combust with each passing second, particularly during the eight-story elevator ride down and the three-corridor walk over. Unlike her own office, Jackson couldn't come looking for her there. An employee needed special clearance on his or her identification badge to enter the lab, and orderlies didn't carry it.

Once Sydney entered the secured lab and the door closed behind her, she breathed a sigh of relief. A few lights were on, and a couple of the workspaces showed signs of life—humming computers, spinning centrifuges, steaming coffee cups—but the occupants had stepped out, and the place was currently deserted. Although no one would question her presence, Sydney was relieved not to have to make small talk. She scurried over to

Casper's workspace in the far-right corner. Opening his refrigerator, she replayed their conversation back at the hotel.

"Go to the fridge. On the bottom shelf, way in the back, you'll find a small vial marked with my name and the label: *West Nile Virus Serum Sample*. Take it and slip it in this bag." At that point Casper had raised the large leather case and opened the main compartment, nothing but a sealed manila envelope inside.

Sydney had taken the bag. "I'm assuming the contents of the vial have nothing to do with West Nile virus?"

"No. It's my protective factor."

"But I thought—"

"There are two vials at my apartment—the two I showed Jackson—but he doesn't know I made a third."

"What should I do with it?"

"You'll take it to Liz and treat her. Then you'll take it to the Hortons and treat them." At that point, Casper had lowered his eyes. "Give it to the children first, then the mother. If there's enough left, treat the father as well."

"But if I use it all up, how will we share your—"

Casper had pointed to the bag. "There's an envelope inside the case. It contains a full description of the prion theory as well as the formula for my protective factor. More factor can easily be made. It only requires a common respiratory virus, a transposon, and the modified protein, all of which I've outlined clearly."

"So what should I do after I've injected the patients? How can I pass the information on without Jackson finding me? It will take a full public disclosure. I don't think I'll have time—"

Casper had grabbed Sydney's shoulders and looked her in the eyes with a frightening reality. "No, you won't. You won't have time. You'll be lucky to treat the patients before Jackson finds you." He then released her. "Maybe I should just do this myself."

"Jackson will catch you before you even step through the door."

"He'll go after you as well."

"But his main focus will be you. He doesn't know I'm involved. *Suspects* maybe, but doesn't know. That should at least give me the time I need to treat Liz and the Hortons."

"And then what?"

Sydney had stared at Casper, realizing his implication. "We need a third person, don't we?" she'd asked. "Someone who can make the treatment public. Someone who can carry on the research. Someone who'll be forced to believe us when they see Liz and the Hortons improve."

Casper had nodded. "And someone Jackson isn't familiar with. Do you know someone like that? Someone we can trust to carry this through?"

Sydney had paused for a moment, but the hesitation hadn't been necessary. It had taken her less than a millisecond to come up with the answer.

"Absolutely," she'd replied.

Stop four: the Hortons. Sydney had made it from the lab on the lower level to 3 North with no sign of Jackson, and she prayed her luck would last. Her minutes were numbered, though. 3 West and 3 North were the most likely places he'd find her, and he was surely aware of that.

She'd wanted to start with Liz, wanted to make sure her friend got treated above all else, but a nurse was at her bedside, and Sydney saw no way to plausibly inject Liz in another medical staff's presence. Although Sydney needed to recruit a third person, the injection part had to be done by her, because there was no time to convince someone of the factor. They might try to stop her in the misguided belief she was doing a patient harm. Sydney needed to treat first and then let the evidence speak for itself.

And she needed to do so without getting caught.

To better conceal herself, she had grabbed one of the surgical hats she kept in the lab. She sometimes wore them to protect her hair while she worked. She'd also donned a white lab coat. Those, along with the respiratory mask, her goggles, and a bustling patient care area, would hopefully force Jackson—and anyone else—to have to look twice to identify her. She only needed a few minutes.

She scanned the hallway one more time but saw nothing but scurrying nurses and a stampeding resident—one of her own—flying into a patient's room. Sydney swallowed down guilt at deserting him in what was obviously a patient crisis, but she could do nothing about that now. No one could know she was back.

Lowering her head, she grabbed a yellow gown and pushed open the Hortons' door. To her relief, the room was empty except for the patients. She closed the door behind her and slipped the gown over her bulky coat.

Mrs. Horton was dozing in a chair against the back wall. She coughed—a cough Sydney well recognized—and stirred. When she noticed Sydney's presence, she sat up and adjusted her mask.

Sydney went to the woman's side and knelt down. "It's me, Mrs. Horton. Dr. McKnight."

"Oh, hi." The woman's voice was a whisper. "I didn't recognize you."

Good.

"You coughed. Are you ill now too?"

Mrs. Horton shook her head but then nodded, and her eyes welled up. "I think so. My throat is scratchy, and my chest is a little tight. But don't worry. I haven't been leaving the room. They've been bringing me food."

Sydney glanced at the door and wondered how she was

going to proceed. She hadn't rehearsed an explanation to Mrs. Horton. Hadn't got past the sheer anxiety of avoiding Jackson to think about how the woman might respond.

She took Mrs. Horton's hands in her gloved ones and stared pointedly at the distressed mother. "Mrs. Horton, I have something that will help you. Something that will help your whole family. One patient has already been cured because of it." Sydney didn't know if Macaby had officially been discharged yet, but the point remained the same.

Mrs. Horton's eyes widened. "What is it? Why hasn't anybody told—"

"It's a very new treatment, developed by one of our researchers. There's little available, but if we can prove it works, we can make more. I'd like to treat your family and you."

"So, we'd be, like, guinea pigs?"

Sydney could tell the woman was skeptical. Why shouldn't she be? Medicine hadn't always had a great track record with the African-American community. *Tuskegee syphilis experiment, anyone?*

"Mrs. Horton, nothing else is working. I think it's our only chance. I'm asking you to trust me on this." Sweat trickled down Sydney's spine, and she resisted the urge to glance at her watch. The effort of convincing Mrs. Horton might take too much time, but Sydney knew she couldn't walk out without saving the children.

The thirty-one-year-old mother stared at Sydney a moment longer. Then she looked at her children, first Jessica, her tiny body fueled by the ventilator, and then Elijah, asleep with labored and noisy breathing. Finally, the woman focused her attention on her husband, who, thankfully, had not yet been transferred out.

"You really think it will make them better?" she asked.

"I do."

"And it won't cause them any harm?"

"No."

"And they'll most likely die without it?"

"Yes."

Mrs. Horton choked back a sob. "Then do it."

Upon her blessing, Sydney jumped up and retrieved the vial of protective factor from the bag. She lifted her gown, reached into her lab coat pocket, and pulled out four of the five syringes she'd placed there.

With trembling hands, she opened the first syringe and plunged its needle deep into the vial. Casper had told her one cc was adequate. Glancing at the small bottle, Sydney prayed she had at least five cc's. She had promised Mrs. Horton she would treat the entire family. What if she ran out of factor before she got to Liz?

The thought made Sydney's hands shake even more, but she could see Mrs. Horton watching her, so she tried to pull it together. Casper had told her to inject the factor intramuscularly. He didn't know what ill effects might occur mixing it with other medications running through the patient's IV line.

Sydney sterilized an area of skin on Jessica's thigh, her quadricep a better choice than her small deltoid, and without another thought plunged in the needle. The infant didn't flinch. Sydney discarded the needle in the sharps container and began to repeat what she'd done to Jessica—only switching her injection site to the upper arm instead of the thigh—on the rest of the Hortons. The air was still and silent, and when Sydney withdrew a cc for Mr. Horton, she also drew up a fifth dose to ensure she had enough for Liz. With relief, she found that she had, although there were mere droplets left in the vial.

When she finished, she tucked the empty vial back into Casper's bag and returned to Mrs. Horton, squeezing her hands once again.

"It's done," Sydney said. "They'll get better."

Mrs. Horton said nothing, but she searched Sydney's eyes,

and Sydney knew the woman desperately wanted to believe her.

Without another word, Sydney tore off the gloves, washed her hands, and left, whizzing past three more patient rooms until she reached the one that held Liz. She didn't bother to look up. If Jackson was there, and if he had seen her, she was determined to treat Liz before he approached her. Or anyone else for that matter.

Liz was sleeping. The nurse was gone. The two other women in the room were on ventilators, oblivious to Sydney's presence. As she pulled on new gloves, she tried to ignore the fact that there was no time to make *them* better. She tried to ignore the fact that they might have children or grandchildren who needed them. Instead, she stood at Liz's bedside and whispered her name.

Liz didn't stir, her breathing already labored. Sydney was horrified by her quick deterioration. Her friend must have been ill longer than she'd let on.

"Liz," Sydney repeated, but still Liz didn't rise from her deep sleep.

Sydney grabbed an alcohol pad and started cleaning Liz's arm, hoping the cold would arouse her friend. When it didn't, Sydney decided to go ahead and inject her. She felt tense and unnerved, and she knew she was running out of time. She still had one thing left to do. The most important, perhaps.

She plunged the needle into Liz's arm. This time her friend did stir but didn't open her eyes until Sydney had slipped the syringe into the sharps container.

"Sydney?" Liz's voice was thick and groggy. She rubbed her arm, obviously confused about the stinging she felt there. "Is that you? What's with the hat? You look like a pinhead."

Sydney smiled underneath her mask and goggles. "Just making sure you're all right."

"Never been better," Liz mumbled through heavy breaths.

Sydney touched her friend's arm. "I have to go. I have

something very important to do, but I want you…" Sydney's voice caught, and she had to swallow down the lump. "I want you to know that you're going to get better. I promise you that. And know that…well…know…"

"Are you okay?" Liz seemed more awake now and tried to pull herself up but was apparently too weak to do so.

"Just know that you're an amazing person, and I've been so lucky to have you as a friend. I never returned the joy and positivity you heaped on me. I never listened as much as I should have. I took more than I gave." Sydney had to stop. If she didn't she might cry, and there was no time for that now. On the other hand, if Jackson found her, this might be the last time she saw Liz, which was a gut-wrenching thought to bear.

"Okay, now you're creeping me out. Go take your cheery bedside manner to some other pour soul." Liz's smile was fleeting. "I'm pretty tired. I think I'll rest."

Sydney nodded, her heart sinking to her knees. She tore off yet another yellow gown and another pair of gloves and prepared to leave the room. With a hand trembling on the door handle, she prayed Jackson wouldn't be on the other side.

Only one more stop to make. Just a short trot to the stairwell and up four flights of stairs to his office.

Can I do it without being seen?

She knew he'd help them. He was the best choice.

Then again, if what Casper had said about fate was true, there'd never really *been* a choice.

16

S ydney took a deep breath and opened the door, every nerve in her body a live wire. One more stop. Mitch's office. Now all she had to do was get there.

Terrified someone would spot her, she kept her head lowered and turned left out of Liz's room. She beelined toward the stairwell, her body close to the wall and its wooden guardrail. The stairs were only a short distance away, halfway between Liz and the Hortons' rooms, and Sydney was relieved she wouldn't have to pass the front counter.

"Hey, isn't that Dr. McKnight?"

Startled, Sydney froze but then quickly resumed her steps. The voice, coming from the counter behind her, sounded like one of the residents.

"What's with the hat?" Sydney heard him say, probably to a nurse. He called out to her. Twice.

Sydney kept walking, but the resident didn't give up, and soon he was trotting down the hallway after her. Only a few more yards now. She was so close, so close to finishing this. She—

A hand touched her shoulder. "Sydney?"

Sydney stopped, hesitated, and turned around. Troy

Palmer, the senior resident she had deserted, the one she had seen dashing into a patient's room less than ten minutes before and the one who'd informed her yesterday of Dr. Burke's disappearance, was looking at her like she was insane.

"I thought that was you. Why didn't you answer me?"

Sydney patted at the ill-fitting hat on her head. "Sorry, just in a hurry." She could almost feel the stairwell door behind her beckoning, and she was desperate to respond.

"I didn't know you were back. I was just about to call Dr. DeWitt. Our patient in room 322, you know, that really big guy? He gave us all a scare. Started thrashing around like a madman, throwing things around the room. I don't know if it's encephalitis from the virus, a response to his meds, or just the way the guy is, but whatever the problem, we finally got him subdued. For now, anyway. Hopefully…"

Sydney barely heard. She had to get going. Jackson might find her any second.

"…won't happen again. Hey, you okay?"

"Hmm?" Sydney cased the hallway, her brow furrowed in a continuous state of anxiety.

"What's with the hat? And that bag? You leaving again? We—"

"I'm sorry, Troy. I need to go." Sydney backed up toward the stairwell. "I shouldn't be much longer."

"But…" he looked bewildered. "What about—"

She didn't hear what he said next. Coming down the hallway was Jackson, dressed in white scrubs. His falsified orderly badge was no longer visible, maybe in light of his extended stay.

"What's going on?" Troy's voice sounded faint, almost like background noise, and though he reached out a hand, Sydney barely felt his touch. All she could see was Jackson, his menacing gaze locked on her own.

"Maybe you should go lie…"

Troy still talking, Sydney still rigid, Jackson still advancing.

He was less than twenty-five feet from her now. He eyed Casper's briefcase in her hand, and his expression went from suspicion to apprehension to anger.

Sydney took another step back. Then another. *Run!* her mind screamed. *Run!*

But Jackson would follow her. He'd find out where she was going. She'd never get to Mitch in time. Never have a way to pass on the treatment.

A crowd had gathered at the counter. Nurses and residents alike were staring at her, no doubt wondering what was wrong with the catatonic doctor.

Jackson was ten feet away now. It was all over. She'd failed. Jackson would catch her, and millions of people would die.

Then something happened, something Sydney didn't comprehend at first. Nurses started running. Troy started running.

"He's doing it again!"

"He's waking up!"

"Have the restraints come yet?"

Even Jackson seemed startled by the commotion, and the sudden ear-shattering shrieks emanating from a patient's room between Sydney and Jackson made both of them jump.

"Call security!" someone shouted.

"We need more men in here!"

Troy had already disappeared into the room of the combatant patient, as did most of the nurses.

"You. Orderly—or whoever you are—get over here."

Rolanda, one of the hospital's best—and largest—general medicine nurses had run up to Jackson, and before either Sydney or Jackson knew what was happening, she started dragging him toward the patient's room. Jackson tried to jerk free, but Rolanda grabbed hold of him again, and the look on her face suggested defiance wasn't an option.

When Jackson still tried to resist, the robust woman chastised him. "What in the hell are you doing? We need all the male staff we can get. Now get your ass in room 322 and help restrain this patient!"

Sydney seized the moment and bolted to the stairwell. Rolanda now called out after *her*, but Sydney didn't stop. She just kept running, through the door and up the stairs, clearing two steps at a time until she reached the seventh floor. Before she burst through the access door, she stole a final glance down the stairs. Nothing.

She ran down a paint-chipped and yet-to-be-renovated hallway, past the secured psychiatric unit, past the outpatient counseling center—now converted to a post-surgical wing, away from the infectious hell of the third, fourth, and fifth floors—and toward the pulmonary offices. She prayed the doors would be unlocked, a fellow or staff member working late, but when Sydney reached the double doors and yanked, they didn't budge. *Crap!*

She pulled out her cell phone. No service. *Double crap!*

She ran back to the post-surgical wing, her heart and lungs operating at full capacity. She needed to find a phone. And she needed to calm down. There was no reason Jackson would come for her there. Even if he'd been able to escape the combatant patient's room, he'd never look for her on the seventh floor. He didn't know about Mitch. He'd assume she had fled the hospital. Besides, he had no proof of what she had done.

Yet.

She found a red house phone hanging on the wall, opposite the treatment room, and although it left her exposed in the hallway, she didn't want to raise suspicions by using one of the phones at the front desk. Some of the surgical staff knew her and would invariably draw her into conversation.

She punched in Mitch's pager number and, when prompted, added the number for the house phone followed by a 111—their signal. Mitch would recognize it and hopefully respond quickly. Although Sydney had initially been disheartened to learn from Crystal that Mitch was on call that night, not anxious to meet up with him considering their less than cordial breakup, she was now enormously relieved. Having the conversation over the phone would have proved difficult.

At the first ring, Sydney snatched up the receiver.

"Mitch?"

"Syd? What's up?" He sounded surprised but also hesitant to hear from her.

"Listen, I need you to come up to your office. Now."

"What's wrong? Are you—"

"Please, Mitch, just come now. It's extremely important."

"Okay, okay, but—"

"Are you coming?"

"Yes."

"And don't tell anyone."

Sydney hung up the phone, hands shaking, heart thumping. She glanced down the hallway at the front counter. No one paid her any attention. In fact, there were only two nurses seated behind the desk, and Sydney realized the entire floor, unlike her own, had an unrushed and non-macabre feel to it, its rooms merely harboring post-surgical patients, none of whom had the Seneca strain. She found herself wishing she was a surgical fellow. No influenza C to battle. No Casper to discover. No Jackson to flee.

But also no means to save Liz.

She hurried back to the pulmonary office suites, where she paced outside the locked double doors and rubbed the mole on the back of her neck like mad. While she waited, she replayed the conversation with Casper back at the hotel.

"Can we trust him?" Casper had asked.

"Definitely."

"Will he believe you?"

"Of course he won't, not at first. He'll think I'm delusional, but once he sees Liz and the Hortons improve, he'll be forced to believe."

"What if he tells someone? What if he goes to the authorities?"

"What authorities? What's he going to say? My girlfriend claims there's a mad scientist at the hospital who's bent on changing the future? No, Mitch isn't stupid, and he knows I'm not either. He'll keep quiet."

"Is he capable?"

"Capable? If you're asking if Mitch is capable of understanding your theory and making more factor, then yes, Mitch is very capable. There's no one better. He's extremely bright, and his sole goal is to make a difference in medicine. Not for fame, either. He truly wants to make people's lives better." Sydney had smiled at that point, thinking about how excited Mitch got whenever he talked about his research, how he prayed he'd be alive one day to see cystic fibrosis patients cured of their disease. Well, he would be curing a disease, all right. Just not the one he had intended.

"Yes, Casper," Sydney had repeated, "Mitch is extremely capable."

And now Sydney was awaiting that capable person, chewing her cuticles, and praying he would believe her, praying he would get there soon.

Elevator F stood almost directly across from the pulmonary offices. A few seconds later, its bell dinged, and a door slid open. Sydney stopped pacing and realized she was like a deer in the headlights, frozen in fear and unable to escape. What if it was Jackson?

It wasn't Jackson, nor was it Mitch. It appeared to be a tired surgical resident, scrubbed, gloved, masked, and hatted. Even on the post-surgical ward the staff took protective precautions. He nodded in Sydney's direction and headed to the patient rooms.

Sydney resumed pacing, wanting to find a more secluded place to hide, but not wanting to miss Mitch. She waited for the elevator to ding. It didn't. She paced. She rubbed her mole. She hyperventilated. She chewed her cuticle. Still no ding. Just when she thought she would have to page him again, a voice broke the air.

"Syd? What's going on?"

Sydney turned to find Mitch and almost buckled in relief. He looked the usual—dark hair slightly disheveled, black glasses, scrub top fitted tight enough to showcase a lean but toned physique—and yet Sydney saw him in a whole new light.

"Quick, let's get into your office." Surprised he hadn't used the elevator, she added, "Where did you come from?"

"I used the B elevators. I was down in the cafeteria when you paged. Haven't eaten almost all day." Mitch pulled a granola bar and a bag of chips from his lab coat pocket as proof, and then walked toward the double doors and pulled out his keys. "After you," he said, holding the door open, curiosity on his face.

"Are you okay?" Sydney relaxed a little when the doors closed behind them. "You seem to be limping."

"Just tired. Always takes more energy to propel this thing when I'm exhausted, you know?" Mitch led Sydney to his office, the same type of partitioned cubicle as her own but with more space, allowing for an additional bookshelf and file cabinet.

He held out an arm, indicating Sydney take the chair. Then he moved a stack of papers from the corner of his desk and sat down, accidentally knocking over a picture frame next to his computer. He didn't bother to pick it up, but Sydney knew what it held. Her. Guess he hadn't cleaned house yet.

Mitch removed his glasses and rubbed his eyes. Sydney was about to explain why she had brought him there when he said, "Man, it's really bad out there. I don't know if you've been listening to the news, but around the world, so many people are sick. Hospitals are overwhelmed, even at surge capacity, and medical personnel are dropping like flies.

Hundreds of them. Researchers, too. Nobody's ever seen anything like it."

Mitch paused for a breath, but before Sydney could cut in, he continued. "Not only is the virus highly contagious, it seems to have a totally different mechanism of action. I talked to Dr. Tillman, one of the guys from the CDC?" He waited to make sure Sydney knew who he was talking about, and although Sydney hadn't seen either Dr. Tillman or Dr. Mayfield since early that morning, she nodded. "He said the CDC has considered raising the virus to a Biosafety Level 4, but that would drastically limit the number of scientists who could study the virus, and we need all the help we can get." In a tone Sydney had never heard Mitch use before, he added, "I'm scared."

"Me too."

Silence between them for a moment. Then Mitch said, "So what did you bring me up here for? And what's with the big briefcase? Got a present for me?"

Mitch's voice carried an edge of sarcasm, but when Sydney said, "Yes," his eyebrows rose in surprise. "What do you mean?"

Sydney moved to the edge of the seat, puffed out her cheeks, and exhaled. Where to begin? Everything had seemed so reasonable in her mind, but now that the words were about to come out, they sounded preposterous.

She looked at Mitch, her gaze stern. "I have something to tell you. Something huge. Something so unbelievable, you're going to think a latent schizophrenic gene has kicked in, but I'm not psychotic. What I'm going to tell you is the truth, and I beg you to let me finish before you pass judgment."

Mitch swallowed, his Adam's apple bobbing up, then down. "Okay, now that you've got me sufficiently freaked out, what is it?"

"It's about Casper. Remember when you said something wasn't right with the guy? Well, you were correct."

"I'm listening," he said warily.

"Casper isn't exactly who he says he is. In fact, he's not even from here. But he knows about this virus. Knows it will completely overwhelm the world if we don't do something about it, and by *we*, I mean Casper, me…and now you."

In the next few minutes, watching Mitch's face vacillate between scorn and amazement, Sydney told him everything, including Casper's origins, the virus's future, and the treatment. At some point Mitch stopped her, obvious hurt in his eyes.

"Are you making fun of me? Is this your idea of a good time? Let's see how far we can push Mitch?" He started to rise, but Sydney put a hand on his leg to stop him. It was his prosthetic leg, and nothing but hardness greeted her.

With her free hand, which now trembled, she reached into the black bag and pulled out the manila envelope. She hadn't yet opened it and wasn't sure of the contents, but it was full and rather heavy.

"Here, look at this." From the envelope, she pulled out a stack of papers, the first of which was an article. Two actually. The two she had seen on Casper's bedroom table linking a prion to the Seneca strain and the deaths of billions of people. Sydney handed them to Mitch, indicating the date, which Casper had since circled.

Mitch scanned them, displaying the same incredulousness that Sydney had when she'd first encountered the papers. He looked up. "This is crazy. I don't know what you expect me to say."

"Just hear me out, that's all I'm asking." Sydney glanced at her watch. A few minutes before ten. She had been at the hospital nearly forty-five minutes. Casper was giving Sydney an hour. If she hadn't called the hotel by a quarter past ten, he was coming after her, something Sydney had strongly discouraged.

She perused the next stack of papers from the envelope

and handed them to Mitch. They contained a short brief—apparently drafted by Casper, though *when* Sydney had no idea—that explained the virus's mechanism of action and illustrated how the infection activated a prion in the respiratory cell membrane and caused complete destruction of the lungs. It further outlined that almost one-fourth of the population was immune because of a mutated version of their cell membrane protein, one that was incapable of folding into a prion. Finally, the brief explained Casper's treatment: the altered respiratory virus that contained the DNA to code for this mutated protein. When given to a patient, massive copies of protective protein could be produced, thereby overwhelming the abnormal prions and allowing the patient to live.

Mitch read through it once, then twice, and although he still appeared skeptical, Sydney could see absolute fascination in his eyes. When he finished, he tried to speak, but nothing came out.

She handed Mitch the last document: a blueprint for the manufactured virus. Or, as Casper liked to call it, his protective factor.

After analyzing the blueprint, Mitch shook his head slowly. The skepticism was gone, and bewildered amazement took its place. He waved the papers in the air. "This is unbelievable. Impossible, even. But man, it makes sense."

Wonderment was in his voice, and his open-mindedness surprised and impressed Sydney. Mitch seemed much more accepting than she had first been. Then again, wasn't everyone?

"I mean, who would have guessed? A prion? Preposterous but at the same time absolutely credible. How is that possible?" Mitch's excitement had forced him up, but as there was really no room to pace, he just shifted his weight on his legs and sat back down.

"So…you believe me?" Sydney was anxious for his response.

Mitch tore his gaze away from the papers and blinked a few times. "I don't know what to believe. I mean, time travel? Come on. But this…well…this stuff actually makes sense." He put the papers on the desk and rubbed his eyes again, his black frames lifted up and out by his fingers. When his hands were back at his sides, he said, "And I know you, Syd. You're the most practical person I've ever met, skeptical of anything that hasn't had at least fifteen clinical trials and twenty board reviews. If you believe this…"

"I do." Sydney vacated the chair and joined him on the edge of the desk. "Because I've seen proof. I've seen a patient discharged because of it. Or at least he will be soon."

Mitch seemed confused, but then his face lit up in comprehension. "You mean Ted Macaby? That's why he's better? He got this…this…" He picked up the last document. "This protective factor?"

"Yes."

"Good God." Mitch sounded both awed and frightened.

"And in case you still don't believe me, you'll have five more patients as proof. I've just treated Liz, as well as a family of four in room 334. The Hortons. Follow them, and you'll see this is real."

Mitch's amazement only heightened. He put a hand on his head and said, "Un*fricking*believable."

They sat in silence for a moment while Mitch absorbed what Sydney had told him. Sydney could almost hear each passing second on her watch. She had six minutes left to call Casper. She had to get moving.

Just as she was about to hurry Mitch along, he said, "You mentioned this somehow involved me. I mean, assuming I buy all this—and I'm not saying I do—what is it you want from me?"

Sydney straightened and spent the next minute telling him.

"You want me to take credit for this theory? That's unethical. I can't do that."

Sydney moved closer to Mitch, their bodies now touching. "Listen, I don't have much time. I need to get going. This isn't unethical. In fact, it's the most ethical thing you'll ever do. Casper has to leave. He can't stay—" Sydney was about to tell Mitch about Jackson but decided against it. Knowing there was danger involved might make Mitch leerier, and they didn't have time for that. "What Casper is doing is unprecedented. We don't know what will happen. But the fact is, he has to leave, and he needs someone to carry this on."

"Why not you?"

Sydney faltered for a moment, again not wanting to tell him about Jackson. If Mitch knew Sydney was in serious peril, he might not go for it.

She switched tactics. "Even though this is Casper's work, it's still only the building blocks. It will be you who'll have to oversee the production of enough protective virus to cover the world, you who will face all the hard work and sleepless nights, you who will be responsible for the results. That burden alone warrants you full entitlement to any positive credit."

Sydney could tell that thought intrigued Mitch, his ultimate dream really, but he shook his head and said, "Still, I can't take the credit, I can't—"

"You have to!" Sydney's tone was almost maniacal. She glanced at her watch as if it were a ticking bomb. "You can't mention Casper. He will only be remembered as the fraudulent attending who stole another virologist's identity. Linking his name to the theory will only invite skepticism. He can't stay here, don't you get that? He needs to leave."

"What about you? Why can't we do this together? I don't understand."

Sydney shook her head. "I don't know. Maybe we can, but

I just don't know yet. Besides, you're the better researcher. This should be your discovery." Another look at her watch. "I really have to go. You need—"

"Are you in some kind of trouble?" Mitch jumped up, and Sydney followed. "Because if you are, I can't—"

"No…it's just…well…maybe. Look, you need to get started on this. You need to make this public as quickly as you can. The sooner it comes out, the less danger I'll be in."

"But I don't un—"

"Just go see Macaby. See Liz and the Hortons. Prove to yourself they're better. In the meantime, make the theory —*your* theory—public. Get it to your attendings, get it on the radio, get it on the news."

"But—"

"I have to go. You can do this, Mitch. You're the only one I *trust* to do this."

"But what about you? Where will you be?" Mitch's voice was pleading now.

Sydney stepped closer and, after a moment's hesitation, embraced him. "Thank you, Mitch. Thank you with all my heart. You were always too good for me. I never deserved someone as kind and as decent as you, but by doing this, *you* at least will get what you've always deserved. This will be your legacy."

Mitch buried his masked face in Sydney's neck and hugged her back so hard she thought she might break. "You're scaring me, Syd. You make it sound like I'm never going to see you again."

Sydney said nothing, knowing she needed to step away but temporarily unable to do so. It was so much safer in this position, and she was terrified of not knowing what awaited her. Finally, with reluctance, she pulled away.

"Good luck, Mitch. I've no doubt you're about to change the world." She placed a hand over his heart. "A Nobel Prize is just around the corner."

Before Mitch could say another word, Sydney picked up the black bag and hurried out of the office suite. Pushing through the double doors, she ran toward the elevator and once it arrived, she stepped inside, closed the door, and pushed the stop button.

Thirty seconds left.

Plenty of time to make a call.

17

———————

Sydney's hands shook as she pulled out her cell phone. Even though she was locked in an elevator with the stop button pushed, she felt little security. She prayed Casper hadn't left yet. Surely he'd give her a few minutes leeway.

Like before, her phone flashed no service, and Sydney's agitation grew. Pacing the elevator, she angled the phone in every direction and tried for a signal.

Nothing.

She thought about getting off, calling from the house phone again, but she didn't want to run into Mitch. What if he'd changed his mind? What if he had decided she was full of crap? No, she would have to call Casper on the way to her car and hope to God he hadn't left yet.

She reached to undo the stop button but then noticed the metal cabinet situated to the left of the door. Emergency phone?

Advancing a step, she opened the small door and found a red phone, devoid of a rotary dial or buttons or any other means to call out. But it would have to connect somewhere. Security? The operator?

She lifted the clunky hand piece and brought it to her ear. It rang, and after four buzzes, a woman answered.

"Operator."

Sydney grasped the phone tighter. "Yes, hi, this is Dr. McKnight. I need you to dial a number for me."

"Doctor, I show this as coming from elevator F. Do you need assistance?"

"No, I just urgently need to make a call."

"Oh, um, okay. Number please?"

Sydney recited Casper's hotel number, and although the operator was clearly confused, she put Sydney through without another word.

The phone barely rang before Casper picked up. "Oh thank God, I was worried something happened."

"It's finished," Sydney said.

"Liz and the Hortons?"

"Yes, all of them."

"And Mitch?"

"He's on board."

Casper's heavy exhalation came through the line. "It's done then. It's really done."

"Yes."

Sydney waited for him to say something else. When he didn't, she worried he might be having second thoughts.

"You're going to change everything, you know," she said, hoping to reassure him. "You're going to save millions—no, billions—of people."

"*If* the factor works."

"It worked on Macaby."

"Yes, but it's too soon to know whether it will last."

"Well, all doubts aside, on Liz and the Hortons' behalf, I thank you. What you did was very noble…" Sydney let her voice trail off as she balled the red telephone cord in her fist.

"I suspect the NIU might disagree with you on that. *Weak* is the word they might choose."

"Weak? Oh no, Casper, you're not weak. You're saving millions of people, and as if that wasn't enough, you're willing to forgo all credit, not to mention the chance to return home. You assume anyone would do that, but they wouldn't. People suck. Everyone's out for themselves. But not you. You're amazing, and you need to know that. Whatever else happens, you need to know that."

Sydney's uncharacteristic outburst silenced them both, until Casper finally said, "You're the one who did it. You faced the danger. Where are you, anyway?"

She told him.

"You need to get out of the hospital."

"Believe me, I know, but I wanted to call you before you headed this way."

"Have you seen him?" Tentativeness in Casper's voice.

"Yes. I'll explain later, but it's safe to say he thinks I've already left."

"Good. Now come to the hotel, at least until he's no longer a threat."

"And then what?"

There was a pause. "I have an idea."

Sydney's hopes picked up. "What is it?"

"It involves the GTD and the creation of—"

"GTD?" Sydney had heard the initials before but never got clarification.

"Gravitational Transit Device. How I got from my home to here."

"You mean it's here? In Boston?" Sydney couldn't keep the skepticism out of her voice. Even after all this, she still found it difficult to completely believe.

"Yes. I was supposed to leave tonight, remember?"

"How does it work?"

"There's no time for that now. You—"

"Is it a wormhole? Just tell me. This is all still so…so…"

"I only know what they told me during my training."

Casper's voice sounded rushed. "It involves the electrical stabilization of a wormhole. Otherwise the tunnel would seal itself off. Wormholes are very unstable, and they require a negative feedback system to continuously cancel out any disturbance. As for the exact mechanism, I have no clue. I study viruses, not physics."

"You think you can use it to help us?"

"*Me*, Sydney. Help me. I won't get you further involved."

"But—"

"My plan involves a tunnel block, but please, I'll explain later. Just come to the hotel before Jackson finds you."

They disconnected and, after a brief pause to collect herself, Sydney unstopped the elevator and pressed the *G* button. As her temporary sanctuary churned and began its descent to the ground floor, she closed her eyes and tried to still her whirling mind.

So much had happened, too much to comprehend, and although she knew she should feel extraordinary relief, there was something more. Something unsettled. Something almost like melancholy. Ridiculous, she knew, just her stressed-out mind not thinking clearly, but yet there was one thought Sydney couldn't bury: Casper. Casper and the realization she might never see him again. The idea seemed impossible after what the two of them had just done.

Yet, what had Sydney expected? Happily ever after? There was no happily ever after. Not for her. Not for Casper. Sydney knew that getting into this. It was the choice that wasn't. Isn't that what she had said before?

The elevator lurched to a stop, the apparatus no longer in its prime. Sydney waited for the doors to open and stepped off, casting a glance down what was mostly a deserted hallway of administrative offices. She rarely took that route to her car, but since the skywalk to the employee parking ramp was located on the third level and the B elevators would have dumped her back onto 3 North, she had opted to access the lot from outside. She wasn't about to risk being seen again. Unfortunately, she was on the south end of the hospital and the parking ramp was near the north. A long hike awaited her.

She passed a succession of quiet and darkened offices, but as the main hospital lobby approached, the noise level increased. So did Sydney's heart rate. Although she doubted Jackson would be camped out in one of the many upholstered lobby chairs, thumbing through outdated magazines, Sydney couldn't shake the feeling she was about to be discovered.

The number of people convened in the lobby at nearly ten-thirty at night surprised her. She hadn't passed this way in days. Why weren't these folks at home? Disgruntled family members, Sydney supposed, unable to visit their loved ones. Which was worse? To die alone or to risk infecting the ones you loved? The Seneca strain's high infectivity and lethality had no precedent. No manual existed. Drawing from Emergency Operations Plans and initiating Incident Command Systems, hospital administrators and managers, as well as public health officials, had been forced to outline their own rulebooks for the deadly virus, including quarantines and access restrictions. As a result, the lobby harbored a surprising number of protestors, armed with masks and gloves rather than posters and picket signs. Unfortunately for the objectors, they were met by a wall of security, making Sydney feel like she'd entered a war zone.

She sidestepped her way around a bellowing man and a tearful woman, neither of whom had much effect on the subdued police officer manning the hallway to the south hospital. Sydney flashed her badge, and he waved her through. Though she had been told about the security guards assigned to the public areas, she had yet to see them, since she entered and exited only from the secured employee parking ramp on the third floor. Their presence was eerie.

More sobbing and shouting erupted behind her.

God, when did all this happen? Have I been living in a bubble?

But what if her son or daughter was hospitalized with a deadly disease? Wouldn't she fight to gain access as well? Then again, given the virus's propagation, most would soon die at home.

Without Casper's protective factor, that is.

Once the commotion in the lobby distanced itself, Sydney's anxiety returned. She scoured the hallway for white scrubs but saw only a lone nurse and a small group of residents exiting the food court. A glance through the cafeteria's large windows revealed a few more employees, their masks lowered as they ate and their faces weary. No white scrubs in sight.

Anxiety notwithstanding, Sydney had the strange sensation she'd just woken up from a deep sleep, and for the first time in days, she felt reconnected to the world. Alive and reconnected. Maybe it was the sense of liberation. Despite her tense muscles and paranoid state, she felt a degree of relief. She was leaving the hospital, about to breathe in fresh air, and when she returned, patients would be improving. Only a few at first, but then more and more as the word spread.

Thanks to Casper, the world would keep turning.

And after tonight, she would never see him again.

Still trying to process that thought, she reached the north exit, the ER only a few steps away. Like the other exit doors, this one was manned by a guard. Sydney approached and showed the woman her badge. Then she dug in her purse, still inside Casper's black bag, and grabbed the pepper spray and keys.

"Heading home for the night?" the security guard asked, sympathy in her voice. "You docs must be exhausted."

"No more than you, I'm sure."

The guard's eyes looked sad. "Yeah, haven't seen my kid too much lately. They got us pulling doubles. But hey, I'd rather him safe at home, away from all this stuff, right?"

"Don't worry, things will improve soon," Sydney said and, for the first time in days, believed it.

She stepped out into the night air and inhaled deeply. The weather had turned cold—it was now the third week of November—and the fleece jacket she had slipped on in the elevator was inadequate. Didn't matter. She was getting out of there.

Clutching Casper's bag against her body, insulin vials clinking together inside, she quickened her step and headed for the ramp, less than one block away and one street over. That was all that separated her from safety. The safety of her car. The safety of the hotel. The safety of never meeting Jackson again.

She wondered what awaited her in the next few days. When would she get back to work? What story would she give people? How long would it take to make more treatment and see a difference?

She crossed the road. Just a few more feet to the parking lot. Unlike the boisterous lobby, the street was unpopulated, and except for an occasional passing car, the wind created the only noise.

When she reached the secured entrance door, Sydney slipped her hand underneath the fleece jacket and once again grabbed the ID badge clipped to her chinos. Swiping it through the sensor, she performed another visual sweep. No one.

She entered the stairwell to the left of the security door. It, too, was empty, and her heavy shoes thudded on the steps. Shivering, she hugged herself more tightly, goose bumps dotting her flesh. How wonderful a hot bath would feel.

After the final step, Sydney entered the second level through an automatic door that whirred opened, disturbing the silence around her. Unnerved, she walked even faster. The number of cars had thinned since she had returned from the hotel, but there were still far more vehicles than usual for that time of night.

Her car rested straight ahead in the far-left corner, its outline shadowy, the floodlight above it dark. Odd. She hadn't noticed that when she'd parked. It was unusual for her to be careless. She normally chose well-lit spots.

She swallowed down a pasty knot and longed for a cool drink. Soon. Relief would be there soon. Just keep walking.

Around the corner, headlights popped into view. Sydney jumped back in fear and surprise, but it was only a van rounding the corner, ascending no doubt to one of the coveted spots on level three close to the skywalk.

Sydney slowed her breathing and crossed to the left side. A Civic, a Taurus, a pick-up. Then there were two sedans, but the lighting, which Sydney could now tell was broken, probably smashed by some kids, had become too dim to identify their makes.

Then her Jeep.

She relaxed and finally felt relief. Confidence even. She'd done it. Together she and Casper had made it happen. Neither of them knew what the next hour would bring, but at least the worst was over.

She unlocked the car door with the automatic opener and transferred the pepper spray and keys to her left hand, while she reached for the door handle with her right.

Something moved.

Something in her peripheral field.

Frightened, she fumbled to open the door. A quick glance to the right told her nothing was there, but panic and paranoia had taken over. Door open, Sydney flung the black bag onto the passenger's seat and scrambled inside. In her haste, her left hand banged the steering wheel, and the keys and pepper spray flew from her fingers. The keys fell to the concrete outside the car door with a jingle, and somewhere her pepper spray went rolling.

"Shit!"

Leaning over the side, Sydney raked her hand on the ground. Nothing. She bent down even farther, her action dislodging the mask from her face and her brain pulsating from the sudden rush of blood to her head. She clawed underneath the Jeep. Something sharp nicked her finger, but she resisted the urge to pull back. She whimpered, the keys still not in reach.

One more deep sweep.

Yes!

Sydney clasped her fingers around the delinquent keys and, forgetting the pepper spray for the time being, shot back up in the seat. Her blood pressure lagged behind, and a dazzling array of stars and lights erupted inside her brain.

Which was why she didn't see him.

It wasn't until Sydney's vision had normalized and she had reached for the door handle that she noticed the man beside her.

She opened her mouth to scream but never made it. Something covered her unmasked mouth. Something soft and moist, like a wet wipe. Only this one smelled good. Lemon… no, not lemon…tangerine?…

Sydney tried to think

Pepper spray…where is it…think…why can't I think?

Then her whole body sagged, and she was falling.

Falling into a tangerine hole.

18

———————

Head throbbing, Sydney awoke to the sound of CNN News. A bland ceiling greeted her, and the panic of not knowing where she was seized her. She bolted upright, deepening her cerebral ache and triggering a wave of dizziness so strong she thought she'd throw up.

When the wooziness passed, she realized she was in Casper's apartment, seated on his couch, hands bound behind her back, fingertips numb and tingling as if they'd been out in the cold too long. Grunting, she wriggled her hands and struggled to free them.

"Don't bother. The cord might seem thin, but it's extremely strong."

Sydney looked up and saw an unmasked Jackson taking a seat on a rickety bar stool borrowed from the kitchen, an amused expression on his face. Despite his obvious joy at her plight, his statement was wrong, because Sydney was indeed able to loosen the binding cord, at least enough to wiggle her fingers and restore circulation. All the while her gaze remained on the man in front of her.

Jackson raised an ankle and rested it on his opposite knee. The white scrubs had been replaced by salmon-colored jeans and a speckled shirt, its neckline peculiar. His jaw was chiseled and set, his eyes slightly squinted, and, if Sydney hadn't known better, she would have guessed he was there for a casual *GQ* photo shoot rather than the abduction of a terrified doctor.

He leaned forward and, in a voice both calm and cold, said, "You and I need to ramble."

Sydney's stomach did a nervous flip. Based on her past verbal exchanges with Casper, she understood that Jackson and she were about to have a chat.

She went to lick her lips. To her surprise, she couldn't. Something covered her mouth. Horrified, she pursed her lips together and peered down. They seemed normal, no occlusive tape or cloth. Yet she was unable to open her mouth.

With Jackson chuckling in front of her, Sydney tried to part her lips. All she managed was the detection of a faint chemical smell. Instinctively, she reached to palpate the area, but her posteriorly bound wrists made the action impossible.

She whimpered.

Another whimper responded.

Startled, she spun to the left and, for the first time, noticed the man seated in the chair next to the couch.

Dr. Burke.

Like Sydney, his hands were bound with a thin orange cord, but unlike Sydney, his hands were tied separately, each to a wooden armrest on the chair, like a king secured to his throne. He looked a mess—suit wrinkled and stained, face flushed, thinning hair tousled and clumped haphazardly over his beet-red scalp. Given his complexion, Sydney suspected the man was long overdue for his antihypertensives.

With frightened eyes, Dr. Burke grunted and pursed his own lips, demonstrating his mouth was similarly occluded. Sydney studied her boss's mouth, but other than a shimmering glean, she saw nothing.

She turned back to Jackson. His expression had shifted

from amusement to anger. "He's still here because of you. If you and Casper had played nicely, Dr. Burke would be safe at home, nothing but a dull headache and a forty-eight-hour memory lapse."

Sydney swallowed, the invisible band covering her mouth suddenly suffocating.

"Now," Jackson continued, "I'm going to remove the sealant from your mouth, but if you scream or attempt to cry for help, you'll have much worse discomfort than bound wrists. Understand?"

At that point, Jackson reached into his back pocket and pulled out a small device. It was black and smooth, and although it loosely resembled a gun, Sydney saw no trigger, only a tiny barrel opening and three square buttons, each with its own silver symbol, near Jackson's index finger.

Her breaths shallowed. Past experiences with Casper's world told her the gadget might be capable of anything. She nodded, demonstrating her understanding.

"Good," Jackson said, but before he could add anything else, a woman entered the apartment. Dr. Burke flinched. Sydney only stared.

The woman, like Casper—and Sydney supposed Jackson though her opinion of him was tainted—was very attractive, with smooth olive skin and dark hair, flawlessly pulled back and clipped with a triangular-shaped silver barrette. Her gray pantsuit, seemingly present-day in design, flattered her lean body, and she had a similar device to Jackson's tucked into a pouch on her belt.

"You took everything back to the GTD?" Jackson asked her.

"Everything important. I burned his articles and discarded the twenty-first century items."

Jackson nodded. Sydney remained frozen, heart racing, breaths still shallow.

The woman walked to the television, turned up the volume, and glanced at Sydney. "She ready to talk?"

Jackson played with the small gadget in his hands, which Sydney assumed was a weapon. "If she's smart, she is."

Burke shifted in his seat. Sydney tried to offer him a reassuring look but was too petrified with her own thoughts to be convincing.

How did I get here? What did Jackson drug me with?

She remembered only moist softness and citrus before her world had gone black. Now she was tied up, facing two beautiful people with clearly menacing intent.

She wrestled with the cord binding her wrists. Was it maybe a little looser?

Jackson bolted up, halting Sydney's hand-wriggling. He reached out and took something from the woman. To Sydney's surprise it looked like a wet wipe, though Sydney doubted Jackson was about to sanitize his hands. He opened the small packet and indeed pulled out a thin, moist cloth.

Walking toward her, he raised the wet wipe and lowered the black gadget. In exchange, Jackson's lovely counterpart drew her own device and alternately aimed it at Dr. Burke and Sydney.

Must be a gun. What else can it be?

Jackson tucked the presumed weapon into the back of his jeans and reached for Sydney's mouth. A cool wetness pressed against her lips. She froze, remembering the wipe that had put her to sleep, but no tangerine scent wafted this time around.

After a few harsh wipes, he removed the towelette and returned to his seat. Sydney rubbed her lips together and then opened and shut her mouth. She was both relieved and horrified to find that she could, but if she thought Jackson's bizarre wipes would be the strangest oddity she would encounter in the next few hours, she was wrong.

"Okay, Dr. McKnight, I'm going to ask you a few questions. If you'd like to remain in your prehistoric world here, along with your boss, I suggest you answer them. Oh, and in case you try to run or scream for help…" Jackson produced the weapon and pointed it at Sydney's forehead. His trigger finger selected the bottom button, making Sydney catch her breath. After a lengthy pause, he redirected the gun to her left and depressed the button. Sydney cried out in horror as a dime-sized hole burned through the upholstery of the couch.

"That's just a small demonstration." Jackson slouched down once again on the stool. "The actual damage could be much, much worse."

A deep groan came from Dr. Burke's direction, but instead of trying to offer him reassurance again—in her guilt, she wondered what he must be thinking—Sydney's frisbee-sized gaze was instead glued to the noiseless and potent weapon. She nodded.

"Good." Jackson stole a glance at his partner who leaned against the wall to Sydney's left, a few feet from Burke.

Sydney's mind fired. *How long have I been here? Where's Casper? Will he come looking for me? Will he risk jeopardizing everything we've accomplished?*

It seemed unlikely given his earlier comment about their actions outweighing the lives of a few people—namely Casper, Burke, and her. At the time, his comment had sounded obvious and indisputable. Noble even.

Not so now.

Sydney wriggled her hands some more. She was sure the cord was loosening.

Jackson started up again. "Imagine my surprise, Dr. McKnight, when our mutual friend Casper smashed my head with a bottle, secured me with sealant, and left. If it wasn't for my fellow travologist, Agent Natala Mann here, I'd still be glued to a toilet. Now what in the world would make him do such a thing?"

The weapon's bizarre barrel was back on Sydney.

"I…I…don't know."

"Wrong answer!"

Jackson's sudden outburst almost catapulted Sydney off the couch. Her cry of surprise drowned out Burke's whimper.

"Easy," the woman named Natala said. "I know you get angry when you're tense, but even with the television, someone might hear us."

Jackson's jaw twitched, and his enormous jugular veins throbbed, but after a moment, he resumed his relaxed posture and tried again. "Where is Casper?"

Sydney remained silent, both from paralyzing fear and from the need to come up with an answer.

"Where is Casper?" Jackson asked again, edging up on the stool.

"I…um…really don't know."

Her captor's fingers tightened around the gun. "Where were you going when you left the hospital?"

Sydney swallowed. Would he really hurt her, or was he bluffing? "How did you know which car was mine?" Her voice came out small and weak.

"I'd seen you park before, once when I was waiting for Casper near the skywalk. You'd found a very good strip near the door." Jackson smiled. "There, see how easy it is? You ask a question, I answer. I ask a question, you answer. Now, where were you going? To meet Casper?"

Sydney said nothing, staring at the gun, recalling the night Jackson referred to. It was the first time she'd ever seen him.

Jackson sighed and shifted his legs. "Okay then, let's switch tactics. What's this?" He held out an expectant hand, at which time his partner walked to the kitchen and returned with Casper's bag. Jackson dug inside and whipped out a vial.

Sydney opened her mouth, then closed it. Why had she kept the empty bottle? "Um…that's, um…insulin."

"Not the insulin! This!" Jackson jumped to his feet and whirled the empty vial marked *West Nile Virus Serum Sample* against the wall. It shattered into countless pieces.

More unintelligible sounds from Dr. Burke. Or was that her? Sydney wasn't really sure.

Trembling all over, she said, "It's for my West Nile research. L-l-like the label said."

Sydney didn't even see Jackson raise the gun. It happened so fast. But she felt the fire. Felt the heat singe through her chinos and into her shin like the tip of a red-hot poker.

She cried out, more from shock and disbelief than from pain. She whipped her leg up on the couch, wanting but unable to rub it. Like the sofa's upholstery, there was a dime-sized hole in her slacks, and underneath that, a reddened and circular wound, thankfully superficial.

"That was a warning. The next will go through the bone."

Sydney looked at him, horrified, and then went back to the stinging lesion. It looked like one of the cigarette burns she'd received in her youth, and although its scar would eventually be indiscernible from the others, she would always remember its origin.

She threw a furtive glance at the door. Could she make it? Doubtful with the weapon in Jackson's hand, not to mention her own wrists tied behind her back.

"Let's try this again." Jackson raised the weapon toward Sydney's face. He stood only a few feet from her now, his expression virulent.

"What was in that vial?"

With wide eyes, Sydney beseeched Natala, still standing against the wall. The woman offered Sydney neither sympathy nor anger, just awaited Sydney's response. To Natala's right, Dr. Burke sat rigid in his chair, his face red and sweaty. He, too, must be praying for Sydney's answers.

But she couldn't give them any, Burke included. If she did, Jackson would learn about Mitch. And Liz and the Hortons. Based on his present behavior, it appeared he'd do anything to stop the word from getting out.

With caution, she returned her feet to the floor and went

back to wriggling her wrists, relieved the two agents weren't in a position to see what she was doing. The cord was looser now, although she still couldn't slip out her hands.

"Don't make me ask again, Dr. McKnight."

Sydney was shivering so acutely, it was as if her heart pumped Freon instead of blood.

Still, she said nothing.

The next burn stabbed her thigh like a fiery lancet. She cried out again—this time from pain alone—and in desperation, she tried to rub at the sizzling area, but her bound hands barely reached past her hip. Tears sprung to her eyes, blurring the growing mass of pulpy, scorched tissue that was once a part of her leg. Worse than the sight was the smell, the scent of her own flesh burning. It made her dizzy to the point of faintness.

Beside her, Dr. Burke moaned and sobbed, the sounds muffled underneath the sealant. Natala said something about "neighbors" and "screams," and the TV grew even louder.

Sydney's wooziness worsened. Bubbling blisters. Burning tissue. CNN blaring. Smell. Pain. Jackson in front of her.

She tried to blink away the blurriness. Tried to stop whimpering. Tried to focus her mind.

Think, Sydney! Concentrate.

Where was Casper? He must know Jackson had her. But she couldn't tell them anything. No. Nothing. Not about Mitch. Not about Liz. Not about the Hortons.

"Do you really think this is effective?" Natala asked Jackson while Sydney tried to suck more oxygen into her world. "We're not animals, you know. You're always at your worst when you're nervous. Reclaim your control."

"But she knows everything. There's a guilt mask all over her. We need to find out who she's told—or worse, who she's treated. Do you realize what could happen if we don't? They didn't send me here to be a hand-holder." Jackson sounded agitated and hyper as he paced the room.

"I'm aware of the implications, but we need to be careful. What about Casper? He's where the real risk lies."

"Well, we don't have Casper now, do we? I thought he'd be here by now. Figured he'd risk everything to rescue his beloved fair maiden, but maybe I was wrong."

Is it true? Will Casper give me up? A rational voice inside Sydney suggested it was for the best, but she refused to listen. She needed someone to help get her and Burke the hell out.

"What about his tracking device?" Natala asked.

"He's managed to create interference, though how I don't know."

Jackson and Natala fell silent for a moment, both staring at Sydney. The cord around Sydney's wrists was definitely looser, and a few more moments of wriggling would set her hands free. But then what? They had guns. She didn't. They had coma-inducing wet wipes. She didn't. She had a palm-sized fire pit on her thigh. They didn't.

And what about Dr. Burke? If Sydney was able to free her hands and miraculously tackle one of their captors, could Burke overtake the other? The idea seemed ludicrous considering Sydney's wound and Burke's attached chair.

Then Natala said something that chilled Sydney's blood even more.

"Maybe we're targeting the wrong person. Maybe our pale young doctor would be more forthcoming if her respected boss were the object of your Triotherm."

Sydney's gaze darted between her two captors. Jackson smiled, a smile that despite its perfection and gleaming teeth was hideous. Sydney wriggled her hands even faster. She was so close now. So close to slipping them free.

Jackson raised his weapon and aimed it at Dr. Burke's chest.

"No!" Sydney cried and bolted off the couch. Before she made it even one step, Natala flew across the room and pushed her back down, igniting another round of agony in her leg.

Natala softened and kneeled in front of Sydney. "Listen, you can stop all of this. You have the power. Just tell us what you know." Her voice was smooth and controlled and much less intimidating than her partner's—the twenty-third-century version of good cop/bad cop.

Sydney shook her head. "I-I don't know anything."

Jackson's gun moved closer to Burke who looked terrified beyond belief. Natala raised a hand to subdue her partner.

"I don't think you understand," she said to Sydney. "This is way above you. You may think that in Casper you've found an answer to your *own* problems, but what about his? Do you realize what your interference is costing him? Do you?"

Natala paused, and despite the blaring of the television—a reporter grilling a scientist about the virus—Sydney was sure Natala could hear her heart pounding.

"Casper is a very kind man. He'd help even a criminal in need, but because of you, he's in for a world of pain. Do you realize that? Do you understand what you've gotten him into?"

Sydney swallowed, Natala's words burning deeper than the broiled flesh on her thigh.

"If you care for him, if you *really* care for him, you'll tell us what you know so we can rectify the problem. Then Casper can return home to his respected and civilized life."

Sydney stared at Natala, trembling, her chest rising and falling with each hyperventilated breath.

"You want Casper to be safe, don't you? You don't want him to have to hide for the rest of his life, do you?"

Natala was right, of course. This nightmare was because of Sydney. It didn't matter that Casper had claimed otherwise. This was Sydney's fault: The future being irreparably changed. Casper unable to return home. Burke sitting in a chair, bound and gagged, close to stroking out. If Sydney hadn't voiced her suspicions about Casper to Burke, the department head wouldn't have dug deeper and learned the truth about Patrick Michael Jones.

"So you see," Natala went on, her voice soothing, "there's really only one choice. Then everyone can go on with their lives. Safely."

Sydney searched Natala's eyes, tempted to nod, tempted to agree. With a few words from her, it could all end.

She snapped to reality.

No. That isn't true.

They wouldn't let Mitch go. They wouldn't let Liz and the Hortons improve. They'd have to kill them. If they didn't, the future would be changed. *Their* future. And that's just what they wouldn't allow.

Sydney looked at Dr. Burke, a rare tear tracking down her face. She wanted to tell him she was sorry, wanted to explain her reasoning. If he knew all that was at stake, surely he'd side with her.

"Why don't you let Dr. Burke go?" she pleaded with both voice and eyes. "He doesn't know anything, and even if he did, Casper said you can erase it with drugs."

Jackson snorted. "That *was* the plan. At least until you came around. But I'd say he's had so many unpleasant memories laid down now that not even the best of our medicines could erase them. Wouldn't you agree, Dr. McKnight?" Jackson used his gun to indicate Sydney's thigh and then redirected it back to Dr. Burke.

Sydney wriggled and tugged on the cord. Although held up at the knuckles, her right hand was close to escape.

"This is your last chance." Jackson's tone was low and venomous, and his gun was less than twelve inches from Burke's chest, his finger on the middle button this time. "What was in that vial and who did you give it to?"

More tears fell, both from Sydney and Dr. Burke. She tried to look at him, but in her guilt, she couldn't.

Finally, with a hitched and unsteady voice, she said, "I'm sorry, I don't know what you're talking about."

The scream that followed cut Sydney to the bone far deeper than Jackson's weapon ever could.

She spun toward Burke and saw a six-inch slash on the left side of his chest, cut cleanly through his suit and underlying white shirt. Unlike her own burn, whose bleeding had been halted by the cautery effect of the weapon, Burke's wound was bleeding profusely.

Dr. Burke writhed and buckled in his seat, unable to lift his bound hands to his chest. Panicked, he stood up and, though seemingly impossible, brought the heavy chair with him. It flailed and whipped around the room until Jackson delivered another bloody cut to Burke's leg, the weapon's beam tearing through Dr. Burke's pants as if they were no more than tissue paper.

"Sit down!" Jackson ordered.

Burke sat—well, fell really—back to a seated position, blood dripping from his chest and leg, his cries and moans muffled by the incredible sealant still coating his mouth.

Sydney sat rigid on the couch, horrified and disbelieving, both by the terrible pain she had inflicted on Dr. Burke and by the unimaginable functions of Jackson's gun.

"Stop! Please stop. Don't hurt him anymore."

"That's completely up to you. Just answer my question. Otherwise, the next slice will cut deep into your boss's heart." Jackson aimed the gun at his declared target, and Burke moaned and shrank back in the chair, blood saturating his clothes and the carpet around him.

"Good Lord," Natala said, but yet she did nothing.

"Now, last chance, Doctor. What have you and Casper done?" Jackson's expression was one of fury and frustration, his weapon steady on Burke's chest.

Sydney inhaled deeply, but struggling as she was, she couldn't slip her hand out of the binding. She looked at Burke, her eyes pleading and apologetic. *I'm so sorry,* she wanted to say. *Please forgive me. This is bigger than us.*

Instead, she lowered her gaze, and with a voice barely more than a whisper—and hardly that of her own—she said, "We did what we had to do."

She closed her eyes and waited.

19

Sydney opened her eyes to a *thump*. Out of confusion, her first thought was the gun, but she knew that didn't make sense. Its burning and slicing had been silent thus far.

She looked at Burke. He was sobbing but still very much alive. Then she saw both Jackson and Natala staring in the opposite direction, and she realized what had happened.

That thump was the door closing.

In its frame stood Casper.

His gaze caught Sydney's, and although she knew he shouldn't have come, she felt indescribable relief, even if just for the few extra minutes it would buy them.

For a moment they all stared at each other, the only sound the annoying blare of the television.

Finally, Jackson said, "Look who decided to join the party mix."

Casper ripped off his respiratory mask and started to speak, but when he noticed Sydney's leg, shock and fury colored his face. He rushed forward, but the Triotherm Jackson thrust in his chest quickly extinguished his stampede.

"Easy, Casper. You'd hate to see the same thing on her leg

happen to her face." Although calm, Jackson's voice could have sent a child skittering.

"What did you do to her?"

"No, my friend." Jackson stabbed the end of his gun into Casper's chest. "The question is, what have *you* done to her?"

Casper paused for a moment, nostrils flaring, gaze going back and forth between Sydney's wounds and her face. In an unwavering voice, he said, "I did what I had to."

"No, what you *had* to do was follow the mission."

"The mission changed."

Without warning, Jackson smacked Casper hard in the face with the hand holding the gun. Casper stumbled back, blood spraying from his lip. Horrified, Sydney jumped up, only to be shoved down once again by Natala. Eyes narrowed in rage, Casper rubbed at the area and then lunged for Jackson, but the gun immediately found its way up to Casper's head.

"Go ahead, give me an excuse," Jackson seethed. "Just one little excuse to neurolize you."

"Calm down." Natala's expression was stern. "Everybody calm down. Beating him up won't solve anything."

"Calm down? Casper might have catastrophically destroyed the whole mission. Why would the NIU have trusted such a weakling?"

"Not everyone pisses boulders like you," Natala said. "Come on, do your mind flexes. Breathe."

"Yeah, well, for all we know, he's just tampered with my bloodline."

"And that's a bad thing?" Natala offered a small smile, as if trying to lighten the mood, but the notion was ludicrous. The gun digging into Casper's head was anything but carefree.

Casper backed up, his hands out in front of him. "It doesn't matter what you do now. Kill me. Kill us all. The damage has already been done."

Jackson and Natala stared at Casper, their anxiety obvious. The brief distraction gave Sydney the opportunity to tug on the cord a little harder. She was so close, her right hand almost out except for the bulge of her thumb, which was now raw and tender from the constant struggle. Her actions caught Burke's attention, and his eyes grew wide as he shook his head.

"And what damage is that?" Jackson's voice faltered for the first time.

"Everything I know about the virus has been made public. Patients have been treated."

Casper's blunt admission surprised even Sydney. How could he be sure Mitch had already released the news? His assertions would only put Mitch in danger, not to mention Liz and the Hortons.

"A researcher has been given my notes, as well as the formula for the protective factor. He's already contacted reporters. You'll hear about it soon." Casper nodded his head toward the still-blaring TV. "So now that it's out, killing us will change nothing."

Sydney stared at Casper, her mouth agape.

Is it true? Did Mitch really report the findings so quickly?

Then again, how long had she been there? She hadn't dared look at her watch in case her wriggling hands were discovered. Had Casper contacted Mitch in the meantime?

Tentative excitement washed through her, and she tugged on the cord even harder. If what Casper said was true, there was no need to hurt them. Jackson wouldn't kill them out of spite, would he? Natala had said they weren't animals.

Except for the TV, the room was silent, Jackson peering hard at Casper as if trying to call his bluff. "You're lying."

Sydney's hand slipped out. Heart thumping, she hardly dared breathe, not wanting her freedom discovered. With Natala still focused on Casper, Sydney again caught Burke's attention and, through eye contact, tried to indicate that the right distraction might allow them to overtake the futuristic agents. Despite their wordless exchange, he seemed to under-stand, although Sydney could tell he wasn't optimistic. Blood continued to seep from his wounds, but the flow had tapered, suggesting the cuts were more superficial than they'd first appeared.

"You wouldn't do that," Jackson said. "Why would you risk facing such a terrible unknown? Why would you risk everything you've worked for?"

"This *is* everything I've worked for." Casper paused for emphasis and looked at Sydney. "Besides, this mission was a horrible mistake. Despite our best measures, we were still discovered."

Jackson remained rooted to the spot, his gun pressed against Casper's head. Sydney could tell he was caught, desperate to call Casper's bluff but not daring to assume it was one. If he killed Casper, how could he discover the truth? How could he undo what had already been done?

Jackson dared a quick look in Natala's direction. "What do you think? Is this rag telling the truth?"

Natala didn't answer right away, her silence replaced by a CNN reporter discussing the toll of the virus on the troops in the Middle East. Finally, she said, "Maybe we should navigate back with all three right now. See what the NIU wants to do."

"Or maybe…" Jackson used his gun to guide Casper toward the couch next to Sydney, "we should take care of his twenty-first century love. Maybe then he'd feel more inclined to tell us the truth."

As Jackson spoke, he shifted the gun from Casper's temple to Sydney's, making her inhale sharply.

"What do you think, Casper? How about a fiery hole the size of my fist through her brain?"

Sydney looked at her blistered and pulpy thigh and imag-ined what the beam would do to her cerebral cortex.

"It's your choice," Jackson continued. "Tell me everything, or she dies."

Casper's face was a combination of anger and fear. "Don't. Please don't."

"It's up to you. Do we let her live? Let her go back to her life? Or does she die?"

"You…you wouldn't let her go."

"Why not? No one would believe her. As long as we get rid of the evidence, she can go back to her lonely little life, and her boss can too."

The gun remained aimed at Sydney's face, Jackson's index finger on the middle button. On Sydney's left, Burke trembled in his chair. To the right of her on the sofa, Casper breathed heavily, his brow perspiring. Sydney shook her head at him, tried to tell him *No, don't do it, he's lying.*

"This can be between you and me, Casper. Tell me what you've done and how we can undo it. Come on. We may have our differences, but you and I go way back. Return to the right side, my friend. It's not too late. Not for Dr. McKnight either." Jackson's voice was more soothing now. Tempting.

Some of Casper's strength and anger seemed to fade. "I… Sydney doesn't…"

That's as far as he got. Natala called out Jackson's name and, with an expression of horror, directed him to the TV, where a young newscaster was making a statement.

"Like I said, little is known at this time, but the researcher, a fellow in pulmonary medicine, claims to have discovered the virus's deadly mechanism of action as well as a possible cure. Using molecular genetics, Dr. Mitchell Price alleges to have treated six patients in all, one of whom has already been discharged from the hospital in good health, and the other five of whom are showing dramatic improvement as we speak…"

The reporter kept talking, and although Sydney was as stunned as the others, she took advantage of their captor's distraction. Alerting Casper of her freed hands, she raised her eyebrows in question. He hesitated and then raised a hand as if to indicate she hold on.

"Is this a hoax or truth?" the newscaster continued. *"We don't*

yet know, but when asked why he kept his discovery a secret up to this point, Price cites caution and the need to avoid unnecessary frenzy. We'll keep you posted on this startling story as more develops, but…"

Looking ashen, Jackson stuttered something about the NIU, something about needing their immediate recommendation on how to proceed. As the two agents locked eyes in astonishment, Casper indicated with a nod that Sydney go for Natala. He would take Jackson.

Sydney's heart pounded. She wasn't sure she could do it. Her leg throbbed, and she trembled all over. But despite having their weapons aimed on Casper and Sydney, the agents were clearly distracted, their conversation escalating.

"How could you have let it get this far?" Natala's composure finally cracked.

"I watched him as closely as I could. He scrambled his tracker."

Sydney's body tensed in anticipation. She could feel Casper beside her on the couch—his concentration, his urge to pounce. The agents kept arguing, Natala blaming Jackson, Jackson blaming Casper and the NIU's decision to use him, his gun now jabbing the air.

Casper's hand crept toward Sydney. *Almost, almost*, it seemed to say.

Sydney's heart beat even faster. She held her breath. Could she do this? Did she have the strength? Did she have the *choice*?

She didn't get the chance to find out. At Casper's urgent nod and with both agents still pointing weapons and blame, Sydney leaped off the couch, sending her best round-house kick Natala's way. She aimed for Natala's hand, and her aim was good. The gun flew out of the agent's hand and smacked the wall, but where it landed, Sydney couldn't tell.

From then on things happened quickly. At the same time Sydney threw herself into Natala, Casper similarly jumped Jackson, but whether he'd been able to grab the weapon,

Sydney wasn't sure. She kept rolling around on the ground with Natala, who, though an inch or two shorter than Sydney and just as thin, was surprisingly strong.

"The gun," Sydney screamed to Dr. Burke. "Get Jackson's gun."

A shocked and bloodied Burke forced himself up, but with the heavy chair still bound to him like some weird upholstered growth, there was little he could do.

Sydney tried to head for a weapon herself, but Natala smashed a fist into her nose with such surprising strength that Sydney fell backward and landed hard on the floor, igniting another jolt of pain through her leg. Before she even had a chance to recover, a second punch landed on her forehead. Something sharp—a ring, maybe—ripped into her skin.

Blood dripped into Sydney's eyes and throat from the two nearly simultaneous blows, and she blinked and choked as if she were drowning. Yet when Natala came at her again, Sydney somehow managed to kick the woman off. As Sydney pulled herself up, she saw Casper and Jackson wrestling on the ground. Although Casper was on top and seemed more in control, Sydney couldn't tell who—if either—possessed the gun.

She started back to find the other gun, but the next thing she knew, Natala was on her again, knocking her to the ground with a bowel-loosening kick in the back. Straddling Sydney—*God she's strong!*—Natala raised her fist but then froze.

Sydney followed the woman's gaze. Despite the heavy chair appendage, Dr. Burke was standing next to Natala, shaking and hyperventilating, wrists bound and reddened from the prolonged captivity. Miraculously—and awkwardly —he held a gun with the fingers of his right hand.

Ignoring her fiery leg and throbbing nose, Sydney inched her way out from underneath Natala. While the agent remained in a frozen crouch, her shaking voice trying to convince Burke to hand over the gun, Sydney started towards

Casper, who still struggled with Jackson on the floor. Judging by Jackson's bloodied face, Casper's boxing skills remained fresh.

Limping and blinking away blood, her corneas stinging, Sydney searched for the other gun. What happened next, she couldn't be sure. One second she was stumbling around, half-blinded by blood, dizzy with pain, desperate to find the gun; the next she was on her face, her legs having been kicked out from underneath her. Her already injured nose and jaw struck the carpeted floor, creating a new gusher of blood and forcing Sydney to open her mouth and gasp for air.

Behind her Natala shouted, "Watch out, Jackson. He's got your gun."

But where's the other one?

Creeping over the carpet, the pain from its traction against her burnt leg almost unbearable, Sydney tried in vain to find it.

Grunting from Casper or Jackson. Agitated moans from Burke. More cajoling from Natala, hoping to keep a terrified Burke from snapping.

The gun. Where's the gun?

Jackson and Casper were still fighting, their bodies too enmeshed for Dr. Burke to take aim. Could he take aim? Would he take aim? Would he accidentally shoot Casper or Sydney? All of these thoughts swirled in Sydney's brain as she searched for the gun.

Where's the damn gun?

Finally, she spotted it.

Behind the couch, half-hidden under its frame. She pulled herself up, struggling to stand. She had to get to it. Had to get to it first.

But Jackson was coming. He'd freed himself from Casper and was also going for the weapon. With one strong arm, he flung Sydney back against the wall and then lunged forward and grabbed the gun. At the same time, Natala shouted to

Jackson in warning, just as Dr. Burke awkwardly took aim at her partner.

Burke never made it.

Jackson raised the other gun. Silently, as if in some terrible B-movie, Dr. Burke buckled to the floor in a sideways posture, the attached chair contorting his body. His reddened face wore a mask of horror: mouth sealed in a grimace, eyes bloodshot and moist, a few strands of thinning hair caught within the lashes. A huge burn smoldered over his heart, much like the one on Sydney's thigh, only this time there was blood, buckets of blood.

Seconds later, Dr. Burke's singed heart made its final few beats, his eyes wide-open in terror.

20

"No!" Sydney cried.

As Natala reclaimed her gun, Sydney staggered to Dr. Burke's side and put a finger on his carotid artery. Nothing.

"No," she said again, this time softly, her word ending in a sob. "Why? Why couldn't you just let him go?"

Sydney placed her trembling hands on Dr. Burke's face. "I'm sorry. I'm so sorry I let this happen to you."

At that point someone turned off the television, and silence enveloped them. Sydney wondered if any of the neighbors had heard the scuffle, wondered if anyone had called the police.

Turning her tear-streaked face to Casper, she saw his own anguish, but he could do little given Jackson had him by the neck, the weapon pressed once again to his head. Soon Natala's gun was pressed against Sydney's. She inhaled another deep sob. All that fighting for nothing. Burke dead for nothing.

No! Not for nothing. Liz. The Hortons. The millions and millions of people they would save.

But the concrete finality of Dr. Burke's death made all those others seem abstract and unreal.

The room remained silent, all of them winded, all of them somber.

Finally, Natala said, "Let's get out of here. Take these two back with us and let the NIU decide how to proceed."

"What about him?" Jackson nodded toward Dr. Burke.

"We'll have to leave him. There'll be lots of questions, but none they can answer. Why couldn't you have neurolized him instead of creating all this blood?"

Jackson, looking more anxious by the second, ignored her question. "You sure you removed all traces of us?"

"Yes. All the equipment as well as Casper's computer."

Jackson nudged Casper toward the door.

"You're barbaric," Casper said through clenched teeth. "Kill a man and then leave him there tied to a chair like some useless object."

"Hey!" Jackson shouted, startling them all and nudging the gun harder against Casper's skull. "You're the one who caused this. You're the one who started this whole nightmare rolling. If it wasn't for your pathetic weakness, your sickening shortsightedness, Dr. Burke could've returned to his life. Dr. McKnight, too, for that matter. Now they'll both end up dead, and for that you've only yourself to blame."

Casper blanched, his face sweaty. Sydney could see he was shaking, and in her muddy brain a coherent thought surfaced: When had he last had his insulin?

Or was his physical transformation merely defeat? Despite Sydney's own despair, her heart longed to reassure Casper, longed to tell him he'd done the right thing. She understood him well enough to know that Jackson's words couldn't have burned deeper than if they'd been branded into his skin with the gun.

Casper closed his eyes, and Sydney worried that a part of him had given up. Casper who'd taken on the future. Casper who'd taken on a deadly virus. Casper who'd relinquished his own freedom.

Now looked beaten and defeated.

***

After that, everything was dark and foggy, literally and figuratively. The agents herded Sydney and Casper out of the apartment and into the pre-dawn night, but not before Casper had insisted on untying and moving Dr. Burke's body to the bed. He said they could kill him right there—he didn't care— but he was damned if he would leave a man lying on the floor like some useless piece of trash. With palpable sorrow, Casper had dragged Burke to the bedroom and heaved his body on the bed. When he'd finished, he pleaded with Jackson to release Sydney.

Jackson wouldn't hear of it. In fact, his exact words were, "Why don't we just kill her now?"

To which Sydney's stomach had lurched, and she almost vomited.

"Come on, Jackson, we're not animals," Natala had repeated for the hundredth time, although by that point, Sydney had strenuously disagreed. "You're not thinking clearly. Dr. Burke's death was unfortunate and unplanned. Let's not make ourselves look any worse in front of the NIU and the Presidential Body. We have enough questions to answer."

"What about the virus?" Jackson had asked.

"What about it? Casper's already disclosed the treatment —or had someone else do it for him—and the news is spreading all over the country. Even if we eliminate the scientist who claimed the discovery, too many others already know. Best to leave and let the NIU decide our next move. If our future still *exists*, that is." Natala's anxiety was obvious.

Although Jackson must have driven Sydney's Jeep to Casper's apartment, he now insisted that she drive them to the harbor, which wasn't an easy task considering her emotional state. Apparently, that was where their gravitational device was docked, although the idea seemed too preposterous to ponder.

Sydney pictured the authorities finding her car at the harbor. She thought of the police investigating her disappearance. She imagined the gossip that would erupt at the hospital. Who besides Liz and Mitch would even care she was missing?

Twice she had to slam on the brakes because of her lack of focus, and twice she was reprimanded by Natala who sat in the front passenger seat.

"Are you trying to get us all killed?" the agent asked, her nerves apparently as shot as Sydney's.

Sydney said nothing, but the plan didn't sound half-bad.

Once at the harbor, the agents pushed Casper and Sydney like cattle along a concrete pier and then onto a smaller wooden dock, weapons pressed closely against their captives' sides to avoid drawing attention, even though the area remained deserted. Casper's soft briefcase bounced against Sydney's body as she hobbled along. They'd allowed her to bring the bag, considering it contained Casper's insulin and syringes, but even though his glucose monitor had beeped during their preparation to leave—Sydney still had no idea where that device was implanted in his body—Jackson wouldn't allow him to take any medication, apparently another means of exuding his dominance.

Like that was necessary.

"Here it is," Natala said, jerking Sydney to a stop.

Sydney stared out at the harbor. Water whipped against a bevy of docked boats, and above them a few brave gulls cawed in the fading darkness, but Sydney saw nothing else. Nothing but boats and water.

"Where?" she asked, in genuine confusion.

"There." Natala gave a nod to indicate something in the foreground.

Sydney still saw nothing. When she gave Casper a questioning look, he pointed to a white fishing boat with blue siding and a small cabin.

Sydney didn't understand. "All I see is a boat."

"Just get in." Natala shoved Sydney forward, apparently tired of her twenty questions.

Sydney clutched the bag to her side and took a tentative step toward the boat. Casper reached out to help her, but Jackson pulled him back. Instead, Sydney was practically dumped over the side by Natala, who once again impressed Sydney with her physical strength.

Did her parents select for that too?

Natala pushed Sydney toward the small cabin. Casper and Jackson followed. Sydney was beginning to think they were all bonkers. They expected her to believe she was traveling to the future in a boat? She almost laughed, that was how comical it seemed. Maybe it was all a demented joke, after all. Maybe she had been captured by a cult and was off to meet their "master."

Once inside, Sydney's hysterical amusement faded. While the outside looked like a boat, the inside most certainly did not. The walls, ceiling, and floor boasted shiny silver with a soft texture. Even the windows gleamed metallic—or at least where the windows were supposed to be. From the outside, they'd resembled tinted windows. On the inside, metal had replaced glass, a metal Sydney couldn't identify.

In addition to the metallic walls sat five chairs—two in front, three in back—a remarkable feat in the small space. Simple in their design, the seats contained headrests, body harnesses, and thin armrests housing various colored buttons.

In front of the seats, Sydney discovered an even bigger surprise. Covering the anterior wall from floor to ceiling flashed the most amazing display panel she had ever seen. Even the bridge on the *Starship Enterprise* couldn't compete. On the left end hung an ultra-thin screen, depicting the harbor and its collection of boats. Every few seconds the image shifted, offering a panoramic view of the outside surroundings.

Dumbfounded, Sydney glanced at Casper, but he offered only a sad smile. Jackson pushed Sydney onto a chair and sat down next to her. "We're not in Kentucky anymore, Toto."

Sydney wondered if this was the "fun" version of Jackson.

The entire front panel appeared to be one giant computer screen, and although Sydney saw no buttons, Natala brought plenty of flashing icons to life. Sydney watched the woman's fingers fly over the screen until dozens of images lit up, all of them meaningless and foreign to Sydney. Various voices accompanied the images and told them the launch sequence was setting, the date coordinator was processing, the analyzer was booting, and dozens more nonsensical phrases.

Sydney temporarily forgot her fear. She still hadn't closed her mouth, which hung open in amazement. "How could this be a boat?"

"It's not a boat," Casper said. "It only carries the illusion of a boat on the outside. It can be designed to fit in anywhere."

Sydney shook her head, not even beginning to comprehend. A female computer voice interrupted her confusion. Unlike Casper's computer, there was no sexual overtone and no accompanying image.

"Departure sequence initiated. Ten minutes to launching."

Like a zap from a stun gun, Sydney's fear jolted back. Natala's fingers commanded the screen as she ordered everyone to secure their harnesses. Given the guns pointed at their chests, Casper and Sydney complied.

Sydney slipped her arms through the straps and secured the belt at the chest and the hips. She then fastened another small attachment that looped over her crotch. The action sent a stab of pain through her thigh, and she had to pause for a moment and catch her breath. She grimaced at the wound, but although big, ugly, and raw, it was still pink—a good sign. Jackson hadn't singed her as deeply as he'd promised.

Oh dear God, it's really happening.

She was about to be plucked from her world and thrown into another, one she couldn't even imagine. What would become of her?

"Nine minutes to launching," the no-nonsense computer voice said.

Sydney could hardly breathe. It couldn't be real. It wasn't possible. Things like this didn't happen to Sydney McKnight. Things like this didn't happen to *anyone.*

She looked to Casper for guidance, her body tense with fear, but he seemed lost in concentration, scanning the small room in what Sydney assumed was a last-ditch effort to find a way out.

She followed his lead. There had to be something they could do. Natala had now taken her seat, and Sydney's eyes searched the front panel around her, but it was pointless. She couldn't make sense of the giant screen. Even if they did manage to overpower Jackson and Natala—which had already failed once—would Casper be able to command the controls?

"Eight minutes to launching."

Oh dear God, dear God, dear God, dear God.

Frantic, Sydney again scanned the small area. Jackson to her right, the weapon in his hand. Casper next to him. Natala in front. Sydney searched the floor, but other than the bag next to her feet, there was nothing, her pepper spray long gone. She started to panic and worried she might lose it completely.

A beeping broke her frenzied thoughts. It was Casper's glucose monitor again. He tapped his wrist and rubbed sweat from his forehead.

We have to do something. We have to do something now.

Sydney froze. Slowly, her gaze returned to the floor.

The bag.

Casper's bag!

Sydney's heart pumped even faster, and a sliver of hope crept into her psyche. She turned toward Casper, her body trembling from a combination of fear and excitement. "Casper, you're shaking. You have to take your insulin!"

He looked at Sydney dully but said nothing.

"Your insulin. You didn't take it yet." She pleaded with her eyes and tapped the bag by her side.

With a shaky hand, Casper rubbed away more sweat. "I know." His voice sounded weak. "I'm afraid if I don't take it soon, I'll black out."

"Seven minutes to launching."

Sydney undid her harness and bolted to a stand. Jackson leaped up beside her.

"What do you think you're—"

"Please! You have to let me give him his insulin. He doesn't know how to inject himself."

"He can take a pill." Jackson sounded rough, but by his expression, Sydney could tell he was unnerved.

"Don't you understand? There are no insulin pills in the year 2009. He's run out of pills and hasn't yet learned to self-inject."

Both agents stared at Sydney uncertainly.

"Please, let me give him his shots. Otherwise, Dr. Burke won't be the only one you've killed."

"I—"

Sydney cut Jackson off. "Please." She glanced at Casper, his tremor worsening.

"She's right," he said through clenched teeth. "I need it now."

Jackson's and Natala's hesitation was obvious. Sensing their medical illiteracy, Sydney knew she held the upper hand.

"What do we do?" Jackson asked his partner.

"Please," Sydney tried again. "He's going to have a seizure and possibly die if he doesn't get the insulin."

"Six minutes to launching."

"Please!"

Natala stood up. "All right, all right. Just do it."

"You sure about this?" Jackson rubbed his chin, uneasiness in his posture.

"What's our choice? God knows we can't bring Jones back dead too. We'll never travel again."

They both stared at Casper, who was now trembling, sweating, and blinking rapidly.

"Do it," Natala said again.

Sydney wasted no time. She dove into the bag and pulled out two syringes and two vials of insulin. With trembling hands, she plunged the first needle into the first vial and drew up the full amount. Then she did the same with the second.

"Why do you need two?" Jackson asked, weapon still in his hand but no longer precisely aimed.

"He requires two types of insulin." Sydney's words were rushed. "Short and long acting."

"Isn't that too much?" Natala asked, but Sydney ignored her.

"Five minutes to launching."

Sydney pushed past Jackson and ordered Casper to stand. "These need to go in your abdomen."

With great effort, Casper stood. He trembled all over, and a string of drool fell from his lips.

"Jesus," Jackson said, looking a little weak.

"Hurry up," Natala ordered, now hovering over Sydney, too, as if Sydney could somehow escape the claustrophobic space.

Sydney looked pointedly at Casper and handed him one of the syringes. Then she ran a hand over her neck and gave a slight nod. "You ready?"

He nodded weakly, dribbling more saliva.

With a shaky hand of her own, Sydney lifted Casper's jacket and shirt and exposed his abdomen. Although she wasn't focused on the two agents, she could feel Jackson to her right and Natala to her left, closest to Casper.

"On the count of three," Sydney said, catching Casper's gaze and shifting her own to Natala and then back again.

"One. Two. Three!"

At that moment, Sydney swung around and plunged the needle deep into Jackson's neck while Casper did the same to Natala, delivering dangerously high levels of insulin into people who didn't need it. Jackson's huge jugular vein was an easy target for Sydney, and he cried out in shock and dismay.

Backing up against the silvery wall, needle and syringe stuck in his neck, Jackson seemed about to faint. He fumbled with his gun, raised it, but Casper lunged forward and grabbed the weapon, and then pressed it against Jackson's chest. Like a crumpled potato sack, Jackson fell to the floor in a heap.

Natala, on the other hand, had yanked out her needle and was frantically rubbing her neck near her trachea. She spat out something incoherent, voice hoarse and eyes wide with fury. She raised her gun toward Sydney, but the woman's temporary surprise had given Sydney the advantage. Like Casper, she wrestled the gun away, although what to do with it she had no idea.

"Neurolize her," Casper shouted, but the command was apparently rhetorical, because he seized the gun from Sydney, and within seconds Natala slumped to the floor like her colleague.

For a moment, everything stilled, but the computer counted on, oblivious to the plight before it. *"Four minutes to launching."*

Spurred to action, Casper commanded the computer to open the door. He dragged Jackson outside of the transit device, his arms and chest straining under the agent's bulk.

"I've neurolized them, but it's only temporary…well, maybe. We have to get them out of here."

Casper returned for Natala, a much easier cargo, and plopped her out on the dock next to Jackson. When he reentered the transit device, he asked, "How long will it take the insulin to act?"

Sydney put unsteady fingers to her temple. "Uh, t-ten, fifteen minutes. Maybe quicker, maybe longer. They'll get shaky and confused, and then they'll start to seize, assuming they can still do that after being neurolized." Sydney's use of the word sounded foreign to her ears, but she thought she finally understood the action of the weapon's top button.

"Most recover from neurolization within fifteen minutes. As long as it doesn't stop their heart." A frown crossed Casper's lips.

"Three minutes to launching."

With feverish intensity, Casper motioned her to sit down. He was about to close the doors.

Sydney eyed the agents' immobile bodies outside, posed like two sun-worshipers in the newly dawn light, the wooden dock rocking slightly underneath them. She couldn't help feeling horrified over what she and Casper had done.

She held up her hands. "Wait."

Sticking her head out of the boat, she looked around. No one. She bent down and fished inside Casper's bag for the cell phone in her purse. To be assured of service, she stepped onto the deck and dialed 911. She could see Casper's agitation, but she couldn't leave the two like that. If Jackson and Natala didn't receive a glucose bolus soon, they might die, and now wasn't the time for Sydney to decide whether she could live with that or not.

Within seconds, she reached an operator and quickly relayed their location and told the woman that medics were needed. The operator was still talking when Sydney hung up. She slipped back into the cabin, and Casper closed the door.

"Hurry," he said. "We have very little time."

Less than seventy seconds remained on the launching indicator. Sydney climbed into a front seat and fastened her harness. Casper searched the blinking display, his manner frantic.

"What are we going to do?" Sydney asked, equally desperate.

"I don't know, I don't know. There's no way to create a tunnel block once navigation has been activated. The only thing I know how to program is forward travel, and that's already been done."

"Shut it off then, and let's start over."

Casper nodded in wide-eyed panic and scanned the screen, his fingers ready to hit something—anything—on the navigation panel. It was the closest to a meltdown Sydney had seen from him.

And then: *"Last and final minute to launching. System is now secured."*

Casper's hands froze in midair, and his shoulders slumped. "Too late," he said in a harrowing whisper.

It took Sydney a moment to register his words. In a shrill voice, she said, "Too late? What do you mean, *too* late?"

"There's no way to terminate the system in the final minute of countdown."

"So, what does that mean? We have to return to the year 2209? We're no better off there than here with Jackson and Natala. Even if they die, someone else will be sent to find us, right?" At the mention of their names, Sydney's eyes darted to the video screen, its panoramic view of the outside world capturing the supine agents in their neurologically shocked slumber.

Casper's face showed clear dread. "But there are no other options.

The clock was now at thirty seconds.

"Please, there must be something."

Casper put his head in his hands and squeezed. He looked both pensive and terrified at the same time. Then his expression changed, and his eyes opened wide. "There is one way, but it's only to be used in extreme emergencies."

"Well, I think this constitutes an emergency! Tell me."

"We still have the option of expulsion."

"*Twenty seconds.*"

"What?" Sydney's tone approached a screech. Whatever it was, *expulsion* didn't sound so good to her.

"It means we have the option to override the system to prevent its programmed return, but we'll be delivered to the easiest electrical access."

"*Fifteen seconds.*"

Sydney shook her head with fury. "What are you saying?"

"I'm saying we'll still travel forward, but we won't know which year."

"So we could end up anywhere?"

"Yes."

Good God! What kind of an option is that?

In her mind's eye, Sydney pictured her apartment. She pictured Mitch and Liz. She pictured space aliens and Martians and freeze-dried food.

And then with her actual eyes, she saw Casper. Saw his anxious yet determined face.

"*Ten seconds.*"

From there, the computer kept counting, and in little more than the time it took a butterfly to flap its wings, Sydney had to make a horrifyingly life-changing decision.

"Sydney, we have to decide." Casper clutched her hand and stared with urgency into her eyes.

"*Five…four…*"

"Do it!" Sydney cried.

In lightning speed, Casper's hands were on the panel. He pushed a succession of buttons, and Sydney prayed he knew what he was doing.

"*Two…one…*"

A whirling noise overtook the shiny, metallic transit device, and at the last second, Casper's finger pushed the final button. He wiped sweat from his brow, and his breaths came out heavy and harsh.

"Expulsion option requested. Expulsion option granted."

Sydney looked at Casper, and he looked at her, and together they clutched their armrests. The transit's liftoff was swift but smooth, like free-falling down a thrill ride in an amusement park. Only this time they didn't shoot down. This time they shot up, crossing over to a place Sydney couldn't imagine, over to a time she couldn't predict.

She opened her eyes even wider, her gaze never straying from Casper's.

At least she wasn't doing this alone.

"The drooling was a nice touch," Sydney said, for lack of anything better, her shaky voice finally breaking their silence. Her hands still gripped the armrest like claws, and her body was so tense she thought perhaps she had petrified during their ascent.

"You think?"

"Hollywood will be calling."

"Who's Holly Wood?" Casper winked.

Sydney pried her hands free and leaned back in the chair, the gigantic computer screen blinking and flashing, its blues, greens, and yellows almost seizure-inducing. She trembled from cold, and the nervous energy in her body could have powered an entire stadium with light. It was difficult to focus, and she worried if she thought too hard about what had happened, she might self-combust and explode into a million pieces.

She wondered if this was how the lone survivor of a plane crash felt, wondered how he clung to his sanity as he weaved through the twisted wreckage, tripping over tangled and singed bodies. Like his survival, Sydney's escape was too inconceivable to comprehend, and she'd have to take it one minute at a time if she herself wanted to survive. One second at a time, even.

Worry—but no longer panic—clouded Casper's face. Sydney realized it was one of the few times in days their mouths and noses weren't obscured by masks or their hands ensconced in gloves.

As if having the same thought, Casper reached up and touched Sydney's cheek, wiping away what was probably dried blood from her earlier fight with Natala. "You really slammed me tonight."

"I'm sorry?"

"Impressed. You really impressed me."

Sydney's skin warmed where Casper touched her, the lone hot spot in a body of ice.

"The insulin was a brilliant idea," he added.

"I just hope they survived." Did she? Sydney looked at her leg. She thought about what Jackson had done to Dr. Burke and decided she would have to get back on that.

"Do you think it will heal?" Casper asked.

"What?"

"Your leg."

Sydney examined the wound again and nodded. "A hospital would be nice though."

Silence once again fell over them, and Sydney watched the years tick off in a glowing, green light. Some years passed quickly. Others lingered for several seconds before giving way to a new one. 2022…2023…2024.

"I'm sorry I got you into this," Casper said, his hands back in his lap.

"I think we both know it's not your fault."

"But you've had to leave your whole life behind—your job, your friends, your family."

He got two of the three right. Sydney had no family.

"So have you, Casper. Besides, there was nothing either of us could do. This whole thing took on a life of its own, and everything happened so quickly that the only option was to move forward. There never was any turning back." She spoke more for her own reassurance than his.

"Kind of like fate."

Sydney shook her head. "No, it just happened. You didn't plan it. I didn't plan it. It just happened. Life's like that. There is no fate. There are no coincidences. One act sets the next in motion, and it's up to us to deal with the consequences."

Casper frowned. "You really believe that? After all that's happened, you still think that's true?"

"Yes," Sydney said, though with less certitude than a moment ago. She concentrated on the monitor.

2053…2054…2055.

Casper dug in his pocket and pulled something out. Sensing Sydney's curiosity, he flashed an insulin tablet her way. "Still had a couple left." He wiped more sweat from his brow. "Better take it now before I get into real trouble."

Sydney went back to the shifting dates on the screen and shivered. "How long does this usually take?"

Casper shrugged. "Depends. Sometimes the wormhole is easy to maintain, and the transit is rapid. Other times, there's so much energy to overcome, it takes longer. Don't worry. It should be soon."

Don't worry?

Sydney's aching body was a taut violin string about to break. In the last twenty-four hours, she'd had more adrenaline bursts, more near bouts of incontinence, and more reality checks than she'd had in her entire thirty-one years. If that wasn't enough, now she was headed—without exaggeration—into the unknown.

She looked down at her clothes. Torn, burnt chinos and a black turtleneck sweater, not to mention her battered face.

How much would she stand out? She thought of what women wore two hundred years ago and how different it was from the year 2009. Where did that leave them in the future?

2078…2079…2080.

Sydney's fiddle string tightened another notch, and she turned to Casper. "How are we going to fit in? I won't know anything or anyone. What will I do? How will I live?"

"You'll know me." A soft smile.

"But I might not even recognize a toaster."

"We'll work it out. Together we'll work it out. We've done all right so far, haven't we?"

His expression was so noble and confident that Sydney didn't feel she deserved to breathe the same air.

Casper grabbed her hand and pressed it between his own. "You know, I'm okay with this. No matter what you might think about fate, I now realize I was meant to do this. My whole life has been based on this moment, from my ridiculous sterile creation, to my cold and unhappy childhood, to my constant obsession with the past. I have no regrets. You need to understand that."

Sydney nodded, wanting to prove she was equally brave, but at the same time wanting to crawl underneath the chair and hide. No matter how tough she used to think she was, nothing had prepared her for this.

"But I'm scared," she finally said, not remembering the last time she'd verbalized such a feeling.

Casper smiled and squeezed her hand even tighter. "So am I, but we'll be okay. I'm a historian. I know more about the past than anyone."

"This from a guy who doesn't remember Hollywood."

Casper laughed. Then he released Sydney's hand, and his face became somber. "Just remember, a lot changed in the United States in the twenty-first century. Wars, cities destroyed, alliances broken—we're not the only superpower anymore. But," he said, noting Sydney's distress, "judging by the dates on the coordinator, we've passed the worst years. We'll be okay. You have to trust me."

His smile was back, in all its genuineness and beauty, and the optimism he displayed calmed her. In some ways he was a lot like Liz. At the thought of her friend, a lump rose in Sydney's throat, and she realized how much she'd miss Liz. She didn't even get to say goodbye. Not really, anyway.

Sorry, Liz. I'd had no time to think, no time to back out.

Maybe that was good. Maybe some of the best decisions were made in the blink of an eye, the kind that allowed no time for egos or self-serving outcomes. The kind that forced people to do what was right. Because of Casper, Liz was alive. Because of Casper, billions of people would live. Liz, the Hortons, Dr. Steinberg and the doctors from the CDC, the street vendor on Sydney's corner, the woman who poured Sydney's double latte, the parents of a future president, the scientist who discovers the cure for AIDS.

Maybe those split-second decisions were what defined people's characters and showcased their true selves, like the woman who runs out on a busy street to save a blind man in the middle, or the man who leaps in the path of a bullet meant for his wife, or the bystander who dashes back into the burning building for one last victim. Maybe that was what separated the good from the bad, the strong from the weak, the heroes from the cowards. Hasn't everyone at some point wondered how they would react if the moment was upon them? Would they run out in the street or stay back? Leap in front of the bullet or retreat? Dash into the building or head for the hills?

At least Sydney had always wondered what she would do. Maybe now she knew.

Or maybe it was all bullshit. Maybe she was just looking for consolation, something to stroke her ego, a platitude to tell her she'd done the right thing, while she waded through a future of unfamiliarity.

She studied Casper. His eyes were closed, and his face was calm, and if he had any regrets, Sydney knew they were only for Dr. Burke and herself. Casper didn't seem scared. He didn't seem to be wallowing in self-pity.

2112…2113…2114.

She reached out and touched his hand. Maybe to see his smile, maybe to see if he was real—she didn't know.

Casper smiled and started to say something, but he didn't get the chance. The transit device's momentum had changed. Sydney couldn't define how or why but knew the motion was different. She looked at the shifting dates. The years slowed down, a final countdown to her rebirth, and finally one persisted, its green light flashing.

Then a month was added.

And a day.

And an actual time.

Sydney's heart pounded as she read the numbers. Never before had she felt so hesitant, so frightened, so ignorant.

Or so alive, so important, so immortal.

Casper unfastened his harness and cupped Sydney's anxious face in his hands. "Are you ready?"

She blinked, not wanting to answer, not wanting to do anything but jump inside those eyes and let them swallow her whole, anything rather than face the inevitable.

But once again Sydney saw Liz in her mind. She imagined Liz leaving the birthing center with her newborn son. And the Hortons attending a professional soccer game, Elijah the starring goalie. And Mitch giving his acceptance speech for the Nobel Prize.

She took a big breath and exhaled. She nodded.

Casper spun around and, with a few swipes of his finger on the large display, commanded the door to open. They both stood, and Sydney followed him to the door, her legs wobbly, her hand clutching his like a vise.

Casper turned to Sydney one last time before they exited. He smiled, and together they climbed out and entered their sunny new providence.

August 4th, 2129, eleven-nineteen a.m.

The End

AUTHOR'S NOTE

This book is a work of fiction, created by me in the 2000s and republished in 2025 as a second edition. The novel takes place in 2009 and was initially published in 2012 by Whiskey Creek Press, well before the COVID-19 pandemic. While I strived to keep the story medically accurate, I took liberties to improve the dramatic tension. For example, an influenza virus with such a drastic mortality rate is highly unlikely, as is a pathogenic circulating influenza C strain. Furthermore, prions have nothing to do with influenza and everything to do with my imagination.

Thank you so much for giving it a read! If you enjoyed it, maybe you would consider leaving a review on your online book site of choice, even if just a sentence or two. Reviews help other readers decide if they, too, might like to give it a go, and your support means the world to me.

ABOUT THE AUTHOR

Carrie Rubin is a physician turned novelist who writes medical-themed thrillers. She enjoys exploring other genres as well and has a novel of magical realism published under the pen name Dannie Boyd and a cozy mystery under the pen name Morgan Mayer. She is a member of the International Thriller Writers association and lives in Northeast Ohio.

For more information, visit:

www.carrierubin.com

BOOKS BY CARRIE RUBIN

The Liza Larkin Series:

Fatal Rounds

Malignant Assumptions

The Benjamin Oris Series:

The Bone Curse

The Bone Hunger

The Bone Elixir

Other Medical Thrillers:

Broken Hope

Eating Bull

The Seneca Scourge

Pen Name Dannie Boyd:

Fractured Oak

Pen Name Morgan Mayer:

The Cruise Ship Lost My Daughter